MY SECRET SNOWFLAKE

KATHY STROBOS

Cover Design: Cover Ever After

ISBN: 9781958894170 (Paperback)
ISBN: 9781958894125 (E-book)

www.kathystrobos.com

Published by Strawbundle Publishing
New York, New York

For my mom and dad.

Also By Kathy Strobos

New York Friendship Series
A Scavenger Hunt for Hearts
Partner Pursuit
Is This for Real?
Caper Crush

New York Spark Series
My Book Boyfriend
Love Is an Art
My Secret Snowflake

For giveaways, updates on new releases, behind-the-scene news and what's going on in my life, please subscribe to my mailing list at https://kathystrobos.com/sign-up-for-my-newsletter/

Chapter One

Iris

I FEEL LIKE A Santa Claus who's eaten too many cookies and is now stuck in a chimney, unable to shimmy up or down. So much for my bright idea that I could easily step on a carton and climb through this open window that's about five feet off the ground. I cling to the windowsill, not quite able to hoist myself all the way over, but I'm far enough off the ground that dropping back down could hurt. My stomach is on the sill, and my hands and elbows are holding me on, the wooden ledge biting into *everything*—splinters are a definite possibility. The box I stepped on to get a leg up is now a crumpled heap below me.

"Are you okay, Iris?" Jazmine asks from below me. "Ow. Ugh. There are so many prickly bushes here. Amelia, you should definitely stay on the path."

"I can see your key card on your desk, Amelia," I say.

Amelia, Head of Human Resources at Dream Company where we all work, is outside on a beautifully gardened gravel path, but her key card is in her hotel room. To save Amelia the 100-euro penalty for needing assistance after eleven p.m., I came up with the brilliant idea that I could climb in through her open ground-floor window, retrieve her key, and let her in. It must have been all the "let's-think-out-of-the-box" exercises we've been doing on this company retreat in Provence with our new parent company, L'Etoile S.A.R.L.

"I probably should have just called the porter," Amelia says. "But then he'll think I'm an idiotic American. And what if he tells L'Etoile? And then L'Etoile thinks I'm an idiot?"

I'm the idiot. What if our L'Etoile colleagues see me hanging here? Oh no. I kick my legs. But I'm swimming in air, not water. *C'mon, nonexistent arm muscles. Pull. This is your time to shine.*

"Can you push me some more?" I bite out.

"I'm trying," Jazmine huffs.

As some cool air brushes over the backs of my thighs, I wince. I have the uneasy feeling that all Jazmine did was push up my skirt. My arms are definitely weakening.

"I think I'm going to fall," I gasp.

"Can I help?" It's a man's voice.

Oh, no. Is my underwear showing? It can't be showing, right?

"Yes, please!" *Hold. On.*

"Sebastian, great timing," Jazmine says.

Sebastian? The new guy in Legal?

Should I shimmy and try to get my skirt back down? I bite my lip and hold on tighter. If I shimmy, I'll look like I'm doing some weird move to the windowsill. Or like I'm a worm.

Some twigs crack behind me as I presume Jazmine and Sebastian switch positions. I don't dare look around. *Please, let my underwear not be showing.*

"Okay if I put my hands on your hips?" Sebastian asks. His voice is a deep timbre behind me, and it's as if my hands *want* to loosen their grip on this windowsill and slip into the warmth of his arms. The smell of Ivory soap mixes with the night breeze.

"Yes, yes," I say. *I can't hold on much longer.* Especially when my body seems to have the completely wrong idea about this situation.

And suddenly two hands grip my hips, and my stomach is over the windowsill. Along the rest of me. *Crash! Ouch!* I *don't* catch myself in time. I'm on the floor.

"Are you okay?" he asks.

No. I want to disappear between these wood boards.

"Yes," I say, adding a cheery lilt to my voice as if I'm totally fine and my knees are not all scraped up—and I adore looking like an inelegant mess in front of a very attractive guy.

I stand and pull down my skirt. It's dark, so *maybe* my underwear wasn't visible? But at least Sebastian is an American colleague. Because my underwear would definitely not impress our French hosts.

I am so mortified. I can feel my cheeks flush.

I turn on the desk light and grab the key. I flash a thumbs-up out the window at the three shadowy figures standing outside, only the face of the man illuminated by the lamp. Amelia and Jazmine have retreated to the pathway, out of reach of the bushes.

"I'm Sebastian," the man says as he steps forward. "I'm not sure we've met formally before."

As if all the women at Dream Company in New York City didn't immediately sigh in appreciation when he joined a month ago. Even I couldn't help noticing him and I'd sworn off dating.

Should we really be doing formal introductions now?

"Iris Murphy," I say. "Thank you. I was definitely stuck."

"It was definitely a pleasure." He flashes me a wicked grin.

I blush. Yes, my underwear was definitely showing. And I'm wearing my white full-coverage underwear—not at all sexy, especially with the cat pawprints. I close my eyes. *Why did I have to wear those?*

Still, given his smile and chiseled cheekbones, those dark-blue eyes, and his wavy blond hair, I'm sure he's seen women in underwear before. Just maybe not granny underwear that looks like a cat stepped in pink paint and then massaged my butt.

"You've earned your good Samaritan points for the day," I say wryly.

"I don't think this qualifies," he says with a slight laugh to his voice. "I couldn't *not* help when it was like a luminous white flag of..."

My underwear was glowing? Great.

"Surrender?" I ask.

"That's not quite what I thought, although it definitely works. Given that HR is right behind me, I'm not going to say anything else." He gives me this half-smile that definitely hints at something more.

"You can't leave me hanging," I say.

"I didn't. I'll be off, then." He backs up through the bushes, back to the gravel pathway that meanders among the cute little cottages at this French countryside resort.

That's more in line with his usual behavior, according to the female office gossip. He's gorgeous but aloof. All work and no play. I smooth down my skirt again. Patrick had the same complaint about me. *My ice princess.* That's what he liked at first—that I wasn't falling over myself to attract him. But that didn't last. I sigh. I leave by the front door and meet Amelia and Jazmine outside.

Amelia takes her key card, saying thank you again and waving good-bye. Jazmine and I walk down the path to our suite in the building next door.

"I can't believe *Sebastian* came to your aid," Jazmine says. "I wouldn't have pegged him as the type to rescue a damsel in distress."

"I wasn't a damsel in distress. I would've gotten myself over the ledge eventually," I say.

Jazmine pats my back. "Of course. Still, sometimes it's good to recognize when you need help. You don't have to do it alone."

"Why wouldn't you have pegged him as the type to rescue a damsel in distress?" Let's not drop that far-more-interesting line of conversation. Does Jazmine also see him as distant?

"I mean, he seems like a great guy, but he doesn't socialize much," Jazmine says. "But I think he was definitely smiling when he passed me. Maybe he's just the ticket to get you over your good-for-nothing ex."

I shake my head. "Should you—as HR—really be advising me to date a work colleague?"

Jazmine laughs. "You know I'm all for dating in the office. If I could only get Aaron to notice me. We're in France, and it's a romantic, moonlit night."

I swoop my arm through Jazmine's. "And I'm happy to be here with you."

Jazmine and I had met at an office public service event this past summer where we'd been paired painting a classroom. *This past summer.* I'd spent all my free weekends flying to Patrick's rock concerts. I hadn't seen my friends or family at all. When I was really down about my breakup with Patrick, she made me the absolute sweetest care package—with bubble bath, a romantic comedy book, hot chocolate mix, and a gift certificate for a Thai restaurant around the corner from my parents' house. I'd moved back home when I had to leave the apartment I'd shared with Patrick.

"I really hope our flights home don't get canceled because of a labor strike, like on our way over," she says.

"Me too. Tessa's engagement party is Saturday night, and I'm both the DJ and tech person. I don't want to miss that." Earlier this year, I'd missed most of my sister's engagement party because of a cyberattack.

My phone beeps.

"Who is that?"

"My brother. Asking if I'm okay. Liam's become such a worry-wart ever since I texted him when I...found Patrick." I still can't quite say when I found Patrick *cheating*. "And asked him to help me move out."

"You're doing much better. And I know you don't want to hear this, but you and Sebastian talking through that window looked sparky tonight." Jazmine pulls out her key and opens the door to our cottage. "Anyway, are you ready for your presentation tomorrow on cybersecurity?"

"Yes, I even discussed it with my new French infosec colleagues. I think I impressed them. I keep feeling like this is some sort of test and not just let's-all-get-to-know-each-other."

"I get that vibe too," Jazmine says. We look at each other and then shrug. I wave good-bye and let myself into my room next to hers.

I pull up Liam's text to send him a picture of me smiling next to Jazmine in front of the Eiffel Tower from a few days ago—to reassure him. But I can't help flipping back to our text exchange from *that* night. I had come home early from a cybersecurity conference, only to find two wineglasses, a trail of clothing, and a closed bedroom door. I'd texted Liam, who was dog-sitting in the neighborhood.

Me: *Patrick…*

But I couldn't type out the words.

So I texted a photo of the trail of clothes. A black dress. Red bra. Patrick's jeans. His lucky black shirt. A black pair of underwear. Boxers.

Me: *Can u help me take my stuff home? Now.*

Liam: *I'll kill him. You can stay there.*

But I couldn't.

A framed photo of Patrick and me staring at each other, love shining out of our eyes, on my desk, had caught my glance. And it felt like a dagger piercing my chest. I still remember the bitter taste of blood from biting my lip mixing with the salt of my tears.

Patrick saying he was sorry—that she was a mistake. The woman objecting to being called a mistake. Saying she was sorry to me and yelling at Patrick. Me telling her it wasn't her fault. Fatma swishing her tail angrily and hissing at them both. The woman helping me pack up and telling me to take the chocolate and the ice cream. I didn't want the chocolate or the ice cream. I wanted my boyfriend, or rather the boyfriend I thought he was.

My stomach clenches. *I'm definitely not ready to fall in love again.*

NO FLIGHT DELAY AND no cybersecurity crisis. And this is most definitely New York City and not Paris or Provence, as my best friend Maddie and I pass the corner pizza store we haunted as kids. The smell of melted cheese wafts over as someone exits out the door, a pizza box in hand. We're actually on our way to Tessa and Zeke's engagement party.

"I have such a good lead on this story." Maddie is a reporter covering the city desk.

The gallery hosting Tessa and Zeke's engagement party is in the middle of the block. In the top center of one narrow brick building, a woman perches on the windowsill, her face and body turned inward, her hand holding a cigarette out the window.

As we arrive at the gallery entrance, our friend Lily rushes up to us.

"I'm so glad you're here. Tessa's terrible paintings are gone. I put them right here"—she points at the front façade— "and I carried in the framed photos—because those are so personal—and I was sure nobody would take the paintings. But they're gone." Lily practically wails the last part.

"We didn't see anyone coming this way carrying paintings," I say.

Lily looks down the street the other way, but it's empty. "I was only gone for five minutes. I got distracted buying Rupert a bulldozer T-shirt for Christmas."

"They'll be fine. They're going to be so happy with the party and all their friends here to celebrate them. And Tessa will probably be relieved that she never has to be embarrassed by them again."

Lily looks torn. "Maybe. Maybe I can pass it off that I 'lost' them on purpose. But they probably have some sentimental value, given that she painted them when she was trying to persuade Zeke she had some artistic talent."

A cab pulls up, and Lily's boyfriend, Rupert, alights. She rushes up to him and explains to him what just happened.

He pulls her in to hug her tight. "Are there any building personnel helping you with the setup?" he asks.

"No," Lily says. "I met the super here, and he gave me the key. Then he bicycled off."

"Maybe you can call him and ask him if any security cameras monitor this area," Rupert says.

"Great idea." Lily smiles at him, and it's one of those smiles you know you're not supposed to see, meant for just the two of them.

I feel very single.

"Maybe we should focus on getting whatever else needs to be set up first, and then if we have time, we can try to find the missing paintings." Maddie pulls me through the front door, leaving Lily and Rupert alone.

I make sure all the electronics work, including my playlist, while Maddie greets the caterers and sets them up in the small back kitchen. Lily and Rupert hang up various photos of Zeke and Tessa over the course of their relationship.

As Maddie and I stand off to the side, surveying the room, Lily joins us just as her phone rings. She hits the button to answer.

After a moment, her eyes grow wide. "In the garbage?" Lily screeches. "Okay, okay. In the back?" She listens for a second then hangs up and shakes her head. "He says he bicycled back to check on me, feeling bad that he'd left so abruptly, and saw the paintings leaning against the window. Apparently, artists leaving paintings outside the building is a thing. There's a rule—any art left outside goes in the garbage in the back. I must have missed his return when I went to the bathroom."

"I'll look," I say. "You stay here."

I slip through the kitchen and out into the small backyard of the building. There's a small iron table with chairs, a standing ashtray, a bike rack, and a *very* large pile of black garbage bags. One rectangular-shaped one in the back could hold Tessa's paintings. I pull aside the first few bags. What do they put in these things? Full paint cans? I need to do that crouch and swing that the garbage truck personnel use. I pull in my stomach muscles, bend slightly, and get a swing going with the next one.

"Hello," says a deep male voice from behind me. One that sounds familiar but I can't place.

I turn around. It's Sebastian—from the office—holding a bicycle. *What's he doing here?*

"You," I say.

"You," he says.

"What are you doing here?" I ask.

"I'm friends with Zeke. We met when we both worked at Capital before I came to Dream." He locks up his bike to the cycle rack. "How do you know Tessa and Zeke?"

"Tessa and I are friends from high school," I say.

"Is there a reason you're rooting through the trash?" he asks.

Great. First, I'm climbing through a window, and now I'm swinging garbage bags. Let's not forget that in between, he saw me giving a presentation on the importance of not falling for phishing attempts—never click an email link unless it's something you're expecting and you've checked that the sender email address is legit and—oh yes, my face blushes—always shred your personal information because hackers will go through your garbage.

"The super threw out Tessa's paintings, and I'm retrieving them," I say. "I think it's that bag in the back."

"I'll help." He dispatches the bags pretty quickly, and I'm not ashamed to admit that I'm definitely enjoying the view of his muscles working underneath that white button-down. He pulls out the last bag.

I rip open the rectangular bag, and it is indeed Tessa's paintings. Thankfully, they're the only thing in the bag. I call Lily. "I found them."

"Great! Phew. I don't think we should hang them," Lily says. "Let's just lean them against the back wall. Too many people are here now."

Sebastian is standing close to me, and when I look up at him, my heart does a little cardio dance like it's become an animated cartoon. His shirt collar is open at the neck, and a ghost of a smile hovers as he gazes down at me with those very-blue eyes.

Get a grip.

I explain the plan to Sebastian, and he nods.

Wait, is this the Mr. Single Sebastian who Tessa has mentioned? My mouth drops open. One of Zeke's friends who has no interest in dating? The guy who is also Rupert's best friend? Lily also definitely said he doesn't date.

"Wait—you're the Sebastian who is friends with Rupert and Zeke and who doesn't date?" I ask and then immediately regret it. Can I just hide in that pile of garbage bags?

What are the chances? It has to be him. He gives off the same vibe at work. *Of course* that's the guy I would be attracted to.

He blushes.

He runs his hand through his hair. "I don't think they have any other friends called Sebastian." He coughs. "And I am happy being single, so I haven't been looking to date lately. But I wasn't aware I was such a topic of conversation."

I make a slight scoffing sound. "Please. Lily loves to matchmake, and you're Rupert's single friend."

So, most definitely not an option. All the better. He's definitely not the type of guy I resolved to date next anyway.

The paintings look undamaged, none the worse for having been shoved in a garbage bag.

Sebastian picks up two paintings, and I grab the other two, following him back through the kitchen.

The party is in full swing when we enter the packed gallery. Zeke's dog is the center of attention of one group of revelers. We discreetly lean the four paintings against the back wall behind the bartenders.

Zeke clinks on his glass with a spoon. "We promised no speeches, but I want to thank you all for coming to celebrate with us. We have the best friends ever, and I look forward to many more years together celebrating life's milestones and enjoying every day together. Thank you, Tessa, for agreeing to be my wife and making me so happy."

"Hear, hear." We all clap as Tessa tears up and kisses him.

"And thank you, Tessa, for reminding me how important it is to step out of my comfort zone and take risks to get what you want."

"Even if it does result in some very bad art." Tessa points to her paintings.

"But a very solid relationship," Zeke says.

There is more glass clinking, and Zeke kisses Tessa. I don't look at Sebastian. We're work colleagues, so I can't just wave and disappear. But it's so awkward to be standing next to him as Tessa and Zeke share a very tender embrace.

Tessa and Zeke break apart, Tessa looking very flushed, and the music starts up again. Oops. I abandoned my music post; Maddie is doing it.

Lily joins us. "Did you two finally meet?"

Sebastian quirks an eyebrow and says, "We work together at Dream."

Her eyes widen, and I can practically see her matchmaking gears clicking in her brain.

"I have to go give Rupert a hard time for missing our squash game again," Sebastian says.

Yup, definitely Mr. I'm-Staying-Single Vibes.

"Thanks for your help out there," I say. "I'm supposed to be in charge of the playlist, so I should relieve Maddie."

"I'll relieve Maddie." Lily turns around and practically runs over to the DJ station.

"Are you taking song suggestions? Do you want Zeke's 'getting ready to go out' song?" Sebastian asks.

"You know that?"

"No, but Rupert definitely does. I'll ask him and report back to you."

"Is Rupert going to share that with you?"

"Are you doubting my powers of persuasion?" His eyes twinkle at me.

"Yes," I say.

"You're on." He heads straight for Rupert. Maybe I misjudged him. He doesn't seem so standoffish now. He's helped me twice, and now he left our conversation open-ended with a reason for us to talk again rather than moving on to someone else, as so often happens at cocktail parties.

I walk over to join Lily and Maddie because DJing really is my responsibility.

Sebastian is grinning at Rupert, and he seems like someone who's a lot of fun. I'm sure he'll persuade Rupert to reveal Zeke's "getting ready for a night out" song. But am *I* ready to pursue this feeling about him and possibly risk getting my heart broken again?

Chapter Two

Iris

I follow the "North Pole" signs lining the hallway to the conference room to participate in the Dream Company's annual office Secret Snowflake gift exchange. The conference room is decorated for all denominations for the holiday season, and Eartha Kitt's "Santa Baby" is playing in the background. A large menorah waits in one corner, ready to glow with light. A Kwanzaa candle display sits on the table, and a red-and-green half-decorated Christmas tree stands in another corner. Wearing an elf hat, which rather suits her, Jazmine is hanging some red bulbs on it. Amelia is supervising—with a tape measure in hand?

"I think they need to be two inches apart," Amelia says. "Set decoration and production design are coming, and I don't want this to look unprofessional. What if Xavier shows up?"

Xavier is the CEO of Dream Entertainment.

"I think he will understand this is more about the *spirit* of Christmas." Still, Jazmine hangs the red bulb where Amelia is pointing.

Amelia checks her list. "I'm going to check on the drinks." She hands Jazmine the tape measure.

"I'm so tempted to stick a purple bulb in the center of this," Jazmine mutters as Amelia walks away. Still, we hang the rest of the bulbs, properly spaced.

I recognize a few people: some from marketing, IT, and the studios. It seems like a good cross-section of the company.

"I plastered the accounting room with posters about this Secret Snowflake exchange, so I hope Aaron signs up—and I draw his name. I can give him a romantic dinner date for two," Jazmine says. She's had a crush on Aaron in Accounting for the past year.

"As long as you're one of the two," I say.

"I would be. Given the $30 spending limit, it would have to be me making a home-cooked meal for the two of us."

"Very clever," I say.

Whoever gets her as his or her Secret Snowflake will be lucky.

We meander over to the center table, which is full of home-baked goods and breakfast pastries. I pour myself a mug of hot chocolate and take a slice of Jazmine's delicious chocolate babka. It's her grandmother's recipe. Croissants and bagels fill out the breakfast spread.

"Isn't there anyone who interests you?" Jazmine asks. "What about Sebastian? He was quick to jump in and rescue you at the retreat two weeks ago. You guys looked cozy together when you were talking that night."

I can feel my cheeks redden. "That was before I saw him at my friend Tessa's engagement party and realized he is the Sebastian who has sworn to remain forever single. I definitely don't want to pursue a guy who wants to remain single. What fun is that?"

"That seems a waste," Jazmine says.

I laugh. "It's such a waste." I take a bite of the babka. "This is so good, Jazmine."

"Thank you," Jazmine says. "Do you know why he doesn't date?"

"I don't know. Lily doesn't know either. Some bro code. Her boyfriend just says Sebastian has his reasons."

"If I wasn't interested in Aaron, I'd take that as a challenge." Jazmine raises her eyebrow at me.

I shake my head. "I take it as a red flag. He was so hurt by someone in the past that he's firmly declared that he's a fortress now."

"Hmm...except that sounds like someone else I know. Patrick wasn't worthy of you, and he's not worthy of being the reason you've taken a hiatus from dating."

"I haven't declared I'm a fortress."

"But you're not dating right now?" Jazmine shakes her head, the bell on her hat jingling.

"That was because of work. I'm definitely looking for a certain type of guy." The opposite of Patrick. What had I been thinking? Patrick always complained when I had to work late on the nights he didn't perform. Now I'm looking for a guy who supports my career wholeheartedly. The plan is to be absolutely systematic and rational when choosing whom I next date and vet him properly before tumbling into any romantic entanglements. "And I live with my parents. I can't exactly bring a guy home and then it's 'meet my parents' for breakfast. And if I call them up to tell them I'm not coming home, they'll give me the third degree about how well I know this man etc."

The room is filling up with more of our coworkers, and we retreat to a corner by the tree. I breathe in the pine scent. Maybe I should buy myself a small tree for my bedroom since I won't be decorating my own apartment this year. Still, the goal is to have my own place by the new year, once I get my bonus.

"What type of guy? Any possibilities from the office?"

"I don't want to date someone at work. Lily has a guy in mind from the library; he often comes in there to read. She just has to think of some way to bring it up."

"I hope you get Sebastian," she says. "You might be just the one to melt the ice fortress guarding his heart."

"If I see him again at a friend's party, maybe I'll try to figure out his deal."

"I can't believe you guys have friends in common and you never met before he helped you through that window."

"Shh. That's a statement very much prone to misinterpretation," I say.

"Or not." Jazmine winks. "There was some definite heat. I was surprised when *he* volunteered to help."

"I think we win the workaholics award," I say. "But that engagement party was the one event we both couldn't miss."

"Well, your free time was also committed to attending Patrick's concerts."

My stomach clenches. I tried so hard. *And for what?*

Amelia announces that the Secret Snowflake exchange is now open for sign-ups and explains the rules. "Happiest of holidays to everyone!"

Everyone claps and whistles. I finish my cake and hot chocolate and throw out the empty plate and cup.

We walk over to the sign-up table. Jazmine pitches her name in the large brown burlap sack first. I write my name and desk location on the lined scrap of paper and then toss it in.

One of the guys from my cybersecurity unit, Hank, comes over. "Have you seen Raphael? I haven't seen him since Kevin called him to his office this morning."

"No. Poor Raphael," I say. "Kevin has been impossible to please lately."

"It's probably a discussion about bonuses." Hank smiles. "Are you actually signing up for this?"

"Yes. Aren't you?"

"No. I'm just here for the free food. Why would I want a gift from someone who doesn't know me? Or to have to spend my time buying crap for someone else?"

"I think you're actually supposed to put some thought into the gifts. Enjoy the food," I say as Jazmine grabs my arm to pull me away into a corner.

She squeezes hard. "Aaron is here!"

A tall guy wearing wire-rimmed glasses walks up to the sign-up table, followed by the rest of the accounting department. Jazmine's posters definitely worked.

Clusters of colleagues mill about, conversations buzzing.

Amelia calls us all to line up to pick our Secret Snowflake from the burlap sack. Jazmine is nearly vibrating with excitement in front of me.

"I love the holidays," she says.

"That's lucky, given that you celebrate Christmas, Hannukah, *and* Kwanzaa."

She smiles. "I know. But I love all the messages of hope, giving, family, and community. Don't you?"

Yes, but I haven't felt very hopeful recently. All I do is work—without much time to see family or friends. At least I'll be able to get home tonight in time to decorate our family bar. But I used to love Christmas. Nothing compares to the joyful anticipation of Christmas morning—and all the family hanging out together.

Jazmine picks first. Then I put my hand in the sack, the rough burlap contrasting with the smooth feel of the paper. We move off to the side before we unfold our crumpled-up pieces of paper to reveal whose names we've drawn. All around us people are chattering, excitedly discovering their Secret Snowflakes.

Jazmine takes a big breath. "I can't believe I'm nervous."

"You should just ask Aaron out."

"He's an accountant. He probably doesn't believe in dating at the office. I need to sneak into his heart so he can't *not* date me. My strategy of running into him whenever he takes a coffee break doesn't seem to be working."

"No. He only seems to think you drink a lot of coffee."

"Well, that I do," she says, gesturing to her bright-pink thermos, now set down on the table near us.

I pat her back. "I can't imagine anyone not wanting to date you. Really."

She unfolds her slip of paper. "Ernest." Her shoulders slump.

I unwrap mine. "Aaron." I hand it to her and take her slip.

"Are you serious?" she asks. "You got Aaron!"

"And now you have Aaron. Happy holidays," I say.

"Thank you. Are you sure?"

"Absolutely."

Jazmine clutches the name to her chest, the biggest grin lighting up her face. I only hope Aaron is worthy of her.

"And Ernest is perfect for me."

"Are you interested in Ernest?" Jazmine playfully punches my shoulder. "Why didn't you tell me?"

"Because I'm not dating someone in the office. But if I was going to date someone in the office, he would be a definite possibility."

He works in accounting. He often has this quizzical expression on his face that is cute. He seems very...dependable. And trustworthy.

"I'll try to find out the scoop on him from Aaron—if I ever actually talk to Aaron," Jazmine says. "But Ernest and Sebastian have been eating lunch together lately. Maybe Sebastian is friends with him?"

"Really? That's perfect. I can ask Sebastian what's a good gift for Ernest and figure out why Sebastian has sworn off relationships." I grin. If I give Ernest the perfect gift, it might spark his notice.

"You *are* interested in Sebastian." She wags her finger at me.

"I am definitely *not* interested. He's exactly what I've sworn off. But I'm intrigued by why he wants to remain single—as another person who's joined the single bandwagon."

"But given that he's friends with Lily's boyfriend and Tessa's fiancé, doesn't that speak well for him?"

"It speaks well for him, but not for a relationship with him. It's bad enough that Patrick plays in bars around the Lower East Side and I periodically run into him. Imagine if I had to see Patrick for years at friend get-togethers." I shudder. At least I no longer have to avoid the lower loop of Central Park. That was really annoying because I like to run there. Patrick cleverly wrote a song with a New York refrain, and the pedicabs love to blare it as they cycle tourists around, and for a while, I just couldn't take it. Now if I hear his songs, my heart doesn't ache like it did. And I don't regret dating Patrick, because even if it did end painfully, I learned things about myself I couldn't have figured out otherwise. What I'm looking for now is someone trustworthy and dependable, someone whose appeal is not on view—a hidden gem, so to speak. No more heart-melting, gorgeous rock stars for me.

"It seems like you've given Sebastian some thought."

"I haven't. Okay, maybe a few thoughts, and then I reminded myself of why Sebastian's all wrong for me, including that—even though you disagree—dating in the office seems like a bad idea to me."

"Sounds like a calculated risk to me. One that's worth taking."

"You *were* listening to our cybersecurity presentation the other day."

"Of course."

My phone beeps. I check it.

> Raphael: *Malware. Someone clicked on a phishing email.*

"Work. I'll see you later."

"You never get a break. Thanks again," Jazmine says. "I will definitely figure out a way to repay you."

"Now I'm worried." I wave good-bye and rush to Raphael's office.

I knock and enter Raphael's office. He points to his monitor. "I neutralized the malware and gave the employee a new laptop, but it's lucky you implemented so much network segmentation. It was isolated to that area. I forwarded you the phishing email so you can add it to our database of successful examples."

"Not like we need any more. What were they trying to steal?"

"I don't know. We've secured the movie database," he says. "That's our most valuable asset. But we should knock some more items off our vulnerability assessment."

"Will do."

I leave Raphael's office and head to the canteen to grab more coffee. It's going to be a long day.

I type as I round the corner into the canteen—right into a hard chest.

"Whoa," Sebastian says as he holds up a steaming paper cup of coffee, the lid now slightly askew.

I pull back. "I'm so sorry. Did it spill?"

"Only a little," he says, retreating back into the canteen and setting down the coffee. Two brown spots dot the cuff of his crisp white button-down shirt.

Great. Now I'm also a klutz.

I grab a napkin, wet it, and dab at his sleeve. He smells of fresh air.

"You smell like you just came in from outside." I look up at his face. I'm standing way too close.

He blinks. "I just met with Bob and then took a walk around the block to clear my head."

"The meeting was that bad?" I ask. Bob is Dream's General Counsel, so that doesn't bode well.

He raises his eyebrows and looks off to the side then glances back. "Just a lot to think about. It seems like you're also multi-tasking." He gestures to my phone.

"Yes. Work's been busy," I say.

He unbuttons his cuff and reveals two spots of red on his wrists.

"You're hurt," I say. "I'm so sorry."

"It's okay, Iris," he says.

The way he says my name makes my heart melt a little.

"I can just roll it up. I'm sure it will come out in the wash," he says. "And I have an extra shirt in my office."

"I'm so sorry. I wasn't paying attention," I say. "You need to run your shirt under cold water immediately so the stain doesn't set. Let me get some ice for the burn. Run both your wrist and your sleeve under the cold water." I walk over to the ice maker and wrap some ice in paper towels as Sebastian runs his shirt sleeve and wrist under cold water.

"The stain has already come out," he says. "Don't worry about it."

I put the ice cube in the towel on his wrist. "But just keep this here for a little bit. I'll feel much better."

His eyes are a very deep blue, and his voice holds a reassuring deep tone. He really is so attractive. And at the engagement party, he was funny, teasing Zeke warmly.

Still, the absolute last person I should be intrigued about is someone who has sworn to remain single.

Jazmine enters the canteen. "You two look cozy." She winks at me.

I shoot her a look. The last thing I need is Sebastian thinking I'm hitting on him, especially when I know he's off-limits. So embarrassing.

"I was typing on my phone while I walked. I bumped into him and spilled his coffee," I say quickly.

Aaron enters the canteen at that moment. Jazmine grins at me and mouths, *Perfect timing.*

"It's a party," she says. "Have you met everyone here?"

Aaron adjusts his glasses and says, "No. I'm Aaron. I work in accounting."

"I'm Sebastian, in Legal. I've seen you around when I've met with Ernest."

"Iris in Cybersecurity."

"Good to meet you all," Aaron says.

I realize I'm still holding Sebastian's wrist and pressing an ice cube to it, and cold water is now dripping all over his shirt sleeve and the counter.

"I think I'm good now," Sebastian says.

I nod quickly, dropping his wrist. I throw the ice cubes into the sink and the wet towel into the garbage. His wrist looks better. The red spots aren't going to blister. Sebastian rolls up his sleeves, revealing very attractive forearms. I've always liked that look on a man. *Off-limits. Not for me. I've learned my lesson.*

He secures the lid to his coffee cup and picks it up.

"Good to meet all of you," Sebastian says. "I'm off."

Jazmine tilts her head at me, indicating I should leave.

"Same. Me too." I follow Sebastian out of the canteen into the carpeted hallway.

He stops after we round the corner, but this time, I manage not to bump into him.

"Didn't you forget something?" he asks, a twinkle lighting up his eyes.

I have my phone. "I don't think so."

"Didn't you want a coffee?"

Great. Now I look like a complete idiot. "I'm awake now. Having scarred you for life."

"I doubt you've scarred me for life. And anyway, the care afterwards was worth the burn." He smiles mischievously at me.

And this is exactly why he's off-limits. Look at how easy it was for him to make that sound flirtatious.

"Do you want my coffee?" he asks.

"I'm not going to take your coffee too." I should ask him about Ernest. "I have a question for you."

And then suddenly my boss's boss Kevin enters the hallway. "Nice to see you have time for socializing, Murphy."

"Maybe you can stop by later to discuss that legal question," Sebastian says.

"Perfect," I say and retreat down the hallway to my desk. Does he actually think I have a legal question for him? Or was he just trying to help me by making Kevin think I was discussing work? Still, the privacy of his office will be much better for what I want to discuss with him.

Chapter Three

Sebastian

I CLOSE THE DOOR to my office and slump down in my chair. L'Etoile may close us down? The expectation when L'Etoile bought Dream was expansion—and it is the exact opposite? So that's why Bob wanted me to get a handle on the financial numbers with Accounting these last two weeks.

Here I thought I'd be General Counsel of Dream in two years and that would finally impress my dad. Instead, an unemployment check may be in my stocking. Maybe I shouldn't have left Capital to work at this start-up. I knew there were risks, but I didn't think I'd be out of a job.

My phone rings. *Dad*. It's like he can sense when I'm vulnerable. Now that he's retiring, he's obsessed with pressuring me to switch from law to finance and work at the private equity firm he built with Neville. It's not enough that he finally succeeded in convincing my sister, Annabelle—though at least she was smart enough to carve out her own spot in London. I've warned her not to trust Neville's son, Nathan. No matter what. Don't be the gullible guy who believed Nathan when he was using Emil's corporate credit card and said he'd accidentally grabbed the wrong card, that he'd pay it back and clear up any misunderstanding. He didn't. Emil was almost fired. I'd found out just in time.

She understands, to some degree, why I don't want to work with Nathan in New York. Only she thinks, after that experience, I won't be duped again. But it's still hard for me to believe what Nathan did. How did he change so much, from the kid I spent hours playing with around the office on weekends while our dads worked?

I swivel my chair around to look out my window at the people walking on the High Line and take a few seconds to regroup. It's cold out today, so only a few people, bundled up, wander along the meandering pathway through the garden that now grows in what used to be an above-ground railroad track. A work of art usually dominates the scene, but the Friends of the High Line must be in the middle of changing the exhibit. I pick up the phone.

"Are you coming home on Friday night?" my dad asks.

"Yes," I say. "How are you feeling?"

"I'm fine," my dad says. "The doctor even said I was doing better. Pepper and I did a whole lap around the Central Park reservoir today. About two miles in total from our apartment. We only inspected every other tree for squirrels. She'd say hello, but she's sleeping at my feet."

"Maybe you should take a nap too," I say.

"I very well might," he says. "Before your mom gets home and puts me to work."

I chuckle.

"Just talked to Astor. He still has an opening at his investment company, and he'd be willing to train you," my dad says.

And with that, our conversation leaves neutral territory.

Has Dad heard that Dream is in trouble?

"As a lawyer?"

"No. As a banker."

"Dad, I'm not interested in being a banker." The Hudson River, visible through the bare branches, is a murky green-gray-blue color today.

"You don't have any power as a lawyer. You're just playing with commas."

"And you're playing with lives. Remember, I watched you for years. Firing people when it had to be done for the bottom line. That's not what I want to do." I try to cushion the rejection. "And commas can be very important."

"Just think about it," my dad says. "Maybe you can be the finance guy who creates more jobs. You can't do that as a lawyer. And I'm just worried that as the lawyer, you're the service provider. You're not the client. I built this whole company, and now Nathan will run it into the ground. Think about all those jobs being lost."

"You need to tell Neville that," I say. "And Annabelle will save it."

Which is why Annabelle isn't happy with my position. *You're just leaving it all to me to save Dad's legacy. And to deal with Nathan, who sees the fund as his personal checkbook.*

"I have thought about it. I went to law school instead of business school," I say, frustrated. "I have to go, but I'll see you for dinner soon."

I hang up and rub my forehead. *Why can't he accept that I don't want to be handed his company on a silver platter? I need to prove myself. By myself.*

And now Bob wants to see me in his office. Again.

The dull throb at the back of my head intensifies.

I grab my revised draft of the presentation for our new French overlord and head out the door. Framed stills from movies produced by Dream line the hallways. Being a part of the movie business is a dream come true, even if it's on the business side as the company lawyer.

One of the women from accounting stops me in the hallway. Her perfume reminds me of Melody's—a citrusy scent. I step back.

"Sebastian. Are you coming to the company drinks tonight?" she asks.

"No," I say.

She pouts. I keep my face straight. She's way too flirtatious. She's like a Human Resources trap, checking to see if I watched the latest harassment training video.

I quickly open the door to Bob's office to escape.

He shoves something in a drawer and looks up, clearly flustered.

I should have knocked. His current demeanor reminds me of a guilty witness.

"You wanted to see me?" I ask.

He pulls out a folder and hands it to me. "Here are my revisions to the contract."

Rubbing his chin, he furrows his brow. "Also, you need to socialize more. People need to be comfortable coming to you with questions."

"Have people said they're uncomfortable coming to me with questions?" I ask, shocked.

"No. Nobody's said that. But I—and you—need to be taking the corporate temperature as part of our job. We need to be approachable so people come to us when they have questions—before they do the wrong thing and then we're in the thick of it, cleaning it up." He says that last part almost bitterly. "Being successful in this company is not just about solving problems in an ivory tower, but also being seen as a resource, as someone trustworthy to whom people will turn if they suddenly suspect they're in a tight spot."

What? I don't give off some ivory tower vibe. Is he trying to come up with reasons to sever me so the company can save money?

"Do you think I'm not seen as a resource?" I ask.

"No," he says quickly. "But you get what I'm saying."

"I do. I certainly hope I come across as a resource and not as the 'guy who says no,' but I will socialize more. From what I've heard to date, everyone is expecting good bonuses this year because we've just been acquired by L'Etoile. People think we are expanding, despite the last two movies flopping."

Bob winces.

"At the box office," I add. I liked both movies, but they didn't seem to be what the market wanted.

"So, it doesn't seem like the employees know yet?" he asks.

I shake my head. "I'll let you know if I hear differently."

"Xavier insists we shouldn't worry," Bob says.

Dream Company was founded by two brothers, who are exact opposites. Colby is the financial brain who runs all business matters. Xavier is the creative one who oversees the movie projects. They seem to get along, but they are two very different personalities.

"Colby says L'Etoile is deciding whether to close us down and just keep the New Mexico office," Bob says. "Xavier is adamant that will never happen. Our presentations to the board about why L'Etoile should keep us is just to force us to look at all cost-cutting options. What's the latest with the board presentation you're working on with Ernest?"

"I'll have it to you by the end of the day." I stand. "Ernest has to make some adjustments to the numbers."

"And remember to let me know what else you hear around the water cooler when this becomes public knowledge around the company. I don't think it's public yet, but people do crazy things when they're desperate."

I nod and then leave and walk down the hallway to my office.

Another *not* reassuring meeting.

Right before I reach my door, Xavier, our co-CEO, dressed in all black including his sneakers, appears in the hallway. Colby's office is at the very end, next to the other senior executives: Legal, Human Resources, Marketing & Publicity, IT/IS. Xavier's office is a floor below with all the other creative people. He's always impressed me as a boss. He's so quick in meetings, and it's just so fun to work with him. And I don't know how, but he knows everybody's name.

"Sebastian," he says. "Great job ironing out that issue with the union. Well done."

"Thanks," I say.

"What are you watching nowadays?"

I stop. "I have to be honest and say I haven't had time to watch much lately because of work."

"What are your friends watching?"

"My mom is watching Hallmark movies," I say.

He wags his finger. "I'd like to greenlight another one of those. I need to brainstorm." He nods, turns around, and heads back downstairs.

He does have his quirky side.

He also seems calm. He's not giving off any vibes of desperation. And this is his dream company. But even if the company is safe, it doesn't mean my job is safe if they're looking to cut costs. Why was Bob so flustered when I walked into his office?

I enter my office and proceed to revise the contract per Bob's latest comments and mull over his vague—and slightly ominous—instructions to haunt the canteen. Maybe I should ask him if there's a specific department he wants me to socialize with. *Do I have to attend the Accounting happy hour?* The folders of work on my desk are piling up. That has to be more important than socializing.

I push up my rolled-up sleeves. My wrist looks fine. *Iris Murphy.* I chuckle. She always surprises me. I will definitely never forget seeing her half-hanging out a window, Jazmine trying to push her in from below. And her very attractive... I cough. I can still see her grinning and waving the key card triumphantly through the window.

As if on cue, a knock sounds on my door, and Iris sticks her head around the door.

"Do you have a minute?" she asks.

"Sure."

Chapter Four

Sebastian

IRIS TAKES A SEAT in front of my desk and crosses her legs. My gaze remains firmly planted on her face, even if she does have attractive legs. It's not like I could avoid noticing them when she was kicking them out the window.

These offices are small, but I'm lucky to have my own space—most of my colleagues sit in open-plan spaces, but Bob argued Legal handles confidential matters so we need privacy.

She says, "I'm sure you've seen the posters for the Secret Snowflake exchange—"

"No. What's that?"

"It's like a Secret Santa exchange, where you pick a name out of a hat and buy gifts for that person anonymously. It's now called Secret Snowflake so nobody feels excluded. Anyway, I signed up and got Ernest."

I wouldn't have picked Iris as the type to sign up for the office Secret Snowflake exchange. She comes across as all-business in the work environment—other than the window stunt and whatever she was doing swinging her hips and tossing around garbage bags at Zeke's engagement party.

"Aren't you guys friends?" Iris asks. "I don't know him, so I was hoping you could suggest some good gifts for him. Within the thirty-dollar limit, of course."

"I'm not really friends with him. We just had a tight deadline on a joint project," I say. "I have no idea what to get Ernest as a gift. Socks?" Ernest is very...earnest. When her face drops, I add, "But I'll think about it."

"Not if socks is your idea of a good gift," she says.

"I heard Lily loved the *Shh, I'm reading* socks Rupert bought her," I say.

"Lily loves Rupert. And they have their own love language." She rolls her eyes.

"You seem skeptical," I say.

"Not of their love. No," she says.

"Just your own? Aren't you dating someone?" Didn't I hear Iris is dating a rock star? Rupert invited me to see a concert, but I had to work.

"We broke up."

I nod. "I'm sorry." It feels inadequate, but something needs to be said.

She shrugs.

"There's a lot to be said for being single," I say. "No one steals the comforter or eats your last banana. You can do whatever you want at night. And nobody complains if you work late."

Her brow wrinkles. "Did you date someone who complained if you worked late?"

"Yes. You?"

"Yes. Even though he worked late too. And then he blamed me when he didn't do this gig because I was free to hang out, and then an agent showed up at that gig and signed another act." She shakes her head. "He stole the comforter too."

"So many perks to being single," I say. We smile at each other—as if in acknowledgment that we're in this together. And there's a flicker of awareness, but it's quickly banked. I'm staying single. Not to mention we're colleagues and our best friends are coupled up. Iris is definitely out-of-bounds.

She also seems to withdraw.

"Anyway, you should sign up for the Secret Snowflake," she says. "They're still looking for some more participants. And the events are fun."

"There are events associated with it?" I ask. "Bob just told me I need to socialize more so people come to me for advice if they suddenly suspect they're in a tight spot. It made sense." But *not* that I give off some unapproachable vibe.

I'm approachable. Iris is sitting in my office, and that woman from Accounting clearly felt comfortable asking me to drinks.

"There's an activity where you make a gift—kind of like a return to kindergarten craft time." Iris laughs. "You should see your face. You look utterly pained at the thought of that."

"Crafting is definitely not my forte."

"What is your forte?"

I stare at her for a moment as I consider how to answer that question in an appropriate way. I want to joke about rescuing damsels in distress, but then I simply respond, "Not picking out gifts for Ernest or strangers."

"You ate lunch with Ernest every day this week. You must have some idea of what he would like."

"How do you know I ate lunch with Ernest every day?" I ask.

She rolls her eyes. "I'm surprised you don't notice all the staring single women. You're one of the best-looking guys in the company, and every day you sit together at the corner table with Ernest. Haven't you noticed that all the surrounding tables are full of women?"

"No." I frown. "Really?"

She leans back as if that compliment was already too much.

I grin. "So, I'm one of the best-looking guys in the company."

She shakes her head and covers her face with her hand.

"I think I would have noticed if you were there," I say. From what I've seen, Iris has her fair share of admirers. It makes sense. She is very attractive, with her silky brown hair and green eyes, but mostly I think it's her smile. She comes across as kind of reserved, but then when she smiles—like she did when she grabbed the room keys—it's so wholehearted that you can't help but smile in return and feel a sense of delight.

"Are you free for lunch today?" Iris asks. "But not in the cafeteria. Because there's no privacy in there. I'm sure I can ask you enough questions to figure out a gift for Ernest."

I'm all for lunch with Iris and getting to know her better—in a strictly platonic manner—even if it is under some false pretense that I know anything about Ernest, but it's probably best to be honest.

"Sure. The only thing I know about Ernest is that he plays golf. Shouldn't I just invite Ernest and you can ask him questions directly?" I ask.

"No, not yet. I don't want to blow my cover and have him realize I'm his Secret Snowflake."

"You take this very seriously," I say, half-teasing.

She grins, and her whole face lights up. When she gives a presentation about cybersecurity measures, she's so serious, almost scary—I definitely don't dare click on any links unless I've first checked that the email address of the sender is legitimate. When she's in cybersecurity mode, she doesn't smile. But then she has this other side to her—the side that climbs into open windows and cares about getting the right gift for someone she doesn't even know.

"Of course. Undercover missions. Super fun. You know, I started out as a white hat hacker."

"I didn't know that," I say. "I feel like I should be worried now. You'll be looking for my vulnerabilities, figuring out where I'm weakest so you can overwhelm my defenses."

She narrows her eyes and pauses a minute, her glance sweeping over my office. I wonder what she sees. My law school diploma is framed on the wall, next to a black-and-white photograph of a snowy Literary Walk in Central Park.

I should bring in some personal knickknacks for my desk, but I've been working so hard ever since I arrived, I haven't really had time to think about decorating my office. There's been so much to learn—transferring from working in the legal department of a finance company to an entertainment company brings some very different issues. But that's a challenge I enjoy. I think I have the hang of it now.

She leans forward. "You seem to have built a rather strong defensive network, and that does intrigue me."

"Why?"

"Because you seem happy being single. That's impressive. And then, of course, why does it make you happy?"

"I explained why before."

"I think that's just scratching the surface."

"Maybe you're giving me credit for being deeper than I am," I say.

"I'm sure there's a deeper reason," she says. "Just as I'm sure that there's an opening somewhere."

I hold her glance. Now her eyes look more hazel than green. "I don't think so." My voice sounds a little sad. *Oddly.*

"Anyway, there are a few other Secret Snowflake–related events. In addition to the crafting activity, I asked HR if we can solicit book donations to benefit Lily's holiday book gift drives at her library. We'll have a Secret Snowflake event where company employees can wrap the books. And then there will be the reveal party. You should also definitely attend the main company holiday event, which is ice skating at Rockefeller Center with little siblings from the Big Brothers Big Sisters program with Alice Walker High School. You're allowed to come even if you're not a big sibling. That program is great. We meet as a group every other week, so it is very social."

Xavier has created so many great initiatives at this company. And he was so happy when L'Etoile bought Dream, thinking it would mean more money for all his projects. And maybe it would have, if those last two movies hadn't bombed at the box office.

"That I can do. And I should sign up with Big Brothers Big Sisters."

Social activities per Boss Request. *Check.*

So what if they all also include Iris? I'm sure we can be friends.

And the fact that I'm already swamped with work?

"Should we meet for lunch at that new gnocchi place?" Iris says.

"No," I say quickly. Too quickly. Iris pulls back. But I'd just taken a huge bite of gnocchi when Melody told me she thought we should just be friends. All taste left, and the bite became a huge soggy mess of dough in my mouth that was impossible to swallow. Like my mouth was a cement mixer. I haven't had gnocchi since.

"How about StuffIt on 10th Avenue?" I ask. "I'll sign up in the meantime. Will you help me pick gifts for whomever I get?"

"I love that place. Definitely." She gets up to leave. "Let's meet in the lobby at one."

I finish the last of my edits on this contract and send it back to my counterparty. An email from Ernest pops up, asking me if I'm free for lunch today. I let him know I'm meeting Iris instead.

My phone rings.

"Iris?" Ernest asks. "The stunning dark-haired woman in the cybersecurity department? How'd you score that?"

I frown. That's a little crass.

"She's friends with Rupert's girlfriend."

"The librarian?"

"Yes."

"Oh, so this is a friend thing?"

"Yes," I say.

"Can you introduce me to her?"

Is Iris interested in Ernest? Because he is clearly keen on her. Is that why she noticed he and I have been eating together in the cafeteria lately? I should do some due diligence on Ernest, given that Iris is Lily's friend. Part of the same friend circle. Like I'd do due diligence on anyone my sister dated.

"I thought you were dating someone," I say.

"I was, but it didn't work out. Mother didn't like her. Is Iris also a bookworm?" Ernest asks.

"I don't know. I don't know her that well," I say. "Why? Do you consider yourself a bookworm?" Books would be a good gift.

"Not really, but Mother is very fond of reading romances."

Not sure how that relates, but okay.

AT STUFFIT, IRIS AND I each order a tinga de pollo burrito and sit with our drinks at a table against a bright-turquoise side wall. Colorful Mexican tiles adorn the counter in the center of the restaurant. Mariachi music plays on low volume in the background. It smells of frying tortillas and simmering tomatoes. Several customers sit at the counter.

"I thought nobody knew about this place. I never see anyone from the company here," I say. It's one of the best deals in the neighborhood. Maybe Bob is right that I need to meet more colleagues.

"I usually pick it up and eat at my desk. And the production guys regularly order from here for delivery."

We compare notes on other affordable options in the neighborhood, and I manage to impress Iris with one that she didn't know of before. The waiter places our two plates down in front of us. We're both silent as we take some time to eat our lunch.

"What made you want to work at Dream Company?" she asks. "Zeke mentioned you were very well-respected at Capital."

"My job there was great, especially my boss, but this seemed to offer more opportunities for promotion," I say. "Bob said he plans to retire in two years, so he'd train me and then I'd take over as the

GC. There was no way I was going to become the GC at Capital anytime soon. My boss would be first in line, plus both the Capital GC and Associate GC are in their late fifties, so they could be there for another ten years. Why did you come work here?"

"Raphael recruited me. I met him at a competition—he was one of the judges—and he seemed like he'd be a great boss. And he is. We work well together, and he gives me much more responsibility than I might have in another job. Especially since as the company grows, the information security team will grow, and I've been in since inception."

She doesn't know. Yet. I think the L'Etoile news is still confidential.

I bite my lip. I finish the last of my chicken burrito. A group of young people walk in, and Iris waves to them. She notes that they're from Production Design.

"Who'd you get as your Secret Snowflake recipient?" she asks.

"Someone named Anita?"

"Pregnant Anita who works in the mailroom?"

"Yes."

"You're lucky. That's so easy. There are so many gifts you can buy."

"If you're familiar with pregnancy and babies. I have no idea what to get her."

"My oldest sister has three kids and my younger sister is pregnant, so I can definitely advise you. And if she has a registry, you can just pick up some stuff off there. Have you given any more thought to what I could give Ernest?" she asks.

"Not really. He has a lot of accounting books around his desk. He often gets a coffee from Starbucks, so you could get him a gift card there."

"That's boring. Does he have any hobbies?"

"Like I said, he plays golf, but I'll have to ask him if he has a secret passion for stamp collecting."

"You shouldn't knock it. People with hobbies are supposedly happier." She finishes her burrito.

"Do you have a hobby?"

"I play video games in my spare time, but it's more like an obsession than a hobby."

"Is that how you got into cybersecurity?"

"Yes. And other reasons."

"Other reasons?" I lean in.

"Other reasons," she repeats.

"But you don't want to share them?"

"It's not that mysterious. My grandmother had a small business. She got phished, and they stole almost all her savings. That inspired me to learn about information security. I started a small side consulting business when I was in high school, where I helped mom-and-pop businesses implement cybersecurity measures. I kept doing that in college and graduate school—until I began working full-time at a company."

"That's so cool. Why wouldn't you share that?"

She shrugs. "Do you game?"

"I played a lot when I was growing up, but I've been working too much lately. And the priority is getting a squash game or run in now so I can stay in shape. I wouldn't consider myself a gamer, though."

That's probably an important hobby for her partner to share.

"Actual exercise is much healthier for you." She shrugs. "Does Ernest read books? Have you ever seen him with a book in hand on his way in the office?"

"Ah, I actually asked him that question, and he said he didn't consider himself a bookworm."

"That's too bad. Books are such good gifts." Iris scrunches up her nose, deep in thought. She looks cute.

"But his mother likes romance," I say.

"He told you that?" Iris asks.

"Yes. You can always give him a gift to give his mom. He lives at home," I say.

"I live at home," Iris says. "Since the breakup."

Way for me to put my foot in my mouth.

"But I'm planning to move out by the end of the year. What did he say he did this past weekend?" she asks.

"Not much." I'm not sure what Iris is expecting. "I think he said, 'I made my Christmas list, and I'd like some pajamas, a coffee thermos, and a new set of golf clubs.'"

"Funny," Iris says.

"Couldn't resist. No. He said, 'Busy weekend, but got in some golf on Sunday. You?'"

"Are you serious?" Iris asks. "What did you do this past weekend?"

"I had dinner at my parents on Friday, played squash with Rupert on Saturday, started reading this book he recommended, had a date on Saturday, went for a run on Sunday, and then worked in the office. What about you?"

"Hold up." Iris splays out her hand like a traffic cop. "You had a date on Saturday? I thought you were committed to remaining single."

"Daughter of my mom's friend. I can't turn my mom down, but in any event, she was also not interested in pursuing a relationship. She just accepted a job in Hong Kong and is about to move there."

"All right, I'm going to make you a list of questions to ask Ernest—and you have to ask them." Iris picks up her phone and types furiously. That looks like a lot of questions.

"Why can't you ask him?" I ask.

"Because then he'll know I'm his Secret Snowflake. There. I just sent it to you."

I open my phone. "How am I going to ask him all these questions? What size boxers he wears? What type of boxers? What? You're not serious."

"I definitely can't ask him that question," Iris says, shrugging but with a mischievous glint in her eyes.

"You can't give Ernest boxers."

"I found some golf-themed boxers for under twenty dollars," she says. "Given that the only thing you've told me he's interested in is golf, that might be the best I can do. Unless you can find another interest."

"Way to put the pressure on. You can't give boxers in the work environment," I say. Boxers! Ernest will definitely take that as a green light. "Why don't you give those golf club sock covers?"

"Do you like socks as a gift? Why do you keep suggesting socks? Have you gone into company lawyer mode?"

"Yes." I cross my arms across my chest. "And I said sock *covers*, as in the things that go over the business end of a golf club. As your counsel, I'm advising you not to give boxers. I'll ask him the questions on your list. Do you still want me to ask him about books?"

"Yes, because even if he's not a 'bookworm,' but he still might like reading a good book."

"I think you created some of these just to make it difficult for me. How am I supposed to ask him what his favorite cookie is?"

She grins. "I admit I wouldn't mind eavesdropping when you interview him."

ERNEST STOPS BY MY office later that afternoon to review the numbers in the CEO presentation. We finish polishing the presentation, and I send it off to Bob. I lean back in my chair.

"It's great you found that extra revenue," I say. *If a bit suspicious.*

As if answering my unspoken question as to how it was missed before, he says, "Colby made a mistake with a bill."

No way. Colby breathes the numbers of this company.

Maybe Bob is right that there is something off lately, but he seemed to be a part of it, with the way he shoved those papers into his desk drawer. Or maybe I'm just being way too suspicious. But I can't just trust everything people say. I've learned that lesson the hard way.

Time to ask Iris's questions. "I was just reading this mystery by Wilhemina Chrissy. Have you heard of it?"

"No."

"Do you read mysteries?

"Not really."

"Thrillers?"

Ernest looks at me. "I don't really have time to read fiction at the moment. I didn't realize you were a big reader."

"I stopped reading fiction for a while, but my friend, Rupert, got me back into it. I guess it's a good way to relax, kind of like a good hobby. Do you have any hobbies?" I'm proud of my segue.

Ernest looks at me like I'm a weirdo. I pull at my collar.

"No," Ernest says. "What is this? Twenty questions?"

"I just realized we eat lunch together every day, and I still don't know much about you." I wince. That sounds ridiculous.

Ernest's eyes widen. "And you want to know what my hobbies are?" He takes a sip of water.

"And your favorite cookies."

Ernest chokes on his water. "My favorite cookies?"

I should flutter my eyelashes at him.

"For Lily's cookie baking party. She wants to know everyone's favorite cookies," I say. "She also wants to know everyone's hobbies and favorite movies, for possible gift exchanges."

Ernest visibly recovers.

"Oh, for your friend Lily's party. Anything with chocolate," he says. "How was lunch with Iris? Why don't you invite her to join us tomorrow for lunch so you can introduce me? I need to establish some sort of connection before I ask her out."

"Don't you need to see if you like her first before you ask her out?" My voice comes out a bit testy, but Ernest doesn't seem to notice. "I'm out of the office tomorrow, unfortunately." Or not. I should *want* to set them up. It's not like I want to date Iris.

"She'll be at Rupert and Lily's cookie party on Sunday, right? That's better. More informal. Thanks again for inviting me," Ernest says.

Lily asked me to invite good single guy friends. I don't consider Ernest a friend, but when he asked me what I was doing this weekend, it felt weird not to invite him when he seemed lonely, especially since Lily had already given the greenlight. But now I'm not so sure Ernest is the good guy I thought he was. And Iris deserves a good guy.

Chapter Five

Iris

A RED LIGHT FLASHES on my screen.

Someone tripped two of my traps in our Alburquerque infrastructure—one trap that looks like the CEO's files and one that looks like his assistant's files. They're decoys. A shiver goes through me. *An intruder is—or was—in the network.* And they're after the CEO's files.

I text Raphael and then try to figure out current status, but he's fast. My chair jostles as he peers over my shoulder at my monitors.

"I think they're out. But I can't yet determine if they took anything," I say. "I need to check if anything was caught or flagged by our monitoring software." I click over to another screen to check our data loss prevention software.

A tall triangular spike.

"Unusual DNS requests," Raphael says.

My fingers fly over the keyboard. Yup, a whole host of domain names we don't know are trying to communicate with our network. A whole bunch of wolves in sheep's clothing knocking at the door and pretending they're here for tea. Not good. Not another attack in which they try to overwhelm our system by using multiple unknown domain name servers. I type a command. No time for tea today. It's lucky I brought my lunch.

"I'll tell Kevin. In the meantime, let's follow our security breach protocol," Raphael says.

I alert Ricardo, my IT colleague in New Mexico. It looks like the CEO's files were targeted, but I'd already isolated that, requiring higher permissions to access. Ricardo notes that any presentations the CEO was working on were probably shared with others, like finance, in addition to his assistant. He mentioned that before, which is why I created a honeypot that looked like the assistant's files. We need to figure out what the hacker took and eliminate their access point.

Raphael calls from the doorway of the bullpen, our fond name for the cybersecurity team room. "Kevin wants to talk to us. Can you come?"

"Ready." I pick up my laptop and follow Raphael into Kevin's office. Two whiteboards are clustered in the corner, but the dominant feature is all the computer monitors, one on Kevin's desk and two on the work surface against the wall.

Kevin taps his fingers. He is a tall, stocky man, imposing, but older. Raphael always complains that Kevin has an IT background rather than cybersecurity, and he is too old-school, refusing to try new approaches. Xavier had colleagues who worked at a film company when it was hacked so completely that they had to shut down the system and work with paper, so he insisted on a cybersecurity team at Dream. That's why five of us report to Kevin, who is dual Chief Information Officer/Chief Information Security Officer.

Raphael and I sit, and I connect my laptop to the screen.

"As we discussed earlier, there's definitely been an intrusion in our system," Raphael says.

Kevin says, "Are you certain?"

"Yes. I set up additional traps, and the hacker tripped two of those," I say.

"You set up additional traps? You didn't think to tell me about them?" Kevin stares at me. It's not a friendly stare.

"She told me," Raphael says. "They're listed in last month's security report."

Kevin grimaces. Raphael and I have suspected the security report assignment is just make-work and Kevin never actually reads them, but nice to have it confirmed.

"Since we are still working on integrating our system with New Mexico, I set up some traps as an additional precautionary measure," I say. That is my job right now—integrating the New Mexico information infrastructure into our information security system. As a start-up, their one IT guy had put in some minimal security measures, like data loss prevention software. But now L'Etoile is ramping up hiring there—in the past month, I've interviewed two more candidates for information security positions to be hired for the New Mexico office. Labor is much cheaper there.

I click to the first introductory slide. It's always best to set the stage with Kevin. It shows how our company has a lock and security alarm on the front door of our building—this would be our perimeter defense—but then we also keep files in locked cabinets, we have passwords on our computers and full disk encryption, and we have locks on office doors. This is what we're doing so far to integrate New Mexico's assets. My next slide explains how the hacker tripped my traps.

We next explain the countermeasures implemented to date. The investigation has been inconclusive so far, but it's early yet. Raphael adds his pitch to hire a forensic firm.

"Look, kids, if the hacker didn't take anything, this isn't a priority, and I'm not going to ask for a forensic team to come in and investigate," Kevin says. "We're trying to keep this location open and keep our jobs. I can't propose that we make some huge investment in this—not to mention, I'm *not* going to admit to our new bosses we have any weaknesses in our cybersecurity infrastructure. There's no funding for hiring a forensic team."

What?

"Is there a question about whether this location stays open?" Raphael asks.

I must look as shocked as Raphael.

"Yes," Kevin says. "New Mexico and New York have both been asked to make presentations about what we offer, justifying why we should stay open. It looks like France just bought us for the movie IP."

Raphael and I sit back in stunned silence.

I'm about to lose my job? Can this year get any worse?

"So, when you were asking me to set bonuses for both a best-case and worst-case scenarios, that wasn't the worst case?" Raphael asks.

"The worst case is we're all out of a job, so there are no bonuses," Kevin says and then immediately moves on. "If someone got in, it must have been because some user clicked on a phishing link. Didn't the New Mexico CEO recently click on a phishing email? How's that campaign going?" Kevin stares at me as if he didn't just hand us coal in our stockings.

Fine. I can be unemotional about this.

"I can push that up the priority list," I say. "I was working on increasing New Mexico's security and facilitating their secure migration to the data center." Which is what Kevin said should be my priority at the team meeting last week. It's still listed as the number-one priority on the whiteboard behind me.

"Isn't it better to admit that we have an intrusion and then leave the decision up to France?" Raphael says. "It's not like Albuquerque is in any better shape. They grew so fast that they only have one guy. And not to be boastful, but he's not in the same league as Iris and me."

"Yeah, but he's half your salary alone. The last two movies flopped, and now France is looking to cut costs everywhere. I don't even know if they think we have anything valuable worth protecting—other than our movies." He stands. "Raphael, I told you I'd give you a half hour, and I've done that. You work on investigating this, and Iris, you should focus on the phishing campaign because that's probably how they breached our perimeter defenses. And I'd like a written update on the migration and a detailed report of any security measures you've taken. All of them. Even if you've reported them to me before." That's our cue to leave.

I close down my laptop and pick it up, following Raphael out into the hallway.

"Apparently we should be looking for jobs," Raphael says. "I'll do what I can, but it doesn't make sense that France wouldn't care about a hacker in the system. Especially when we can't tell what the hacker was looking for. Or what, if anything, they stole."

"It definitely doesn't make sense," I say. Kevin is normally cautious and conservative.

"Wait. Are you looking for another job?" I ask, shocked. I hope not. Working for Raphael has been a dream come true. He is the perfect boss. Kevin, not so much. Which means this job definitely isn't as great for Raphael since he reports directly to Kevin. "I can also stay late to help you investigate, even if we can't do everything we want to or hire a forensic team."

"Let's do what we can. It's our reputation in the industry on the line as well," Raphael says. "I'll try to figure out what was exfiltrated, while you work on installing additional security measures and containing the damage."

"Okay," I say. "And I'll also create more test phishing emails. Maybe with fake job offers."

"That might be too tempting, once this news gets out," Raphael says.

Raphael thinks this could be true. My stomach sinks.

The rest of the information security team mutter "morning" as I return to my desk. A small wrapped gift sits on my chair. I'm not feeling the Christmas spirit right now. I stick it in my drawer. *No bonus. No job.*

The room is now buzzing with activity.

Hank, his baseball cap on backwards, stops by my desk. "I heard New Mexico was hacked. So much for Raphael saying you were one of the best. He should've assigned the integration to me."

Just *brilliant.* Instead of being concerned about our company security, he's happy I failed. But then, Hank was hired by Colby as a favor in return for the use of his father's apartment for a shoot. Apparently, Hank's dad said that Hank spends so much time glued to screens that there must be some useful computer skills he can learn. Unfortunately, we were the ones who had to teach him.

"It's always a question of when, not if." I nibble on my thumb-nail.

I work on putting in additional controls and shoring up any weak spots. It's a triage challenge, and figuring out this kind of intricate puzzle is one of the things I love most about working in cybersecurity. And it manages to stop my brain from looping on the hamster wheel of thoughts about whether I'm about to lose my job.

Jazmine pops by my desk. "You've been head down all day. The little siblings are arriving soon. Are you eating dinner at your desk tonight?"

I look up from my monitor. It's dark outside already.

Does Jazmine know about the closure possibility? She's in HR, so she should be one of the first to know. She seems way too cheerful if she does.

Maybe Kevin was just making it up as an excuse. He probably doesn't want to admit to France that we were hacked—and that we don't know what they stole. Kevin is trying to scare us. He did ask Raphael for bonus best-case scenarios, so that's still a possibility.

I shouldn't panic yet.

We've mitigated the attack as best we can. Raphael's still trying to figure out what was taken. I send a memo detailing my countermea-sures to Raphael. At least I finished that.

"I can't. I have to help my parents decorate the bar. You're wel-come to come if you want. Some other friends are coming."

"I have plans, but I saw a gift on your chair when I passed by to see you earlier. What did you get?"

"That's right—I forgot to open it." I unwrap my secret snowflake gift: hand-knit fingerless gloves in a dark green. Wow. That's a great gift for me. I look around the room. Was it just a lucky guess by my Secret Snowflake? Seems too coincidental. The gift has to be from someone I know.

"Those are really nice. They look handmade, so someone who knits must be your Secret Snowflake," Jazmine says. "I sent my secret snowflake gift via interoffice mail, and I want to pop by Accounting to see if Aaron has any reaction to it."

I really need to figure out a gift for Ernest. Not boxers. I was just teasing Sebastian. *His face*. I almost laugh out loud. "What did you send?"

"I found him an accountant mug, like you suggested." She shows me an image. Written on the mug is: *An accountant: the person in the business most likely to know what is actually going on and least likely to be able to do anything about it.*

She continues, "I want to see if it's out on his desk. But I might need cover because he sits in the back of the room, so you need to come with me. I have a good excuse: I can promote the ice skating at Rockefeller Center with our little siblings next week."

"Okay." I stretch. "Do you have a plan for how to check out his desk?" And maybe this will give me a chance to talk to Ernest.

"Nope," she says. "But two heads are better than one. And I do my best work under pressure."

"Did you guys get a chance to chat in the canteen?"

"Not really. We talked for a few minutes, and it seemed to be going well, but then Kevin came in."

Kevin really was on an anti-Cupid mission that day.

Not that Cupid should be aiming any arrows at Sebastian or me.

As we leave the Cybersecurity bullpen, I spy the box of snowflakes we're supposed to hang up as holiday decorations later. "Why don't we also say we're there to hang up the snowflakes? We can ask Reggie if we can help him."

"That's a brilliant idea," Jazmine says. "See? I knew you'd come up with something."

We go down the hall to Maintenance. Jazmine explains her mission to Reggie, even admitting that she has a crush on Aaron. Reggie is happy to support our scheme.

We hurry across the floor to the Accounting bullpen. The only thing distinguishing their space from Cybersecurity is that Accounting doesn't have a Nerf basketball hoop set up over the supply closet door.

We enter, and a bunch of people look up—including Aaron and Ernest.

Jazmine claps her hands. "Hi, I'm Jazmine. I came by to see if any of you want to sign up for ice skating with the little siblings next week. It's open to all company employees, even those who aren't currently volunteering with the Big Brothers Big Sisters program."

"Is that still on?" asks one guy from a corner—the opposite side from Aaron.

"Yes." Jazmine walks towards Aaron, straight down the middle aisle between the desks.

"But how can they afford that? We're looking for cuts everywhere."

Kevin isn't exaggerating. My stomach dips. Hurray for today's emotional rollercoaster.

"Xavier says that L'Etoile is just testing us and we won't have to make the cuts," Jazmine says.

"They booked it a while ago," Aaron says. "Xavier is paying for it out of his pocket. He said he's not going to disappoint those kids."

"Does that mean Xavier will be there?" Ernest asks.

"I would think so," Aaron says. "I'm already signed up because I just joined the Big Brothers Big Sisters program."

Jazmine grins at him. "Excellent. I'll see you there."

"Are you both going?" Ernest asks.

"Yes," Jazmine says.

Reggie arrives with a stepladder and a box of snowflakes. "Is it okay if I hang up the snowflakes now, or do you want me to wait?"

"We can help," Jazmine says quickly. "We should start back here. By Aaron."

"I'll help too," Aaron says. He comes over to grab the stepladder as Jazmine picks up a box of decorations. They begin working together and chatting. I feel so proud.

Ernest comes over. "I'm Ernest. Can I assist you affixing those snowflake decals to the windows?"

I nod and glance at him out of the corner of my eye. Ernest is definitely attractive in his own, understated way. And the fact that there's no immediate spark, like I feel with... Nope, not going there. I'm looking for hidden fires that smolder and burn for a long time, not instant sparks that blaze out quickly.

"I can't believe the company is spending money on this when we're not even sure if we're getting our Christmas bonuses," one employee grumbles.

Accounting definitely thinks Dream Company is doing poorly. I should cancel my appointment tomorrow to look at rental apartments.

But I really want to move into my own place by the new year.

"This isn't an additional expenditure," Ernest says. "We have these in stock from last year. And it's better to keep spirits up than just give up."

Go Ernest.

Ernest smiles at me, and we take the decals over to the window. I liked these snowflakes so much last year that I bought some for our bar.

"Do you have any special plans for the holidays?" he asks as we plaster decals to the windows. His breath smells of coffee.

"Just hanging out with family," I say.

"That's what the holidays are all about," Ernest says.

"Do you have plans?"

"Mother lives with me, but we're going to Florida for a week between Christmas and New Year's."

Mother? "Together?"

"Of course. I can't leave her behind."

"Is she ill?"

"She's a battle ax. She'll outlast us all," he says.

Okay. That's a bit more dedication to his mother than I expected. But it's admirable. Still, a battle ax mother-in-law is less than optimal. Not that I should even be thinking about mothers-in-law.

I stand back to make sure we're spacing the snowflakes correctly. Ernest mostly seems to be sticking one next to wherever I last placed one. Amelia is going to have a heart attack. I move to the last windowpane. He follows.

"Are you visiting family in Florida?" I ask.

"No. We just want to go somewhere warm. She raised me as a single mom, so I like to give her a vacation for the holidays. It was so much work for her to make Christmas special for me when I was a kid."

"That's so sweet," I say, meaning it. Ernest seems like a good guy—the type of guy I should be looking for.

I could give him a Florida guidebook.

"What are you planning to do there?" I ask. This is the perfect way to trigger some more gift inspiration.

"I'll play some golf, but other than that, we'll just sit on the beach. I'll probably do some work remotely."

Those golf socks might be a good idea too. And suntan lotion.

And he's another workaholic like me. Perfect. Right?

Somehow the image of me sitting next to Ernest on a beach, our laptops open in front of us, his mom in the next lounge chair down, is not giving me goose bumps of delight.

But it probably just feels this way because we're office colleagues. Our interaction might be better in a less formal environment.

"Are you busy on Sunday? My friend, Lily, is hosting a cookie party, and you're welcome to come if you want," I ask. Lily will be so proud of me for going back into the dating pool, even if this is just dipping my toe in there.

"I'd love to come," Ernest says.

"Great. I'll email you the information," I say.

We finish up, and I excuse myself to get back to my desk, leaving Jazmine and Aaron talking. But not before I notice that Aaron is using Jazmine's mug for his coffee. Jazmine notices at the same time, and we smile at each other.

I pop my head into Raphael's office as I pass by.

"Have you found anything yet? Did they take anything?" I ask.

"Some things," he says slowly.

"What?" I ask.

"Well..." He stops and looks really torn.

He folds up a piece of paper on his desk. "I can hear the little siblings in the conference room down the hall. And aren't you helping your parents tonight? I'm leaving soon to see my mom."

He's changing the subject.

"Yes. How's she doing?" I ask.

"She's doing a bit better on this new medication," he says. "You should go. I told Kevin what I found, but since he asked me if I'd told anyone else, maybe I shouldn't tell you. I told him I had not *spoken* to you of what I'd found." He emphasizes the word "spoken."

"Now I really want to know," I say. "But that's kind of weird to ask."

Unless highly confidential or personal data was stolen. But then we'd be in full-blown mitigation mode, informing data protection authorities. And we're not.

Raphael says, "You'll figure out the clues. It's not urgent now. I told Kevin, but his response was...off."

Raphael is also being cryptic, though. I stare at him, my head tilted, but he waves me off.

"Anyway, I'll cover this weekend, so I expect you to take this weekend off. I know you have your sister's event and your friend's party," Raphael says. "Next weekend is yours to work."

"If you need me, I can work this weekend, but I'd really like to make my sister's wedding celebration." I still felt guilty about missing her engagement party because we were dealing with a cyberattack. It was one of the reasons I organized this wedding celebration.

"There's honestly nothing you can do this weekend. I've figured out what happened. And you'll find out Monday." He shoves *The*

Code Book into his backpack. "Thanks for recommending this. I just finished that story in Fifth Century B.C. about how the Greeks shaved the hair of the messenger, wrote the message on his bald head, and waited for his hair to grow back before they sent him to Miletus with the instruction to revolt against the Persian King."

Another change of subject. He won't tell me what happened. Okay, I'll play.

"A bit more time back, then," I say with a wry smile as I leave to return to my desk.

Back in the bullpen, my little sibling is waiting by my desk.

"You're biting your nails again," Faith says. Her mother named her after Faith Ringgold, the artist.

I look down at my hands. "I'll have nothing left, after this week."

First, the weird attack. Then the possibility of Dream shutting down. We're in the middle of several productions. Would they be moved to New Mexico? Here I thought I'd hit the jackpot with Dream. My stomach feels queasy. And now the weirdness with Kevin—and Raphael. What can't they tell me? Am I about to be severed? Raphael would give me more warning, wouldn't he?

"Bad week?" Faith asks.

I force my shoulders to relax and roll my neck. "It's okay. Let's look at your schoolwork."

"I have to find the subtext in *Animal Farm*," she says.

More subtext. More hidden layers. And a dystopian reality.

I focus on Faith and put my questions to the side. *Later.*

I'll figure out the clues. Raphael left me a trail.

Chapter Six

Iris

I EXIT THE SUBWAY at Delancey and Essex, and the chill in the air bites my face. Delancey is a four-lane intersection, and the light to cross is red—like Kevin's instruction to me not to investigate further.

The tree next to me is bare. It looks so barren—like it's closed for the season, in hibernation waiting for spring to start. Jazmine's earlier words about my being a fortress echo in my head. *I'm not being a fortress.* And it's not like I can date right now anyway, given my workload and whatever is going on at work. I feel like I've been on hold—or moving backwards—ever since I moved in with my parents. Now I'm really at a standstill, if I may not even have a job.

I wrap my scarf tightly around my neck.

The bright luminescence of the corner stores illuminates the shadowed sidewalk outside. The glass façade of the Essex Market next to me glows in blue and looks like a video game maze. At least if the bar gets decorated tonight, that's checked off my list. Raphael obviously didn't think we needed to be all-hands-on-deck this weekend, but if we're going to be under attack in the coming weeks, I need to clear any personal obligations out of the way. A faint whisper of protest—*but the holiday parties are so fun in December*—rears in the back of my mind. It's good that both my sister's party and Lily's cookie party are this weekend so I won't miss all the festivities.

On the green light, I cross over, walk down Essex, past the graffitied former Essex Retail Market, and then turn down a side street. Next to a modern white façade with oval windows is another building bedecked in graffiti and red-and-white "no trespassing" signs, metal bars covering broken windows. As I pass, a light hanging over the front door switches on—to deter loiterers. I must have ventured too close. Why was Raphael afraid to tell me—did he venture too close to something he shouldn't have? But what?

A right turn, and I'm on one of the more picturesque blocks of the Lower East Side, filled with unique shops, bars, and restaurants.

A neon pink restaurant shed, covered in colorful graffiti, stands out. That is, until Sticky Rice, with all its multicolored paper globes hanging from the tree in front, comes into view. A red cloth triangle awning stretches out to the tree like a magic red carpet. All those bright colors never fail to cheer me up.

Holiday decorations already entice from the store windows. A lit-up snowman occupies one window, while a garland of blue and white balls frames another entrance. All my Christmas decorations are in our basement storage room. Originally my plan was to have my own place by the New Year, but now I've cancelled tomorrow's appointment to look at apartments.

My family's bar is on the first floor of a building about a third of the way down the block, next to Café Katja. Up ahead is the bar's blinking neon sign. As I walk in the front door, the warmth envelopes me, and the low buzz of conversations punctuated by laughter gives it a happy vibe. One garland is already looped up on the wooden bar. Dad must have hung it.

I breathe in the welcoming scent of pine and apple cider. That smell of dry ice from last night's concert is gone. It's not like I can ask my dad to stop using dry ice, but it brings back memories of Patrick and those first weeks when we were falling in love as I watched him performing on stage, emerging from billowy dry ice clouds. But the love—like those clouds—was just an illusion. My dad swears dry ice has no smell, but it definitely does for me. I take another deep breath of the balsam-scented air.

Christmas music plays, adding to the festive cheer. The bar is crowded—as expected on a Friday evening at seven p.m. My dad is pulling pints. He still loves pitching in and chatting with everyone. I make my way to the bar, through the patrons milling about, drinks in hand.

"Any of my friends here yet?" I ask.

"Tessa and Bella," he says. "They're in the basement fetching the decorations. You should also find the fake belly pillow in the Santa costume box. It's nice of you to dress up as a pregnant woman."

"Great." I make my way through the crowd and open the door next to the bar that leads into a hallway. It's relatively quiet in here, the bar noise muted by the thick walls. Upstairs is our living space. I open another door and head down the steep stairs to the basement. I can hear Tessa and Bella laughing.

The basement is well-lit, as a working part of our bar/restaurant where all the deliveries are received and stored. It even has one of those metal gravity conveyer belts to deliver supplies down from the street. As a kid, I thought it was the coolest thing.

Tessa, a tall woman with blonde hair, and Bella, shorter with riotously curly black hair and glasses, stand between banks of iron shelving in the back of the storage area. They've located the three boxes labeled *Bar Xmas decorations*. We hug hello.

"Maddie and Lily are coming too," I say. "We probably have more people than we need." I open the Santa costume box and pull out the fake pillow.

"Well, when your dad offers a free dinner, you know we're all showing up," Tessa says. "This event always feels like the unofficial start of the holiday season."

"How's your latest book coming along?" I ask Bella, who is a romantic comedy writer. "I need a feel-good book right about now."

"I'm stuck." Bella pushes her red-framed glasses up her nose. "I can't decide about the second lead. Should he be perfect? Or clearly no candidate for her affection?"

"No triangle," Tessa says. "I hate second-lead syndrome. I get so sad when the guy I like—the one who has no red flags—gets passed over. And I definitely didn't like it when I thought I might be the second lead in my own romance with Zeke, although maybe I did have some red flags, but only if you didn't know the context."

Bella pats Tessa on the back.

This is my goal for the new year—only green flag guys.

"But it does create tension if the second lead is perfect and you wonder if the protagonist might go for him," Bella says, twisting one of her curly strands uncertainly.

"I'm here," Lily yells out from the top of the stairs.

"We're coming up," I say.

Tessa and Bella each pick up a box, and I stick the pillow on top of the third bin. We meet Lily at the top of the stairs, and I leave the pillow on the steps that lead upstairs for pick-up later. We proceed single file through the narrow hallway back into the bar.

"That shirt is perfect for a librarian," I say. Lily is wearing a shirt that says *Books are a Uniquely Portable Magic.*

"I'm getting quite a collection. They're perfect to wear to work." Lily pulls me aside. "That guy I wanted to set you up with—he came in to the library with a girlfriend. They were holding hands while reading." Lily pouts.

"That's okay—but so cute, right? You and Rupert should double-date with them."

She playfully punches me. "I want to sextuple-date with you and all my girlfriends and their guys."

"We're getting there," I say.

"Should we do the windows first?" Lily asks. "Or wait for the guys?"

I say, "It's only going to get colder. Best to do it now."

Lily lifts the two stepladders my dad left by the table as Tessa grabs the box of snowflake decals. I carry the garlands through the bar—with some good-natured ribbing from some of the regulars.

"Watch out! A tree fairy is coming through," one yells from his barstool.

"At least she's not carrying a hawthorn tree," yells another, "with the fairies gathered round waiting to abduct a human who's caught their fancy."

"Be careful with what you say," I reply, "or I might just hang the mistletoe above your barstools."

They both laugh.

At the front window, Tessa is supervising the application of snowflake decals to make sure we get proper coverage—unlike the very uneven arrangement we ended up with in the Accounting Department.

"Hey," Maddie says.

Maddie made it. I hug her tightly with my one free arm, the other still full of garlands. Maddie's reporter schedule can be similar to mine, with the sudden need to work long hours covering a story in her case, or in mine, responding to a cybersecurity incident.

After wrapping fairy lights around the garland, I hand one end to Tessa and the other to Lily. They're standing on stepladders at either end of the window. The shabby chic wooden letters spelling "JOY" look great in the window. We all go outside to admire our handiwork.

The front window finished, we gather at the table to make festive centerpieces for each table. "All I Want for Christmas" plays over the sound system.

As I'm winding fairy lights around a little tree and hiding the battery in a gift box at the bottom, I look up to see Sebastian arrive with Rupert and Zeke.

His glance meets mine, and I flush. His blue scarf brings out the color of his eyes. Hopefully my friends didn't see my reaction, given his committed single status.

"Hope you don't mind that I tagged along," Sebastian says to me. "I thought you might want someone who's not part of a couple. Plus, Rupert insisted."

Lily is definitely matchmaking.

"Definitely," I say. "The more, the merrier."

We put the men to work hanging the snowflakes from the ceiling and stringing fairy lights.

We finish making centerpieces and distribute them to each table. Tessa hangs an elf laundry line, filled with little green trousers and jackets attached with red wooden clips, on the front side wall.

The last project involves hanging the mistletoe.

"Sebastian, you should hang it," Rupert says, "so you know where it is and can avoid it at the next concert. I'm willing to be the test case underneath." Rupert pulls Lily next to him and kisses the top of her head.

"As if you need mistletoe." Sebastian takes the mistletoe and turns to me. "Where do you usually hang it?"

"By the bar in the front corner by the window," I say. "I'll show you. I can hold the ladder steady."

Sebastian follows me to the front. He climbs up the ladder and hangs the mistletoe on the hook conveniently left from last year. He steps down.

As he stands close to me, I whisper, "Have you heard the rumors about how badly the company is doing?"

He nods. "You?"

"Twice today," I say. "From my boss and Accounting."

"Accounting too? That's not good."

"Has Ernest said anything?" I ask.

"Ernest initially said the last two movies were flops, but we could weather that storm financially. I understand the negative attitude is recent—and the pressure is coming from France."

"That's my understanding too," I say. "So much for the infusion of cash."

"But do you know of problems anywhere else within the company?" Sebastian's blue eyes look concerned. "Bob seemed concerned about something, but he gave no details."

I bite my lip. Do I share that we've had an increase in intruder attacks—and the latest, most suspicious intrusion? He is the company lawyer, so Raphael must have informed the General Counsel—Bob—if not Sebastian.

"Someone tripped two of my traps today. A hacker was in the system. Raphael told Kevin today, but Kevin didn't think it required an all-hands-on-deck reaction."

"The impression Bob gave me was that people did something stupid in response to a threat," he says.

"Thanks," I say. "We definitely haven't done anything stupid in response. But Kevin didn't want us to hire an outside forensic team and didn't want us *both* working on it—which *is* a stupid response. Raphael and I are fully on it."

"I didn't mean that." He flushes. "That was a poor choice of words on my part."

"Sebastian, you're losing your touch." Rupert grabs several pitchers of beer from the bar. "You're standing right under the mistletoe."

"It's his subconscious at work," Zeke says, holding a tray of drinks, "saying 'save me from my single status.'"

Sebastian looks up at the mistletoe hanging right above his head and blushes sheepishly.

"I'm just trying to protect Iris and me from all your public displays of affection," Sebastian says gamely.

"But you haven't moved. Do you want a kiss on the cheek?" Zeke asks.

"Definitely not from you," Sebastian says.

"I'll kiss you—on the cheek," I say.

Sebastian's glance meets mine, and my pulse picks up, my body fizzing.

"I must have been good this year," he says, his lips curving up.

"Or very bad," I say.

He smiles. *A mischievous Sebastian would be a lot of fun.*

"No, I definitely must have been good," he says.

He stands very still, his arms at his sides, as I take a step towards him and lean forward. Our glances hold as I get closer. It feels like he's holding himself in check. I swallow. His eyes focus on my lips, and the warmth of his exhale brushes my cheek. His breath smells of mint. My lips press against his smooth skin, and I'm enveloped in the pine and fresh cold air scent of him. And then I pull back. For a moment, it's just us, gazing at each other, and for me, questioning, wondering—*is there something here?*

The sound of a distant siren slices through this...moment. I step back but also pull him with me—away from the mistletoe. All these sparkly lights are going to my head.

"Now we've broken in the mistletoe," I say.

Maddie walks by to go outside, pointing to her phone. She must be working on an article for *The Intelligencer*. My dad announces that our dinner is ready.

We swarm the table, and I make sure to sit far away from Sebastian. My father comes out with the stew. I stand to help, but he motions for me to sit back down.

Did Sebastian feel anything?

Maybe.

But...

My stomach churns.

The thought of starting another relationship and being betrayed again... I can't.

"Are you in charge of the games for your sister's party tomorrow?" Tessa asks.

"Of course," I say.

Maddie finally comes in from outside and sits down next to me. People often mistake us for sisters. She also lives on the Lower East Side, so we hang out the most—or we did. It feels like my friendships are slipping away as I give in to the demands of my career and put in the time to be the best I can be.

"Are you organizing one of your amazing scavenger hunts?" Maddie asks.

"One quick neighborhood scavenger hunt just on this block, and then we'll play Icebreaker Bingo," I say. "Everyone has to mingle and ask personal questions to find the person who best fits the description in a square. For example, a square could say 'someone who has a dog' and you have to find that person to cross that square off."

The rich smell of chicken tomato stew makes my stomach rumble. Tessa is ladling servings into bowls.

"By the way, my little sibling from the Dream Big Brothers Big Sisters program mentioned that her high school doesn't have a library and she'd like to build one. They're supposed to have one under New York City law, but there's no funding for a librarian," I say to Lily. "Does your library ever give away books to school libraries?"

"I can ask. Sometimes we sell books that are donated to us," Lily says. "I think it may be best to partner with another public school. I've seen that be successful."

"I'll donate my books," Bella says. Tessa volunteers Miranda, our artist friend, to create a poster and a small painting to raffle off to buy new books.

"That would be great. We can put up a poster here requesting donations of used YA books for that library," I say. "And I can also put some up at the office. I'm sure our CEO, Xavier, will support it, even if the company can't donate right now."

"Since we're requesting only new books for the holiday gift drive for the neighborhood kids in need and for the women's shelter near us, I can put your poster up and add a box for used book donations in the library," Lily says.

"Thank you guys so much." I blink back a stray tear. I'm touched by everyone's willingness to pitch in. I knew they would, but I've missed being with them—and this cozy feeling.

"Faith is going to be thrilled," I say. "She's obsessed with Booktube. I'm getting her an embosser with a "Read by Faith" stamp from Etsy for Christmas."

Rupert's head picks up. "Do you have one of those, Lily?"

"No. That's a great gift for a bookworm," Lily says.

I glance at Sebastian. "Yes, if only my Secret Snowflake was a bookworm too."

"Didn't you like the socks Rupert gave you, Lily?" Sebastian asks.

"I love them. They're very cozy. I'm wearing them right now," Lily says.

Sebastian smirks at me. I tip my head in acknowledgment. Point for him. I take another bite of my chicken stew.

"That kiss... Is there something between you two?" Maddie whispers.

I nearly choke on my food. Uh-oh. There's a reason Maddie is such a good reporter.

I shake my head.

She gives me a disbelieving glance, her eyebrows raised.

"Your stew is going to get cold," I say to her.

Dad's stew is good enough to distract anyone, even a reporter like Maddie. The conversation turns to everybody's favorite December activities, like Lily's cookie party. Most of us avoid the Rockefeller Center area like the plague because it's so crowded with tourists.

Zeke whispers something to Sebastian—while glancing at me—and Sebastian shakes his head. I miss whatever is being discussed about this year's shop windows.

"The trick is to go early," Maddie is saying.

There's barely anything left of the stew, which pleases my dad to no end. He loves it when people devour his cooking.

"Should I clear the tables for dancing?" my dad asks.

As we stand to clear the dishes, Sebastian thanks my dad for dinner and says he has to go.

"I promised my mom I'd watch a movie with her tonight," he says. He doesn't even look my way as he says this.

Another guy tied to his mom? Interesting.

"See?" I whisper to Maddie. "Nothing is going on."

"Except that he came all the way down here—and your dad's food is good, but I'm sure his mom would've served him dinner," Maddie says.

Fair point.

"Isn't he the one who loves being single? I think he's running now because he's scared," Maddie says, her head tilted. "Under the mistletoe, he was definitely looking at you like he wanted something more than a kiss on the cheek."

Chapter Seven

Iris

My phone beeps.

> **Maddie:** *I still think there could be something between you two.*

So much for Maddie believing me last night when I said I'd sworn off types like Sebastian.

Three dresses from my sisters lay strewn on my bed, and two more hang over the closet door—one with ruffles. What was Rose thinking? My latest outfit—a black top and jeans, which would have been my go-to outfit—didn't make the fake pregnancy belly look real. The black top is too thin. I need a dress with a thicker fabric. I should have never agreed to dress up as a pregnant woman so Dahlia wasn't the only pregnant woman at her party. Rose dropped off a selection of her maternity clothes yesterday—mostly the ones Dahlia didn't borrow for her own pregnancy—but these outfits make me look like a bear in hibernation, which is probably why Dahlia didn't take them. I finally settle on a blue dress that actually looks good when I try it on. It doesn't look quite as great with my black sneakers, but I'm planning to win some of the party games tonight, so sneakers it is.

Fatma is sniffing the clothes and looks like she is about to curl up for a nap on top of one dress. I move them to the side so she has her own space on my bed. My room is in the top of our house, in the back overlooking the garden.

I pick up my phone to text Maddie—that maybe there's something between her and Nick—when my phone rings.

"I desperately need breast milk storage bags. Can you do me a huge favor and stop by Baby Love on the way to Dahlia's party and pick some up for me?" It's my sister Rose.

"Okay," I say.

"You're a lifesaver. I'll text you a picture of what I want."

Fatma has now curled up right in the middle of all the clothes on my bed, completely disregarding the space cleared for her. Of course. I'm going to have to remove all the cat hair before I return these to Rose.

As I ENTER BABY Love, I blink. *Is that Sebastian standing near a whole bunch of pregnant women?*

It definitely is. Some saleswoman seems be giving a product presentation, and he's listening intently—with an I'm-so-out-of-my-comfort-zone expression on his face. I stifle a laugh.

Oh no. *I look like I'm six months pregnant.* I really should have thought this through. Our bar and block are safe, but wandering around the city looking like a pregnant woman is a different story.

I need to slip by without his noticing me—but the product presentation has been set up smack in the center so I have to go through it to get to the rest of the store. If only I had a massive scarf or some way to hide my face. I could pull my coat up to hide my face, but that would probably only attract attention. This pregnancy coat makes me look like a huge bear. I might have to brazen it out and pretend I'm carrying a backpack under my coat.

"Iris!"

Too late. I've been caught. Sebastian is jogging over.

"Iris. Wow. I'm glad to see you here." He looks down at me and his eyes widen, his brow furrowing, but he snaps his glance back to my face, manfully covering up his obvious confusion.

He continues, "I have no idea what to get Anita, and there's a scavenger hunt competition at two. But I need a partner who actually knows something about babies. Maybe we can win something for Anita."

No. Hanging out with Sebastian is not a good idea. Especially when I'm attracted to him.

He's not my type anymore. I'm looking for a nice guy who doesn't give off rakish vibes. Who doesn't make me think he's a lot of fun when he's mischievous.

"Did I shock you into silence?" Sebastian asks, a teasing note in his voice. "I've certainly never stepped foot in here before." He makes a *tss* sound like he's just been burned by a hot flame.

He is Mr. Single.

He takes another quick glance at my middle area and wrinkles his brow. How can I explain this? I should say no to hanging out and not explain. Just leave him wondering why I'm dressed like I'm about to go on an Artic expedition.

"I can't do it alone," he says. "I don't know anything about babies. Two hours of your time. Tops. This is a huge opportunity to win something big for Anita without spending more than the thirty-dollar limit. That is ridiculously low. You promised you'd help me shop for her."

"I did promise. And I gave you my sister's baby shower list as gift suggestions."

"That's not the same as actually helping pick out stuff. And I repeat, two words: scavenger hunt. And you're here."

He obviously listened to what Maddie said last night. Still, I'm impressed he picked up so quickly that I'd totally be into a scavenger hunt. And I do want to figure him out. This is a perfect opportunity.

"Fine. But..." *How am I going to explain my belly?* "I'm dressed as a pregnant woman. My younger sister didn't want to be the only pregnant woman at her party because none of her friends are even considering having kids yet. Because they're all in their twenties." Dahlia has always known she wanted a big family. She babysat start-ing at twelve and now works as a daycare teacher. Her dream is to start her own daycare. "To be honest, it started out as a joke, but then Dahlia seemed really touched by the idea. And it seemed easy enough. We had the belly from when my brother played Santa Claus at our bar."

Dead silence greets my statement. And then finally, he says, "I don't understand. What do you mean?"

"I have a huge costume belly strapped to my abdomen. I look like I swallowed a pillow or a basketball or a baby elephant."

"A baby elephant is oddly specific," Sebastian says.

"It is. Maybe I just *feel* like I swallowed a baby elephant. And it's hard to get it to look right without the straps showing."

"That's perfect. We'll look that much more legitimate participat-ing in the scavenger hunt."

"What do you mean? Do you have to be pregnant to participate in the scavenger hunt?"

"No. I checked the rules, and you don't. But...this will just look better," he says.

"You don't mind that you'll be walking around with a pregnant woman?" I ask.

"Why would I have a problem walking around with a pregnant woman?"

"Someone may think you're the father."

"I'd take that as a compliment," he says. "But seriously, this will be perfect for the scavenger hunt."

"What if we run into friends of yours?"

"If I see any of my male friends shopping in Baby Love, they'd be the ones running to hide, not me. They would have some serious explaining to do."

Sebastian in casual weekend clothes is even more attractive than Sebastian in work clothes. He still looks so put-together. It makes me want to rumple him up.

Off-limits.

This is a work mission.

Definitely not a good choice.

I'm not ready for a new relationship.

Pregnant me will probably serve as quite a repellent. It's good that I'm dressed this way. I take off my coat.

"Wow. You really do look pregnant," Sebastian says.

"Yes, but I would have preferred the 'swallowed the basketball' pregnancy look. This looks more like I swallowed a beanbag," I say.

"No, it's a cute bump."

Oh, no... Now he thinks I was fishing for compliments. About my fake pregnancy bump. Because that's definitely what I want him to compliment. *Way to go, Iris.*

"Do you think you can move with that?" he asks. "We may need to hustle for the scavenger hunt."

"It's just a pillow. I can definitely keep up."

"I brought a backpack so we can stow our coats in there."

See? He's taking this very seriously.

Today is all about the scavenger hunt. And I like that. I'm competitive too. Patrick was a bit of a slacker at times, and that drove me nuts.

I shake my head.

Focus on the mission.

Sebastian shrugs off his coat and his sweater, revealing a T-shirt that shows off his muscular physique underneath. I can't believe he's just wearing some worn T-shirt. I force myself to stop staring at the actual muscle definition in his biceps. We're work colleagues. And friends. I sneak one last peek. Lily did mention that he was a champion squash player in college.

I take off my coat, and Sebastian stuffs it into his backpack with his sweater. It takes up so much room that he can't fit his own coat in as well.

"I can wear my coat," I say.

"No. Don't worry. Mine's pretty light." He ties it around his waist. "Your stomach looks so real. Wow. What is it made out of?"

"It's a really firm pillow. You can touch it. Crazy how real it looks, right?"

A tender expression passes over Sebastian's face as he touches, very gingerly, the pillow. Seeing his narrow fingers splayed on my "belly" definitely does something to my insides.

"Don't worry. I can't feel your touch," I say.

He blushes. Actually blushes.

"What?" I ask.

He shakes his head. "No. I just realized it would be something to bring a baby into this world."

He looks a little shell-shocked.

Poor Sebastian.

"Maybe you'll have to rethink your forever-single status?"

He raises his glance to mine. "Maybe." He looks down at his watch. "That sales lady said the competition kick-off is at the back of this first floor, by the toilets."

We walk to the back of the store. It's easy to spot the competition, such as it is. This definitely isn't some marathon with a bunch of lean running machines. It looks more like a penguin huddle. One woman looks like she could give birth any minute now. *Would that be good or bad publicity for Baby Love if someone gave birth during its scavenger hunt? And does employee job training include delivering babies?*

The saleswoman is giving instructions. "So figure out the clues, take a picture of yourself with your answer, and report back here in forty-five minutes. We've mixed up all the clues so that you shouldn't necessarily run into other contestants. And then we'll have the one-handed stroller opening contest."

"Are you sure we're allowed to compete when we're not pregnant?" I whisper to Sebastian.

"I checked the rules. There's no requirement to be pregnant. And we are competing on behalf of a pregnant woman who could use all this stuff. This is her first baby. And I don't think she and her husband make that much."

And what if Dream Company does close? Then she won't even have a paid maternity leave.

"On your mark. Get 'set. Go," the contest coordinator yells.

A determined look grips Sebastian's face. He rips open the envelope and reads the clue:

"*You're my very best friend, it's true! Doo doo doo doo, doo doo. Every day when I make my way to the___.*"

"What on earth," he says.

The look of shock on his face is priceless. I giggle.

"It's the rubber duckie song, from *Sesame Street*. It's a tub. C'mon, let's find the baby bathtubs and take a picture with them," I say.

"Of course. The rubber duckie song. If only I still had that on my playlist..."

"C'mon. No time for sarcasm."

"See, I knew you needed to come," Sebastian says. "I would have been thrown by this first clue."

We study the store map listing the department locations. I take a photo of it. Other couples head off.

"It's definitely an advantage if you've shopped here before and know the store layout," Sebastian says. The bathing section is on the second floor. We hurry up the stairs, passing another couple on the escalator.

"So did you ask Ernest my questions?" I ask as we get to the top.

"Yes," Sebastian says. "He likes chocolate in his cookies."

"Over there!" I point to the back of the store. A big rubber duck sign indicates the bathing section. We jog over there. "That's what you got?"

"He doesn't read or have any hobbies. Golf socks are the way to go," Sebastian says.

We skid to a stop in front of the tubs.

Sebastian holds up a plastic tub while I take his picture.

"You're grimacing," I say. "Smile."

"This is not a photo op," he says.

"You don't want to scare the sales associate," I say.

He makes a funny expression, and I snap the picture. He quickly puts back the tub and opens up the next clue.

"*What a bright time, it's the right time, to rock the night away. Jingle bell time, it's a swell time, to go gliding...*"

Sebastian asks, "Is there a holiday department?"

"One of those gliding rocking chairs. My sister swears by it." I check the map. "This way."

"You really are an expert," he says.

It's lucky that this is not a date, because my knowledge about babies and child-rearing would probably scare away even the most ardent admirer. He'd worry I want kids immediately.

Sebastian follows me as I weave through the various departments to bring us to the glider chair section. About twenty chairs are lined up in rows.

"Dinner at my parents' house is all about breastfeeding, potty training, and sleep training." *Stop talking about kids.* What am I do-ing? It's like this fake pregnancy belly has activated all my maternal desires.

"Does it make you feel left out?" he asks.

I glance at him, surprised at such a perceptive question.

"Sometimes. Mostly because I can't contribute to the conversation. And I'm envious that my sisters are sharing these experiences together. But I'm definitely *not* ready for children yet," I say. Phew. That should dispel all impressions to the contrary. "Especially if there's as little sleep involved as my sisters say. I need to be more established in my career. It's hard enough to be a woman in cybersecurity. I need to be in a more senior position with more control over my schedule before I have children. I'd like to actually see them."

Another couple is trying out the gliding chairs. The husband takes a picture of his wife reclining in the chair. We say hello.

"Your turn to be in the photo," Sebastian says.

I sink into the chair, which engulfs me like a Venus flytrap plant. My pregnancy belly rises, nearly smothering me. I try to push it down. Sebastian catches himself laughing and hands me his backpack to cover it. I stand quickly. He takes a selfie with the chair.

"Is it okay?" I ask, adjusting the belly.

"I'm not sure. It might be a little off," Sebastian says. "Let's move out of here discreetly and go behind that post over there so we can fix it."

I keep the backpack in front of me.

Sebastian puts his arm around me, walking close to block the sideview. His warmth and closeness give me a gooey feeling inside. A protected feeling. Sebastian does it so easily. It's so different from what it was like with Patrick. Sometimes Patrick forgot about me in the rush of greeting his fans. And Patrick was not that affectionate in public—he didn't, understandably, like having his love life dissected by fans and the media. Neither did I. Especially when someone posted a particularly unflattering photo of me. But he also acknowledged that he wanted to be respectful of his fans' feelings because some had crushes on him.

We pass by the other couple. The wife looks like she is about to take a nap in the rocking chair.

We move in tandem over to the mirrored pole. I put down the backpack.

"It's just a smidge off, don't you think?" I ask. I'm in front, Sebastian behind me in the reflection in the mirror, my dark hair contrasting with his blond. We look good together—almost like we are a couple. I rub my wrist, which has been giving twinges of pain lately, and adjust the pillow slightly.

"All good," Sebastian says.

We turn around to find another one of the competing couples.

"Oh, you guys are so tall and striking," the wife says. She stands next to a bouncy chair while her husband snaps a picture. "If you don't have this, I highly recommend it. We used it so often for our first. Is this your first?"

"Yes," we say in unison.

"How'd you guys meet?" She rubs her belly. "I just love hearing how people met."

I glance at Sebastian in consternation. *We didn't concoct a story.*

"We met at work," Sebastian says.

"Were there sparks immediately?" the woman asks.

I definitely thought he was attractive the first time I saw him.

As I'm about to say no, Sebastian says, "Definitely a spark, but we were work colleagues, so it took a bit of maneuvering. Good luck with the competition. Lovely to meet you."

"Well handled," I say. We walk away as Sebastian pulls out the next envelope.

"It's always best to stick as close to the truth as possible." He reads the next clue out loud.

Were there sparks for Sebastian when he first met me? The kernel of truth is probably just that we're work colleagues. I glance at his face, but he's opening the next envelope. He reads aloud the clue:

"*Nobody who did this Charleston dance in the 1940s ever ended up in the ER.*"

"What could that be? Should we google names of Charleston dances in the 1940s?" I ask.

"There's the Charleston stroll," said Sebastian. "Ending with ER, that would be a stroller."

"Good sleuthing. How do you know about the Charleston stroll?"

"Dance classes in high school. My mom said no son of hers was not going to know how to dance. I can't say I've found it incredibly useful yet, but at least I'm finally able to answer a clue on this scavenger hunt." He grins. He looks so boyish and happy.

"I'm sure your dancing skills have scored you points with women," I say.

Sebastian's lips curve up. "Maybe." He leans forward and whispers into my ear, "But I know not to kiss and tell."

I shiver as his breath tickles my neck. I refuse to let him see that he's affected me.

"I'm relieved to hear that." I change the subject. "My dad loves the waltz. We sometimes have waltz nights at the bar. Very crowded waltz nights. I hope they ask you to do the Charleston stroll at the end. As proof we didn't just google the answer."

"Maybe for bonus points?" Sebastian looked at her. "It's a lively dance, but it doesn't require a partner. I prefer dances with a partner."

He's definitely flirting. Which isn't fair.

He grabs my hand, and we race over to the stroller section. I take a picture of Sebastian behind a stroller. Wow. It's not that I want kids immediately, but he does look sexy wheeling around a baby buggy.

I rip open clue number 4.

"*You used to cuddle with your husband, but now you cuddle with this.*"

"That's rather depressing," Sebastian says. "What could that be? Is that the baby?"

"No, it's a pregnancy support pillow. What section of the store do you think that will be in?"

"Bedding and décor?"

"It's harder figuring out the location than figuring out the clues," I say.

"Speak for yourself. I would have had to google almost everything, and I would've never figured out this one," Sebastian says.

"Let's ask an associate."

The sales associate directs us to the maternal accessories section. We jog over there. I hold up the body pillow. The snakelike pillow shaped like an upside-down U is two-thirds of my height.

Sebastian looks stunned. "Is there even any room for the guy in the bed once that's in there?"

Sebastian in my bed, those blue eyes staring into mine...

I swallow. "Not much. It's good training for getting used to sleeping on the couch, in the crib, or in the car. It's musical mattresses. My older sister showed me how she can actually curl herself into the crib sometimes. But now they've bought a bed. They went to the mattress store with their six-year-old, four-year old, and the baby, and they asked for an extra-long twin mattress. The sales associate asked who it was for, and they pointed to the four-year old. And then they explained that it needed to be extra-long so her husband can fit in the bed as well. I don't know how they do it. I really need my sleep." I'm blabbering. *Idiot.*

"Me too," Sebastian says. He takes a photo of me with it, and as he adjusts his backpack on his shoulder, his shirt rides up, showing very trim abs.

"Got it," he says.

I hope he didn't catch me leering at his stomach.

"I had no idea. This scavenger hunt is like a crash course in parenting," Sebastian says. "Maybe they should've limited it to actual pregnant people before they scared the non-pregnant off. Anyway, next clue." He opens the envelope and reads the clue.

"*Throw your heart over the **fence** and the rest will follow. Or safety first?*"

"These are such odd clues. But the word 'fence' is bolded, so that's the key word. Playpen? Safety gates?" Sebastian asks.

"That clue is kind of poetic. Let's go with safety gates, because that incorporates safety *and* a fence."

We answer the rest of the clues and report back to the saleswoman at the entrance to the store. Another couple is there already, but we still might have a shot at placing for one of the top three prizes if our answers are correct. We hand in our sheet and show our photos. The store manager checks off our answers. She hands us a gift bag just for participating. It's filled with helpful products, so Sebastian is basically set for gifts.

We sit down and wait for the rest of the participants to return.

"That was fun," I say.

"Thank you for doing it with me," he says. "I thought you'd like it since you like organizing scavenger hunts. What is the scavenger hunt you organized for your sister's party?"

"I picked some of my favorite things about our block, like the colorful paper balls outside Sticky Rice and the metal sign of a stag rearing up outside Café Katya. When I was little, my dad used to tell me it was Rudolph the Red-Nosed Reindeer's dad. And I'm sure you saw the bright neon graffitied sidewalk shed. So I made up some clues, with those landmarks as the answers."

"You should organize a scavenger hunt for Rupert and Lily with book themes. That would be perfect for their engagement party," Sebastian says.

Rupert must be planning to propose soon.

"That's such a good idea. I'll have to think about how to do it," I say.

We place second and win a $25 Baby Love gift card.

"I'll give this to Anita. Meanwhile, I'll buy her some other gifts under the thirty-dollar limit," Sebastian says. "Do you have any suggestions for something not on her registry? I'd like to be more original than that."

"I was sure you were going to buy some socks," I say, teasing.

His mouth tips up at the corner. "Socks are always a good gift."

"Books are also always a good gift," I say.

Sebastian decides to buy a few books plus some socks, especially because he can buy a bunch and stay within the thirty-dollar limit. I pick up the breast milk storage bags for my sister.

"What's your favorite children's book?" he asks.

"*Corduroy*," I say.

"Corduroy, huh? You liked the little bear finding a home?"

"Even though he was missing a button." I glance at him, my brow furrowed. "I'm not sure you should read too much into it."

"Well, we're all looking for someone to accept us, faults and all."

"But I always buy *The Book with No Pictures* as a gift. It's hilarious to read aloud because it requires the adult to make all sorts of funny noises."

"I'll buy both, then," Sebastian says.

We join the line to check out.

"I signed up for Big Brothers Big Sisters," Sebastian says. "I'll meet my little sibling this week. Thanks for suggesting it."

"That's great," I say. "It's one of my favorite activities. I signed up when I saw how much fun Jazmine was having. And now she's roped me into helping decorate their gym for the winter dance."

"I'd be happy to do that too," Sebastian says.

"Are you sure?" I say, teasing. "Can I text her right now?"

"No."

"You're already out?"

"No, I'm in. But don't text her right now, or she'll wonder what we're doing together."

What are *we doing together?*

"I have a feeling she won't think we're just two friends hanging out," Sebastian says.

There's my answer. *Just two friends hanging out.*

Sebastian pays for his Secret Snowflake gifts. As the cashier hands us our receipt, a voice calls Sebastian's name.

"Looks like there *is* someone you know at Baby Love," I say.

Sebastian turns around and then turns back to me quickly. "Oh, no. The building gossip. Unbelievable."

"Sebastian, is that you?" A distinguished-looking elderly woman walks up to us, her head swinging back and forth to take in both of us—and my belly. "Sebastian, your parents never mentioned you were married."

"It was very sudden." Sebastian puts his arm around me and pulls me close. "But Mrs. Pinok, let me introduce you to my wife, Iris."

My mouth drops open, but I quickly close it.

"Your wife," she repeats.

"My wife."

Sebastian's wife.

Tingly... *No, stop it*. Nope. We're friends.

His hand rubs my arm, and his body is so warm next to mine. I don't dare look at him, afraid I might reveal that his words definitely affected me.

"You're about to become a father?" she adds with a pointed look at my belly.

"Hello." I hold out my hand. Mrs. Pinok shakes it. "Nice to meet you."

"My parents can't wait to be grandparents," Sebastian says. I look at him in surprise.

"Oh, yes, well, there's nothing more exciting than grandchildren," Mrs. Pinok says. "Well, congratulations."

"Anyway, we're late for a party." Sebastian removes his arm from around me—*no! why?*—and pulls my coat and his sweater out of his backpack.

As Mrs. Pinok says good-bye, we both put on our coats. He places his hand in the small of my back. We wave good-bye and exit the store. Sebastian chuckles.

As soon as we're down the block, I ask, "Why did you tell her I was your wife?"

"Did you want me to explain to the building gossip that you're wearing a fake pregnancy belly and we're competing in a scavenger hunt to win gifts for our pregnant colleague?"

"No. But if she gossips..."

Sebastian shrugs. "How interested can anyone in the building be? It would be most exciting for my family. My parents would be thrilled if I were married and having a baby. Unfortunately, neither my sister nor I are dating."

I say, "I can't believe you just let your neighbor think I was pregnant."

Sebastian grins. "You have to admit that her shocked expression was pretty priceless."

"But what are you going to tell your mom?"

"My mom will get a kick out of it. I don't think she likes Mrs. P. much anyway. How old are your sister's kids? What we need to do next is borrow one of them and ride the elevator in my building."

I laugh. "My sister would be grateful for the babysitting, but we'd probably have to borrow all three."

"Great, we can just tell Mrs. P. that you have children from a previous marriage but that my mom is delighted by all the grandchildren."

I laugh.

"And what happens when you meet your real wife?" I stumble over the words *real wife*. "And then she runs into Mrs. Pinok, who tells her about your prior pregnant wife."

Sebastian stares at me. "That's quite a scenario you came up with there on the fly. I don't think we need to worry about that. I'm not planning on getting married anytime soon. And I'll figure out something to tell Mrs. P. before that happens. Do you feel better now?"

"Yes," I say.

Sebastian bites his lip. "I'll tell her we were doing market research as a fake dating couple for a Hallmark-style romantic comedy Dream is producing."

"Okay," I say slowly. "There's a lot to unpack in how quickly you came up with that. And how do you know about Hallmark romantic comedies?"

Sebastian shakes his head. "Why does everyone always ask me that? My mom watches them. I bet Mrs. P. does too, even if she would never admit to it."

Sebastian reaches out and tucks down my collar. "So, you're heading off to your sister's now? I can't persuade you to grab a cup of hot chocolate as a thank-you?"

As I reach up to smooth my collar, our hands touch, and that shiver of awareness jolts me again.

And then I hear myself saying, "Do you want to stop by my sister's party? It's at my parents' bar. It's only a few stops away."

No. No. This is not a good idea. But we're friends.

"Sure, I'd love to drop by. It's generous of you to dress as a pregnant woman for your sister. You have two sisters?"

"And a brother. My older sister said she wants to drink and she doesn't want to be pregnant again, ever, even fake."

We stand at the corner, waiting for the light to change.

"What about you? Any siblings?"

"My younger sister Annabelle," he says. "Let me just call my mom and warn her I told Mrs. Pinok my wife is pregnant."

As Sebastian calls his mom, we cross the street so we're now in Union Square Park. It's already dusk at 4:30, and the metal benches sit empty by the forlorn patches of grass. Across the street is an imposing building with columns that probably used to house a bank. But what's most distinctive about 44 Union Square is the glass dome on top, which is supposed to represent a turtle. It looks just like my pregnant belly.

Sebastian smiles at me as he chats to his mom. "Hi, Mom. I'm at Baby Love to pick up a gift for my Secret Snowflake. Anyway, Iris, one of Lily's friends, agreed to do the store scavenger hunt with me, and she's dressed as a pregnant woman. And Mrs. Pinok saw us. So I said Iris was my wife, and now she thinks you have a grandchild on the way."

His eyes light up. I wish I could hear his mother's reaction.

We walk towards the subway entrance, the glowing green ball on top of the pole indicating it's open. Sebastian pulls his coat tighter.

"Yes, I may have let her think that." He explains his market research cover idea. "Iris is fun. She works at Dream with me. She's in cybersecurity." He stops at the top of the staircase leading down into the entrance. "Okay, Mom, I have to go. I just wanted to give you a heads-up. We're entering the subway."

His mother says something more on the phone.

"No, Mom. I'm sure she has plans." Sebastian turns to me. "She wants to invite you to our family holiday celebration. It's December 14."

Chapter Eight

Sebastian

Iris is definitely tipsy. Her glass looks like it is filled with orange juice, but apparently it's not without alcoholic content. She's dancing with her sister in the back of the bar near the stage, waving her hands and singing at the top of her lungs. She keeps reaching down to fix her prosthetic pregnancy belly. It looks lopsided once again, like she really is carrying an octopus who slid sideways. The tables have all been cleared to the sides. A happy haze has enveloped the bar.

I sit next to her great-aunt, taking a break. She is very stylishly dressed, looks to be about eighty, and seemed sweet. Not a smart move. She can drink me under the table. I'm definitely feeling the effects of too much alcohol.

As she sips the second vodka gimlet she's ordered since I've been sitting here—I said "no more" for me—she says, "Darling, we used to have martinis at lunch and go back to work. Your generation has no idea."

Iris is back.

"Sebastian!" Iris grabs my hands.

"This one is a very good one, Iris," her aunt Viola says. "You should hold on to him."

Iris leans into me, and her soft hair brushes against my cheek. I can smell the flowery scent of her shampoo. I put out my hand to touch a strand but pull back just in time. I blink. I need to order a coffee or something.

"Shh," Iris whispers loudly. "Sebastian is not mine. Sebastian is a monk."

"He's a monk?" Viola's eyes widen, and she looks at me in horror.

Iris nods very seriously. Very exaggerated. And she leans in. "Why are you a monk, Sebastian?"

"Why are you hanging out with a monk, Iris?" her aunt says. "There are so many men in the sea. Go enjoy your youth. I'm worried about you. You're pretending to be pregnant. You're here with a monk. Darling, what's going on? Don't give up on men just because of one bad apple." Viola now has her hands on Iris's cheeks.

"I'm not a monk," I say.

"He's not a monk, Iris." Viola slips off her stool. "I'm going to let you two talk. Give me that pregnancy pillow. It's not doing you any favors."

"I'm not taking if off in public." Iris leans back against my leg. And I want to pull her onto my lap.

"A coffee. Strong," I say urgently to the bartender.

"And I'm wearing it because Dahlia asked me too. Although I think all her friends are thrilled to be aunties."

"He says he's not a monk. I'm sure he's seen a stomach before." Her aunt has that pregnancy pillow off in a matter of seconds. She winks at me. "I used to sell clothes. I'm very good at undressing and dressing women—and men." Her aunt sashays over to a table of older men in the corner.

Iris is still leaning against my leg, but then she plops down on the bar stool left vacant by her aunt.

She drops her elbow on the bar and rests her head on her hand and stares at me. "Who broke your heart?"

"My best friend." I rest my head on my hand, mirroring her position.

She frowns. "That's not a very nice best friend."

"Right?" I ask. "I thought we were perfect for each other, but she didn't."

"Did you date?"

"We dated for about six months, and then Melody said she just wanted to be friends. That she thought we worked better as friends and she wanted to keep me as her friend."

"Oh. I'm sorry."

"I still don't understand. We had the best time together. I felt like we were completely in sync. How could she think there was a relationship out there that would be better?" I pause and take a deep breath. "Still, seeing her choose Wim as her fiancé definitely made me realize we were *not* quite as in sync as I thought."

I also am not quite sure why I'm telling Iris all this, but it seems safe somehow. And it feels better to get it out. It's not like I want to discuss it again with Zeke and Rupert. They've heard it all before. Once. When she first broke up with me. And we all got drunk at my place.

"Do you still like her?"

"Yes." I shrug. "Getting over it."

"That's hard."

My mouth dips down, and I look away. "It's brutal. But I'll be happy for her." I shake my head.

Iris just gazes at me, her brown-flecked green eyes melting my defenses.

"But it's not like we have the same relationship anymore. I'm a friend now, and I'm definitely second place to her fiancé. Obviously. I'm coming to terms with it." I down the coffee the bartender serves me.

"And you haven't dated anyone since?" she asks.

"I have, but I didn't feel that same about them—and then, breaking up is brutal. It's not like I *like* telling someone I don't want to date anymore."

"Hmm." Iris's gaze is so soft.

"Have you dated anyone since Patrick?"

She shakes her head, and a shadow crosses over her face.

I want to make that shadow disappear. I shift on the hard wooden bar stool.

"So now you can definitely tell me what you were going to say when you hoisted me through the window?" she asks.

"No. I can't," I say.

"But aren't we more than work colleagues now?" she asks.

"Yes, but we're friends. And what I thought was..." Definitely inappropriate. Definitely not in the friend territory.

She leans forward. "Was?"

Rose comes up. "It's time for the games to start—while the DJ takes a break."

"You were saved by Rose." Iris stands. "I don't know what Elban was putting in my orange juice, but I definitely think he's making them way too strong. I need a glass of water. Do you want one?" She goes behind the bar and pours one for each of us. She rings a bell hanging from the side of the bar, which causes everyone to stop talking, and then she turns on a microphone. "Let's give a hurray for the happy couple." The crowd cheers. "And now let's start the games. The scavenger hunt is outside, so take the clue sheets by the door and go for it. The cold should sober us all up."

We all grab our coats.

"I can't compete because I know all the answers," Iris says, "but you could do it."

"I'd rather hang out with you," I say. "And you already told me some of the clues, so maybe we can just walk down the street and you can give me a personal tour."

We walk side by side down the street.

The chill is definitely sobering me up. I pull up my collar. My ears are freezing.

She shows me the metal stag outside Café Katja and the colorful globes outside Sticky Rice.

"What's great about this block is that all the family businesses look out for one another, kind of an 'all for one, one for all' dynamic," she says.

"That's special—and rare," I say.

"Do you think so?" she asks, turning to face me. The soft glow from the streetlight frames her face. Her huge eyes look both quizzical and sad.

"Yes. That's definitely not what happened in my family business between the other founder's son and me. His attitude was more 'all for me,'" I say, the bitterness still evident in my voice.

"What happened?"

"I worked there after college, and I reconnected with Nathan, the son of my dad's partner, but I thought he was still the kid I played with on weekends in the office while our dads were working. And the thing is—he was still that kid. I'd dismissed as innocent the fact that when we were ten, he suggested we raid the company pantry. We found these amazing desserts and ate them. My dad was so angry with me—he'd ordered those specially for an employee celebration." My gut clenches. That shame. *Why am I telling this story?* I cringe. "I felt terrible, and I thought Nathan felt the same. And I forfeited my allowance for weeks to pay for the new cakes. But I learned my lesson that company property was definitely not mine for the taking."

"What happened when you reconnected?"

I turn away. This story really doesn't reflect well on me. But it's also made me a better lawyer—because I want to figure out the truth and not trust first impressions.

"Nathan definitely had not learned that lesson. We were all working on a deal late at night, and he said he'd take us out for drinks to celebrate our finishing. But the bartender accidentally handed me the receipt after Nathan paid, and I saw this other employee's name listed. It looked like he'd used Emil's corporate card. I confronted him. He said he'd grabbed the wrong card by accident, and he'd pay it back and clear it up. I believed him."

"But he didn't?" Iris asks.

"No. I overheard Emil in my father's office denying that he had used the company's corporate card, and I backed him up. That was also when I realized I wanted to be a lawyer. I found past expense reports signed by Nathan to show that was Nathan's signature on the receipt. Nathan had submitted the receipt as a corporate expense, pretending to be Emil, but I followed up with IT and they were able to prove that Emil wasn't logged in at that time. Apparently, Emil had complained about Nathan's lack of a work ethic, and Nathan wanted him out."

"That's great. You saved the day."

"But I almost didn't. I should have known."

"But you did step in in time," she says firmly, almost as if she knows how much I've regretted trusting Nathan. "What happened to Nathan?"

"His dad told him he was out until he could show he'd grown up. He took that as a win that he didn't have to work in an office for the rest of the summer."

"He sounds like Hank."

Dahlia rushes up with her answers.

"I made this too easy," Iris says as she checks them off.

"No. It was perfect. A trip down memory lane." Dahlia hugs her. The sister resemblance is unmistakable. She has the same silky brown hair and green eyes.

"I heard you saw the cat pawprint underwear," Dahlia says.

"Meet Dahlia," Iris says. "We give each other silly gifts every year. That was last year's Christmas gift."

"Great gift," I say.

"Well, let's see if you like this year's gift." Dahlia grins.

Iris swats at her playfully. "Don't mind her," she says.

We all pile back inside the bar. Iris turns on the microphone again.

"The next game is Icebreaker Bingo. I'll hand out the sheets. When I ring the bell, you can start. The first one with five in a row wins the prize. You can only use a person once as an answer, and that person has to sign your card." Iris hands out the sheets to all her sister's friends and then rings the bell to signal the start of the games. "Go!"

I scan my sheet.

"I'm putting you down for 'is single.' You can put me down for the same," she says. "Everyone else may be paired up here except for Uncle Harvey over there." An older man sits snoring in the corner, a green tasseled pillow under his head, very close to where I hung the mistletoe. I definitely won't be going near him.

"What about your aunt?" I ask.

"If she is, she's not going to admit to it. I think she always has an admirer on hand."

"Let's do it together," I say. "We need 'speaks another language.' That's Arjan, Dahlia's husband, or any of his Dutch friends here."

Iris grins at me. "Sharp."

We join the circle of friends around Arjan, and he writes his name in the blank square. There's a lot of good-natured joking and camaraderie. This feeling of warmth from Iris's family reminds me of my own. Melody's family does not give off the same warmth, especially her mother. That one Thanksgiving dinner I attended was an extremely formal affair. I brought flowers, but they didn't match the color scheme, so Melody swooped in and put them in the second bathroom. They weren't even good enough for the first bathroom. After Melody broke up with me, Rupert tried to console me by saying, "At least you avoided her mom as a mother-in-law."

"'Kills houseplants' is Rose, my older sister, or her best friend," Iris says.

"My younger sister is the same," I say. "My mom has learned to give her only succulents." Annabelle would like Iris.

We ask Rose to sign our card, and she asks Iris to sign hers as a cat person.

"Definitely. Fatma will be insulted if she's not part of this," Iris says. "Do you like cats?"

"Yes," I say.

"But you don't have one?"

"Maybe someday."

The bell rings.

"What?" Iris looks around to see who won. "Already?"

"That was quick," I say.

"Insider advantage," Iris mumbles grumpily. "It's my sister's best friend." It's cute that Iris is so competitive. Iris awards Rose's best friend a bottle of wine.

A tall guy who looks very similar to Iris joins us, standing very close to her, feet hip distance apart. He puts out his hand. "I'm Iris's brother, Liam. I don't think we've met."

Very protective vibes. Given the way Iris was treated by her last boyfriend, I'm not surprised.

"This is Sebastian," Iris says. "He's Rupert's best friend."

Her brother's stance relaxes...slightly. Nice to know that Rupert is liked here.

"And we work together. We're just friends," Iris adds.

That's right. We're just friends. Even though I'm a little less than flattered at how matter-of-fact she is when she conveys this information.

"Work colleagues. Right. That's why you brought him while dressed as a pregnant woman?" her brother asks.

"It does sound odd when you point that out, but work colleagues can be good friends." Iris pats Liam's back. "Someday, you'll learn."

"Where's Maddie?" Liam asks.

"She's covering a story," Iris says.

"Are you in cybersecurity too?" Liam asks.

"No. I'm a lawyer. We're really just work colleagues," I say.

This does not seem to impress her brother. If anything, he seems to look at me with even less favor. *Why am I claiming we're just work colleagues?*

"And becoming good friends," Iris says.

I smile at her. "Yes, definitely."

"Do you game?" Liam asks.

"Um, not really," I say.

"All right, I believe you, Iris," Liam says.

Is *not* being a gamer a fatal flaw?

Liam says, "Hey, come meet my friend who works for Shooting Stars—I thought you guys should connect. He just moved back from LA."

Liam waves to a tall guy who joins us. It turns out he works in creative, but he's very excited about Shooting Stars opening a studio in New York and has nothing but praise for the CEO. We chat for a while, until Iris looks at her watch.

"Oops. I lost track of time. I have to announce the next game." Iris grabs my hand and pulls me away, back towards the bell above the bar. "Do you want to be my partner for the three-legged race?"

"Yes," I say. Definitely.

She announces the "three-legged race down the aisle."

"Dad will be the timer. Everyone, line up behind the starting line. Mom will hand out the scarves, and you'll all have a few minutes to practice."

She hops off the bar stool and grabs my hand. "C'mon. We definitely have a shot at this."

Most of the women are taking off their heels.

Iris's mom hands us a scarf, and I bend down to tie our ankles together. Iris's skirt ends just above the knees, and I feel like I'm peeking at forbidden skin as I slide the soft fabric around her ankle. I place my foot next to hers and finish tying the knot. I look up. Iris is very still. I swear the vibe is more than "just friends."

I break eye contact first and pull my leg to make sure the knot holds. Then I stand, and Iris wraps her arm around my waist and says, "Let's take a few practice steps. Tied foot together first. One, two, three."

I'm off, and she falls slightly against me. I hold her up. She looks up at me and laughs.

I say, "Sorry, let's try again." All around us, couples are practicing. It's a pretty narrow space in this front part.

More steps. We have a rhythm now.

Aunt Viola rings the bell. "Practice time over. Line up."

We're fourth in a line of couples. Rose and her husband are first. They race to the stage in seconds. The next two couples do well but not brilliantly.

"I think they've been practicing at home," I say.

Now we're up. Iris's dad blows a whistle, and we're off. Iris is counting out loud, "One, two, one, two." And she's speeding up. We're leaping now. Like flying reindeer. Or unwieldy elephants.

"One, two." Iris counts the pace.

"Go, go," I say, my arm gripping her body in a death lock.

And we're across the line. We bend down at the same time to catch our breath, knocking elbows.

Her dad yells our time. "Iris and Sebastian for the lead."

Iris hugs me, and we jump up and down together. Her head is thrown back, laughing, and the feeling in my chest is like joy bubbling out of a champagne glass.

I give her one last hug and release her.

"Hurray for the singles," says Rose.

"That signals good long-term potential there," Aunt Viola says.

We move off to the side and sit on the stage.

"At least you've now garnered Aunt Viola's sign of approval. She's usually very stingy about granting it. She liked Patrick, but not for long-term." Iris sighs. "She said, 'You should definitely date him, but try to hold back a bit of your heart.'"

"And did you?" I ask.

"Maybe. Maybe that's also why it didn't work out."

She reaches down to untie the scarf. Her fingers brush lightly against my leg.

"It's stuck."

I crouch down too. Iris's skin is flushed, making her green eyes all the brighter.

Our hands touch as I reach to help.

"I think you're only making it tighter," I say.

"Our leaping didn't help," she says.

"It helped us win. That's what's important," I say. The knot is impossible to loosen.

"Exactly." Her eyes crease at the corners as she chuckles. "Even if we're now attached for life."

Our glances hold, and my hands still. She just seems so alive. And there's that scent of flowers around her.

"Do you guys need scissors?" Rose asks. "Here."

I take the scissors and focus on cutting the scarf. We both step away from the crumpled fabric and don't look at each other.

The last game is a ring pop hunt, and Iris sprints off to take a ring pop from the top of a light fixture. I can't help but tease her. She looks so intent on winning.

"I think there's one behind the stairs going up to the stage," I whisper.

Iris glances back. "Are you sure? Then why aren't you getting it?"

"I want you to win."

She finds the ring pop there and is on to the next possible hiding place.

"If you really want me to win, go look for some ring pops and bring them to me," Iris says.

"Is that allowed?" I ask.

"Nothing in the rules forbids it," Iris says.

"But it's so much more fun to follow you around," I say.

Iris plucks another ring pop from between a napkin holder.

"You don't seem to be taking this competition seriously." She pokes me in the chest.

I laugh.

"You must have been a terror to your little sister," she says.

"My sister can more than hold her own," I say proudly.

"Will she be at Lily and Rupert's party tomorrow?" she says.

My lips turn down. "She's in London now. Plus, she's annoyed with me, so we haven't talked recently. I miss her."

"Just call her and tell her that," Iris says. "I'm sure she misses you too."

Aunt Viola rings the bell. Liam is the winner. He raises his beer to Iris. "Usually, Iris wins the Easter egg hunt. Thank you, Sebastian, for distracting her."

I tip my head. Iris gives me a mock glare.

"I'm calling it a night. I need to sleep." Dahlia pats her rounded belly. "But thank you all so much for coming to celebrate our wedding. Sorry we eloped, but I never wanted a big wedding. And this party was absolutely perfect for me. Thank you, Iris, for organizing this."

Her husband Arjan adds his thanks, and a bit of teasing back and forth among all the friends follows.

Iris smiles at me. "I'm so relieved I could be here with my family and Dahlia's friends."

And then the party is over.

"Do you live around here?" I ask. "I'll walk you home."

"That will be a very short walk," Iris says. "Home is upstairs. I keep meaning to get my own place, but now with the uncertainty about what's going on at work, at least this gives me a chance to save some money. I was initially hoping to buy an apartment with Patrick, one that our neighbor wants to sell. But that's probably not in the cards now. She said she'll hold off on selling it for a bit. It has the most amazing hardwood floors and this terrace that I love."

I should go then, but I hesitate.

Iris says, "But you can help me gather up the votives we placed outside in the garden."

Is she also reluctant to part? After today, I feel like we've developed a relationship—a friendship—that I hope will grow.

We slip out the back door to the small garden.

Iris shivers, and I take off my sweater. "I run hot."

Iris glances at my chest. "Clearly. Thanks." My sweater envelops her, but it looks good.

"You have a swing," I say.

"Dad put that up for us. And now the grandkids use it."

We gather up the votives and put them in a cabinet by the back door.

"I'll still walk you home," I say.

Iris unlocks the door next to the bar, and we're in a narrow hall-way behind the pub. We hike up the steep stairs to the second floor, and she pauses at the threshold before another door.

"I have to open this carefully because my cat, Fatma, likes to try to escape. She thinks she makes a good bar cat." She swings open the door carefully—no cat—and we enter a large kitchen. Iris flips a switch, illuminating a table. The lighting is dim, and I swear Iris sways towards me. We stare at each other. Our lips are inches apart. Her breath brushes my cheek. I smell chocolate and orange juice. I reach out to touch her waist. Gently. Her gaze shifts to my lips. I shift closer. Her eyelids flutter closed. I want to kiss her. Her soft body is heating mine, and I pull her even closer. I dip my head. But something holds me back. And then her eyelids open. I swallow. She's so close. I'm so attracted to her.

We pull back at the same time.

"Well, you're home. I should go," I say.

"You should go," she says. She ducks her head. I take one last look at her head, angled down, her shining brown hair, and leave. She deserves a better guy than me.

A guy who can't trust his judgment. Who read Nathan complete-ly wrong. Emil almost lost his job—and his reputation—because I believed the wrong guy.

And then read Melody wrong. Thought it was all going great. *That we shared the same values.*

A guy who's not still torn up about whether he can figure people out.

I say good-bye to her family and walk outside.

I wrap my scarf tighter around my neck. The cold air feels like icicle-nosed mosquitoes prickling my face. The wind takes my breath away.

I'm in trouble. I like Iris. But it didn't work out with Melody. And my judgment was completely wrong about Nathan. Am I reading Iris correctly? Does she like me enough? Could it work out with her?

I'm happy being single. None of the highs and lows. And then there is the incontrovertible fact that both my best friends are dating her best friends. We will definitely continue to see each other if we break up. What if the breakup doesn't go well? Will they have to choose sides? Will I be invited to some events and excluded from ones she attends? Rupert definitely chose me in the break-up with Melody.

I am torn.

Chapter Nine

Iris

LILY AND I STOP in the mall between the north and south lanes of traffic on Broadway, sharing the very large umbrella she luckily remembered to bring. The rain pelts down, making the red light ahead appear blurry. The sound of the raindrops hitting the umbrella drowns out every other sound except for the car wheels slick-slacking in the puddles. We're on our way to Fairway to pick up cookie-decorating supplies for Lily's festive holiday baking party today.

"No. You don't understand. I leaned in and closed my eyes. And I waited for him to kiss me. And he didn't. I almost kissed him. I'm so mortified. He's the monk. I even called him the monk." I wince just thinking about it.

"He knows you were drunk," Lily says.

"I was drunk, but that's no excuse. I'd sobered up a bit by then. Ugh. I can't believe I did that." I shudder. "And I forgot to give him back his sweater." It smelled so good. I had to make myself take it off and put it in a bag to return. I need to nip these feelings of attractions in the bud now.

"Are you sure he didn't lean in too?" Lily faces me.

"I don't know. I don't think so. He'd just opened up to me about why he was single. I can't believe I went to kiss him...and now I have to work with him."

"And you have to see him at my cookie party."

"Is he definitely coming?" And why is my heart racing at the thought that I might see him again? This is bad. "You need to make sure we don't end up together. I invited this guy Ernest from work so I can get a better feel for him."

"You did? I'm excited to meet Ernest, then. And of course Sebastian's coming, but he'll be late because he had to go into the office first," Lily says. "But wait, he told you about why he is committed to being single?"

"Yes."

"I think that's significant. He usually blows off that question."

"It was a we've-both-had-too-much-to-drink moment. I don't think I can read anything into it."

"I've always thought it was because his standards are too high—as if he's searching for some perfect woman. Was it anything like that?"

"Mm, not really," I say. It did sound like he'd idolized Melody to some extent. And he certainly seemed to hold himself to high standards. He seemed to be really beating himself up over the fact that he'd trusted his friend.

The light turns green. Lily scoops her arm through mine.

"But what if you guys *do* date? That will be so much fun. You guys would be perfect together. And he's a good guy, so there's no way he'd cheat on you."

"Ernest also seems like a really good guy," I say weakly.

I definitely shouldn't have told Lily. I expected her to give me a good common-sense talking to, that Sebastian is a fortress and I shouldn't get my hopes up. But she's so happy in love that she's blinded by it. Maddie will give me the hard truth that I should steer clear of liking him.

We enter Fairway and head straight for the baking section. We pick up green, red, blue, white, and pink sprinkles. I grab some silver stars while Lily adds molasses to our shopping cart. We find the rest of the items from our list and check out.

We walk back outside and up Columbus Avenue and across 79th Street to Rupert's apartment, our progress illuminated by brightly glowing stars hanging from the lamp posts. I pull up my hood to keep my head warm in the freezing rain.

"Sebastian dropped a hint that Rupert is thinking about proposing," I say. "He said I should organize a scavenger hunt for your engagement party."

Lily beams. "Rupert's definitely planning something. I think he's waiting for my dad to come back for the holidays first, but he's asked me some casual questions about rings recently. As if he'd be randomly thinking about rings. He said his assistant asked him about it for her daughter. I thought he'd ask one of you guys."

"He hasn't asked me," I say. "But I wouldn't be much help. Do you have a preference?"

"Not really," Lily says. "That's what I told him. It's the meaning behind the ring that matters. But obviously not something too showy. I want to be able to wear it to work at the library, and I don't want to feel self-conscious."

"That makes sense," I say.

Lily asks me what games we played at my sister's party, and I tell her about them. But I can't help thinking about Sebastian. I should be thinking about Ernest, but all I can think about is what

Sebastian's reaction will be when we see each other again. Will it be totally normal? Or awkward? And which is better?

MIRANDA AND HER BOYFRIEND have been assigned to make the sugar cookies, while Zeke and Tessa are making hedgehog cookies. Tessa probably is the most skilled baker among the seven of us. Maddie is making chocolate chip cookies because we all love her recipe. I'm making gingerbread cookies.

"We're thinking Memorial Day weekend for our wedding," Tessa says. "We found this loft space in Brooklyn where we can hold the ceremony and reception."

"We want to arrange lots of cool New York City activities for all the guests," Zeke says.

Mr. Devi arrives next. He's brought a pan full of samosas, and my mouth waters just thinking about eating them later. He bows out of cookie making but takes a seat on the couch next to Mrs. Potter, who is co-director of the local community garden with Lily. The way Mr. Devi and Mrs. Potter look at each other makes me wonder if there's something more between them. Lily tried to set them up, but even though they each told her they have no interest in getting married again, they look very comfortable together. Mr. Devi is teasing Mrs. Potter, telling her he is sure he saw some poison ivy in her garden.

Maybe friends to lovers will be their new trope too.

No Sebastian yet. Maybe work is keeping him.

I texted Raphael to make sure I didn't have to come in—once I heard Sebastian was going to be here and I was looking for an excuse to avoid him—but he said it had been handled and even he wasn't in the office this weekend. *What did Raphael find? How could we not need to do more?* My curiosity is killing me.

Did I just switch the salt and the baking powder? I check the recipe again. I did it right. I line up the rest of my ingredients so my distraction doesn't result in inedible cookies. Lily would never let me bake again.

Next up is to add the flour into the rest of the dry ingredients, but I'm not careful, and some puffs out, covering my front in a fine layer of white dust. Great. I add the rest of the ingredients, mix the batter, and then separate the dough into two halves and cover it in plastic wrap to let it sit. Now to wash all the dishes and clear my space so I can roll out the dough. I head to the sink.

"I'll wash those for you," Zeke says. "I've just finished ours."

"Thanks." I pile the dishes on the counter.

Rupert greets someone enthusiastically in the hallway, and then Sebastian stands in the doorway to the open living room and kitchen area.

I'm spotted with flour and wearing a huge apron. Not exactly my best look.

He half-smiles, looking quite comfortable.

"Sebastian, maybe you can help Iris?" Lily winks at me. She gives the impression of a sweet librarian, but she definitely has a mischievous streak underneath. So much for helping me avoid Sebastian at her party.

Sebastian flashes me a quick glance.

"Oh, sure," he says.

He hesitates a moment before walking over. He bites his lip like he's thinking about what to say. Cute. But this is so awkward. I know

I should apologize—before he tells me again that he's not interested in dating.

"I'm here to help." He smiles as he joins me at the counter

That's good. He's acting normal.

"Do I need an apron?" He gestures to mine.

"You didn't bring your own?"

"I'm not sure I own one." He holds up his hand. "But I do cook, before you get the wrong impression."

"You're just tidy," I say.

"I could probably use an apron," he says.

"If only I knew who your Secret Snowflake was," I say.

"Let's see if Ernest brings his own, if he comes," Sebastian says. "If not, you could buy him an apron."

"How did you know he's invited?" I ask.

"I invited him," he says. "Wait..."

"So did I," I say.

He glances at me, his eyebrow raised.

"You're okay with aprons but not underwear?" I tease. "Doesn't that send a domestic message?"

"Aprons are as safe as socks," he says.

"Interesting. I have to get the cookie cutters from the pantry. I'm so jealous that Rupert has a pantry."

"I'll come too."

The pantry is a large walk-in closet lined with shelves. It could be in a magazine spread. As I reach up to grab the tin, which is, of course, on the very top shelf because it's probably not used often, Sebastian says, "I'll get it."

He reaches over me. Way too close. What is he doing? I hold my breath. I don't dare turn around because he'll be right there.

The warmth from his body recedes. I grab the rolling pins.

"Hmm," Sebastian says from behind me. "Your apron's coming untied. Let me fix it."

His hands brush my back. That memory of his hands on my hips...and the almost-kiss last night when I leaned in. My cheeks heat up.

Aprons are definitely *not* in the same category as socks.

"All done," he murmurs so close to my ear that it gives me shivers.

My body has not received the message that this is *not* allowed. I need to tell him I'm sorry, and this closet seems as good a place as any. Especially since it's private.

I turn to face him.

"I'm sorry," I blurt out. "I know I leaned in to kiss you, and I know you want to remain single. I'd just had too much to drink."

"No need for apologies," he says. "I'd also had too much to drink...and I also leaned in to kiss you."

He leaned in too. It wasn't just me. *Thank you.*

"I'm obviously attracted to you..." he says.

He's attracted to me?

He continues, "But given our circumstances, I don't think it would be a good idea to have a relationship—or even a fling." And his gaze briefly flicks to my lips again.

And then I focus on the second part of that sentence. A fling. Lovely.

"Yeah, definitely not." Although as our glances meet, and he's so close, I am tempted. We're both single, and we could act on this attraction. But then I'd probably really fall for him and be left pining.

"As I said before—"

Oh, no. I definitely don't want to be told again that he's committed to remaining single.

"I got the message. Don't worry." I hand him a rolling pin, although seriously, dude needs to move on past this best friend. Especially if she's engaged. "You can roll out the gingerbread dough first."

He blinks and takes the rolling pin.

I slide past him and return to the counter. I'm sure the dough has had enough time to warm up. It certainly feels hot in this kitchen.

Sebastian rolls up his sleeves. Attractive forearms. Again. This feels like torture. And he can actually roll out the dough, especially because he's putting a bit of muscle into it. I could happily watch him all day. Yummy.

"Where'd you learn to roll out cookie dough?" I ask.

"Mom. I told you, she's a big Christmas fan," he says. "The Hallmark movies are already on, and I have a standing invitation to come over every Friday and watch with her."

"And do you?" I ask. He doesn't strike me as the Hallmark movie type.

"Usually. My dad's health isn't great, so I'm trying to spend more time with them." Sebastian looks down. "But it's tricky. Because we often end up disagreeing, and that certainly doesn't help his heart."

He looks so vulnerable and lost.

"It's good to still spend time with them." I gently cover his hand with mine. He looks up and smiles wryly.

"It's weird to contemplate losing your parents," he says. "Not that he's that ill, but the doctor says he needs to exercise more. My mom took that as an excuse to get a dog, so now he has to walk it."

"Is it working?"

"Surprisingly, yes. My dad takes long walks around Central Park with Pepper, and he's made a whole new circle of friends at the dog park. It's a whole new life for him. He was a private equity partner, and he worked hard his entire life. He was kind of at loose ends when he retired. But now he's fundraising for a renovation of the dog run. He takes it very seriously. He's running it like he used to run his company. My mom had a dinner party the other night, and he solicited donations like he used to pitch for investment capital."

"I always wanted a dog too, but my hours are so erratic at work that I've been holding off. Also, I'm not sure Fatma will tolerate a dog."

"Don't tell my dad you want a dog. He'll have you at the pound in no time."

I smile. "How come he hasn't persuaded you to get a dog?"

"He's focused on trying to get me to work at his fund. But that's probably next on his list."

"Why don't you want to?"

"I'm not sure family and business should mix...just like friends and business don't mix."

Does that mean he's against dating in the office? Is that why he doesn't want to try dating? Or is he still not over his ex?

"Should I bring anything for your parents' party?"

He shakes his head. "Just brush up on your Hallmark movies, given our cover story."

"Is Mrs. P. going to be there?" I ask.

"Probably. And please don't bring anything. My mom can't wait to meet you because she's consumed with curiosity about the woman whom I wandered around Baby Love with, pretending to be a couple. She thinks there's something more."

"I'm coming to show her there's not?" I ask, completely confused.

Sebastian reaches out and brushes my cheek with his fingertip. His touch reverberates down to my toes.

"You had some flour on your cheek." Sebastian's glance meets mine and holds it. "I've already said there's probably something more. You don't agree?"

I hold his glance. "You're crossing the line." I draw a line in the cookie dough.

"No flirting?" he asks.

"Not if you want me to play fair," I say.

Sebastian's eyes light up. "I'm not sure I want you to play fair."

My lips curve up. Playing dirty can be a lot of fun. And it may be a safe way to explore this attraction between us. Unless he is *really* committed to remaining single. I need to remember that Lily and Tessa both described him as "Mr. Single." I could get hurt if I pursue this.

Sebastian picks through the tin of cookie cutters, laying the options out on the counter.

"No demon cookie cutters in here. Only angels. I'll have to make my own demon." He takes a gingerbread man cookie cutter and lightly presses it into the sheet of gingerbread dough. With a knife, he adds a cape and horns. "To not playing fair."

I press a cupid cookie cutter into the dough, its arrow aimed at Sebastian's devil. "To not playing fair."

He makes a few elves and some gingerbread men. I make a tree, a star, a few gingerbread women, and then a whole bunch of hearts.

"Another heart?" he asks.

"Getting worried?" I ask.

"No." He makes a snowman. "My heart is ice. I'm safe."

"No way." I cut out a sleigh just as Jingle Bells plays in the background over the speakers. "Your devil is perfect for my sleigh." I place my sleigh shape on the cookie tray under his devil. He adds a gingerbread man and woman next to the devil on the sleigh.

We carefully lift the rest of our cut-out shapes onto the tray and then add the sprinkles. He covers his devil cape with red sugar powder, which I then sprinkle all over my hearts. We take turns adding green sprinkles to the trees. Blue sprinkles make my star pop.

I make a heart in the leftover scrap of dough.

More people have arrived, gathering in the living room, chatting and catching up.

We put our tray of cookies in the oven and return to roll out another batch.

"Hi, I thought I'd join you guys." Ernest faces me and puts out his hand to shake. "Thanks again for inviting me."

Excellent. Ernest is the type of guy I should be going for—even if it feels like a chaperone just crashed our tête-à-tête.

Sebastian has made it clear he's not in the market for a relationship. It's time to focus on Ernest.

Chapter Ten

Sebastian

Ernest.

Perfect, right?

Lily sent Ernest over, as requested, and I should retreat. Especially because I can't seem to resist flirting with Iris—despite all my very noble intentions to normalize last night's encounter and bring us back to friends and colleagues. I was doing okay initially, but then I sabotaged it.

Iris laughs and holds out her flour-covered hands. "I'm not sure you want to shake my hand. I'm so glad you could make it."

Ernest says, "I'm so glad you invited me."

I know I told Lily to send Ernest over, but...

"I thought you like cookies with chocolate," I say grumpily. "Maddie over there is making chocolate chip cookies, and she doesn't have a partner."

"Yes, Lily suggested I join Maddie, but I explained that you had both invited me and it would be rude not to join you," Ernest says.

Ah, so Lily definitely didn't listen to me.

"We can probably borrow some chocolate chips and use them as buttons for the gingerbread men," Iris says.

No. Does she really want Ernest here?

"You don't like chocolate chips with your gingerbread?" Iris asks me. "You just frowned."

"I like a lot of chocolate chips in my chocolate chip cookies," I say. "We shouldn't take any away."

"I'm happy to stay here," Ernest says. He washes his hands and sits on the stool next to Iris.

"Do you want to roll out some dough?" Iris asks. "Did you bring your own apron? Do you need an apron?"

Well done.

"No, I'm content to watch you guys. I'm not much of a cook," he says. "Mother does the cooking at home."

I swear I can see Iris crossing aprons and cooking utensils off any Secret Snowflake gift list. But maybe she should by buying gifts for *Mother* too.

"You can still make cookies with us." Iris gestures to the selection.

"I'll happily pick out cookie cutters." Ernest also picks up a heart.

Really?

"So, no cooking. What do you like to do in your spare time?" Iris asks.

"What spare time?" Ernest asks. "Just kidding...but work has been crazy lately, especially with all the concern about cost-cutting and competing with Albuquerque. It's insane. It's not like I can conjure up cheaper office space."

"But you were the one who made the suggestion that we work from home and have a desk rotation for days in the office," Iris says.

"How'd you know that was me?" Ernest asks.

"Our boss cited it in our Monday team meeting as an innovative example, suggesting we should emulate it." Iris rubs her right wrist.

She rolls it around. She did that yesterday too after she handed out the bingo sheets at the party. "So, no hobbies?"

"You and Lily are very into hobbies," Ernest says, his brow furrowed.

"We are?" Iris looks quizzically at me.

I shrug. "Remember? Lily wanted to know what everyone's hobbies are, in case she decided to give out party favors."

Iris nods, an appreciative glint in her eyes. "Of course."

"Knitting," Ernest says.

"You knit?" Iris asks.

Ernest knits? He could've told me he knit.

"Yes, but that's a secret. Just between us," Ernest says. "Mother taught me."

"And me," I say. "I'm still here."

"Why are you still here?" Ernest asks, teasing. "Shouldn't you catch up with Rupert?"

I should. I should definitely leave them to it.

Ernest turns to Iris. "I bet you're surprised?"

"My ex knitted. Briefly," Iris says.

Is being a knitter good or bad?

Rupert and Lily join us.

"Did I tell you that Rupert woke up at six a.m. and went to a Target in New Jersey on Tuesday to get the new release I wanted?" Lily asks. "He was waiting there when it opened at eight a.m. I thought he'd gone for a run, and then he surprised me with breakfast in bed and the latest Wilhemina Chrissy novel."

Lily beams at Rupert.

"You couldn't pre-order it?" Ernest asks.

Way to dampen the celebration of Rupert's romantic impulsiveness.

But Iris smiles at Ernest. Does she agree with Ernest's more practical position?

I practically slap myself for caring but catch myself just in time and rub my forehead. Whatever she's interested in, it doesn't matter.

"I did pre-order it, but that doesn't always guarantee its arrival on release day," Rupert says. "I thought this was safer."

The buzzer rings, and Lily and Rupert excuse themselves to greet the next guest.

My phone timer rings. Iris reaches for the potholders, but I volunteer to do it.

"Does your wrist hurt?" I ask.

"Too much clicking on my mouse last week during that investigation," she says. "I have a brace I can wear this week."

"You need to be careful with that," Ernest says. "Mother had carpal tunnel pain when she worked, and it really hindered her."

I take our first tray of cookies out of the oven.

"Is that a Santa with a red cape? Did his hat break off?" Ernest asks.

"Definitely not a Santa," I say.

Iris smiles at me and says, "More in the Grinch family line."

"Did you make the hearts?" Ernest asks Iris. As she nods, he says, "I'll have to eat one."

"They're still hot." I scoop the hearts off the tray with a silicone turner, away from Ernest's hand reaching out, and place them on the wire cookie rack.

Iris makes another heart in the dough, and Ernest suggests that he give it a try after all. He takes the heart-shaped cookie cutter from her and places it right next to the heart she just made.

Ugh.

She's making a snowman on the other side of the dough. I quickly place a Christmas tree-shaped cutter there before Ernest can place a matching snowman.

But he's still making hearts. Nonstop.

I can't watch this.

And I shouldn't.

I need to stick to my original position that it's better to be friends, given how entangled our lives are.

"I see Rowena just arrived. Rupert's cousin," I say. "I should go speak to her."

Iris's brow furrows, and I think she looks disappointed. But she recovers quickly. I hesitate for a moment, but Ernest makes another heart.

I put a snowflake cookie cutter into the dough next to it.

"Don't forget to make some snowflakes," I say and leave. Ernest is chattering away again.

Rowena is studying the book titles in Rupert's library in the living room and drinking from a mug. They're going to have to add more bookcases if Lily moves in.

"No cookie-making for you?" I ask Rowena, joining her.

She turns and smiles and gives me a huge hug. "Sebastian. I've missed you. Where have you been hiding yourself?"

"Work. And now there are concerns that Dream may close, so moving may have been a mistake." But I've learned a lot about working for an entertainment company.

"I'm sorry to hear that," she says. "I thought Dream was doing well. I enjoyed the last film we saw."

"It flopped at the box office, unfortunately," I say. "Anyway, let's not spend more time on that depressing news. Still keeping your boyfriend mysterious?"

She frowns. "He failed the camping test."

Rowena is co-CEO of Strive Developers with Rupert, so she always fears men are dating her for her money. She takes them camping as a first date to see if they express disappointment because they expect more of a high-flying life with her.

"I'm sorry. But don't you take them camping as a first date?"

"He was too smart to fail that first date, but eventually it became clear." She narrows her eyes as if she's envisioning a million ways to torture him. The thing is, I'm sure the guy also liked Rowena for Rowena. I don't see how he couldn't.

"I told you we should have fake dated and made both our families happy," I say.

"Too happy. They'd have us married and miserable in no time. But..." She tilts her head and studies me. "'I told you?' Is that offer no longer on the table? Are *you* falling for someone?"

Falling? Nailed. *Rowena is so quick.*

"Hardly. But you've turned down the offer enough times that I've given up," I say.

She narrows her eyes at me, but when I shrug, I think she takes me at my word. "I need a refresh of my hot cider. Let's get some for you too."

I follow her across the living room to the bar. I'm careful not to look over to the long stainless steel kitchen counter in the back to check on whether Iris is still making cookies with Ernest. Rowena would spot my interest in a second.

We each pour cider into a mug.

"I saw Melody at the Gala the other night." Rowena pauses, as if she's confirming I'm okay hearing about Melody. *And I am.* Apparently. Even Rowena seems to sense this.

Am I finally over Melody?

And I need to stop saying that I'm committed to remaining single. Iris literally winced when I was about to say it again—until she stopped me. When Melody first ended our relationship, I meant it, but over time, it's become more a reflex than something I really mean.

Rowena says, "Melody looked good. She does like that life."

"What life?" I ask.

"The life of attending New York City galas."

I shake my head. "Melody's not like that. She's from a small town, and she always said those parties intimidate her."

"She *wasn't* like that. She likes them now. She was holding court among several women. She definitely knows how to maneuver in that crowd now." Rowena's tone is decisive. "She's changed. A lot."

"She has to—to help her fiancé," I say. We move to stand at the full-length windows that look out over the rooftops of the Upper West Side, round water tanks dotting the landscape. It's definitely a different view up here.

"Well, yes. But she also chose that fiancé."

"I think she fell in love with him. I'm not sure it was a fully rational choice."

Rowena grins at me. "You're a romantic too—like Rupert. But I wish you would stop wasting your time pining for her. I was actually hoping that maybe you *had* found someone earlier."

"You never liked Melody," I say.

"Not particularly. That's true." Rowena shrugs. "But I also think she realized you were not going to follow in your father's footsteps, and that's why she dumped you for Wim—not because of you personally. She still has this warm tone when she speaks of you."

"You did tell me to take her camping when we first dated."

"You should have." Rowena shakes her finger at me.

"Melody definitely did not want to go camping," I say. "Anyway, at least she didn't dump me for my best friend." That was high school—and brutal back then.

"You've really made some terrible love life choices," Rowena says.

"Thanks," I say.

"Maybe you should use Grandpa's help. He and Mr. Devi keep trying to set me up."

"Doesn't sound like they have a great track record. Plus, my mom is already on this full-time."

I can't help looking over at Iris. *Could Ernest stand any closer?*

Chapter Eleven

Iris

I FEEL NOTHING WHEN Ernest stands close to me. None of the shivers or the racing heart like when Sebastian stands near me. I sigh. Stupid hormones. They have terrible taste in men. Pretty boys, as Liam would say. They seem to only ignite with the spark of attractive men who appeal to many women.

Like the woman Sebastian is standing very close to right now. He looks relaxed and comfortable with her. He said they were good friends.

And she just put her hand on his arm again.

"I think the timer just went off." Ernest taps my arm.

"I'm sorry," I say. "I wasn't paying attention."

"You looked like you were a million miles away."

"A tricky cybersecurity incident at work," I say. That *is* what I'm usually thinking about. And what I should be thinking about now. Instead of the way Sebastian laughs and how it sounds or makes me feel. Or the feel of his hand in the small of my back.

I pull on the festive red-and-green mitts and remove the cookies from the oven. Tessa puts in her tray next.

"The hedgehogs look great," I say to Tessa.

"That's admirable of you," Ernest says to me. "To be thinking about that on the weekend when we may all lose our jobs by Christmas."

"Is it really that bad?" I ask.

"I don't know. I think our finances are okay. I mean, they took a hit when we didn't make a profit on the last two movies, but our streaming revenues are still solid. It doesn't make sense to me that L'Etoile bought us only for the IP. They definitely didn't give that impression at the company retreat in France."

The company retreat. That seems like a lifetime ago.

"Why bring us all out there and do all those team-building exercises if they intended to lay us off?" he asks.

Unless the whole point was for them to determine who to keep and who to get rid of.

I stare at Ernest. "That's true. But Kevin is really freaked out about it."

"I think at worst, we'll have to cut a few positions. I doubt they'll close us down. I'm not looking for another job yet."

"That's good," I say. He sounds very sure.

I move the cooled cookies from the previous batch to a platter and then scoop off the cookies from the hot tray and put them on the cookie rack.

"When are you leaving for your Florida vacation?" I ask.

"You remembered," he says.

"Of course," I say. Does he think I have no memory? We just talked two days ago.

Ernest looks very earnestly at me.

But I can't help but be distracted because Sebastian is back, with the dark-haired woman in tow. It's like all my senses are on high alert.

"Would you like to go on a date with me?" Ernest asks.

I blink. That's not what I was expecting.

"I'm sorry. I don't date coworkers," I blurt out, not thinking.

The thing is, I can't date Ernest. I *should* date a solid, dependable guy. But I feel no chemistry between us. And it's especially obvious when Sebastian shows up and my body sparks like a live wire.

It's not that nausea is desirable, but I also don't want to feel nothing.

"I'm so sorry," I say again. "I just think it's a bad idea."

"No. That makes complete sense." Ernest waves his hand as if to stop me from talking about it.

"But of course, we can be friends," I say. Lame, I know.

I think he mutters that maybe he *should* look for another job, but I'm not sure. And it's not like he'd do that, right?

Anyway, I don't want to say anything more in front of our audience.

"I want you guys to meet Rowena, Rupert's cousin, and one of my best friends," Sebastian says, standing next to me.

Hello, hello, hello, says my body.

Chapter Twelve

Iris

I ARRIVED AT THE office early this morning, desperate to ask Raphael what the hackers exfiltrated, but he is nowhere to be found. His door is closed, and he hasn't responded to my texts. His assistant hasn't arrived yet. However, I already had a visit from the company ergonomic specialist to make sure my chair is at the right height for my desk and I have proper back and wrist support. She noted I was wearing my wrist brace. Who called them—was it Sebastian or Ernest?

Meanwhile Kevin also emailed that we shouldn't worry about customizing the migration, just try to get everything moved over to our cloud server as soon as possible. Every week, it's a different instruction. Last time, he insisted we take our time and demonstrate our expertise. Nonetheless, I've mapped out a new approach, and now I'm waiting for my New Mexico colleague to arrive at the office so I can run it by him. That unfortunately gives me plenty of time to think about Sebastian and Lily's party last night and wander by Raphael's door.

Lily assured me that Sebastian and Rowena have more of a brother/sister relationship. I was afraid Lily would tease me for asking. After all my talk about not being interested in Sebastian, I was suddenly very keen to hear any details about Rowena. But Lily also took pity on me and pretended it was a totally normal question on my part—one that anyone would ask about a work colleague. Right.

Because I definitely need Sebastian to tell me again that he's not interested.

I should be the one saying *I'm* not interested.

A collective gasp shudders through the open desk security operations center. Jin Ae has her hand over her mouth as she says, "Raphael left."

I click over to my email.

To: Raphael Singh
From: Raphael Singh
Date: December 9
It's been a pleasure working with all of you. I have left
Dream Company as of today.

What? Raphael just left? I re-read the email as if I'm missing something in those two sentences. The other faces around the room mirror my stunned reaction. Why?

But Raphael was going to tell me what had been exfiltrated.

Was Raphael fired? He can't leave.

"Should we go ask Raphael?" I ask Jin Ae. Raphael's office is next door. And I'd like to say good-bye.

Jin Ae nods, and we walk out of the room. I open the door into the office next door. Nobody is there. It's completely cleaned out. How is that even possible? No trace. I walk in and check the cabinet behind his desk. No books.

Raphael is gone.

This is strange.

This is very bad. I bite my nail. A pit of unease grows in my stomach. One of the reasons I love this job so much is that Raphael is a great boss.

Jin Ae and I look at each other.

"We have a team meeting scheduled for tomorrow morning," Jin Ae says. "Wouldn't he have said something if he was planning to quit?"

"Maybe he received a great job offer somewhere else and didn't want to disappoint us by telling us he was leaving?" I ask. I don't believe that. He did say maybe we should start looking for jobs. But he would have told *me*. I'm his second-in-command.

As we shut the door, Kevin is walking down the hallway.

"Iris, just the person I'm looking for," he says. "Let's meet in my office."

He turns around. Jin Ae raises her eyebrow at me. I shrug and slip off my wrist brace and give it to her. I don't want to show any weaknesses in front of Kevin. I follow Kevin back to his office.

The whiteboards are all wiped clean—as if we're starting all over again.

He sits behind his desk as I take the chair in front. He steeples his hands and stares at me. Raphael often complained about this, speculating about whether this was some intimidation tactic. Raphael said he always just leaned back and waited for Kevin to talk. I follow Raphael's advice, although if Raphael was just fired, maybe that's not the best idea. Other than for my job interview, this is the first time I've been alone with Kevin in his office. I've been in many meetings with him but never without Raphael.

"I'm promoting you to fill the position of Deputy CISO now that Raphael has left."

My eyes widen, but I try to control my surprise. "Thank you. Why did Raphael leave?"

"He couldn't hack it." Kevin huffs out a raspy laugh. "Sorry for the bad pun. We had a difference of opinion, and it seemed best that we part."

That didn't sound good. Was it the investigation? And why so suddenly? And I'd have the same opinion as Raphael. What did they disagree about? Could I ask? But Deputy CISO—this is a huge opportunity, especially as a woman. I won't have to move laterally to another company for the Deputy CISO job. Raphael was the one who pushed for my hire, definitely not Kevin, as far as I could tell.

"I should let you know that Hank asked for the job."

"Hank?" Hank is the worst—someone who pretends to know everything but in reality knows very little. And he doesn't do the work he needs to do, which means all the other team members have to pick up his slack. "He doesn't have the expertise. I'm second-in-command to Raphael."

"That's not going to stop Hank. And normally, I'm a big believer in the ability to learn on the job, but we can't afford that. Your skills have always impressed me, and you've proven your loyalty." He paused. "You know about the corporate battle going on right now. There can be no problems—but if there is an issue, I need to know. Immediately. No surprises. I don't care how bad it is, it's only going to get worse if I don't know about it and can't do damage control." He stares at me, daring me to disagree.

"I'm happy to agree to that." *I think.*

"Did you do any further work investigating the hack? Any clues? Did they take anything?"

A shiver of unease snakes through me. Kevin *knows* they took something.

"I was doing the damage mitigation while Raphael was figuring out if they exfiltrated any data." And already I'm *not* saying that I know Raphael figured out what they took. Unless Raphael...I don't know what to think. But I can't analyze it now.

Best to distract.

"The hacker was very clever in how they breached our defenses," I say. "You didn't hire a white hat hacker to probe our defenses, did you?"

He blinks. "No. There's no money for that." He looks at the empty whiteboard.

Did he just lie?

"Hank was in here immediately once he heard Raphael was gone," he says. "I'm surprised you let him beat you here. I hope your reflexes are quicker in an actual cyberattack."

He wanted me *to immediately run to his office and ask to be promoted upon hearing that Raphael left*?

No way.

But Raphael's departure has caught me completely off-guard. Not that I can admit that.

"But I just had to take gender sensitivity training." He stares at me. "And apparently women are less likely to ask than men. The thing I like about you is that you get things done, no drama. You're such a go-getter that I'm not sure that applies to you, but then again, you didn't rush here for this promotion. The thing, is if you want to be deputy CISO—"

"I do," I interject.

"Then you have to be able to push for things and take risks. You can't just think you're going to get the budget you need because the CEO will see your good work and reward you. Other departments will be asking for money, and if you don't ask for it, they'll have an easier time cutting your budget without even having to say no to you. If you don't ask, you've already got the no."

Thank you for mansplaining that to me, Kevin. But it's still good advice.

"I certainly pushed for our cybersecurity budget earlier this year."

"Maybe that isn't the best example." He pauses. "In any event, this is an interim promotion. You'll keep your current desk. Hank wants the chance to prove himself too. Ultimately, one of you will be promoted permanently to Deputy CISO."

"Don't you know our strengths and weaknesses by now?" I ask. Kevin has to know Hank would be a disaster.

"Blunt and to the point as always," Kevin says. "I do, but he may have some hidden strengths."

Deeply hidden.

"I'm not going to report to Hank," I say.

Kevin stands and leans over the desk, putting his two hands at the edge next to me, like he is getting ready to do a push-up. Leaning over me.

He is a big guy.

It is so physical. I shrink back.

"Are you threatening me?" he asks.

My mouth opens. His posture is menacing, and he's using his body like a bully.

I straighten my back. "No. I'm just stating a fact."

"If you think that's going to influence my decision, it won't."

This conversation has gone off the rails. What is happening here?

"I doubt Hank will want to report to me either," I say. *How to save this?* "I'm looking forward to the challenge, and I appreciate the confidence you've shown in me."

He settles back in his seat. "See that it's warranted. How's the phishing campaign going?"

"Good, so far. We have a high compliance rate. Very few people have clicked on the emails." Other than Hank. He clicked on two.

"That's great," he says. "And are you going to the ice-skating event this afternoon?"

"I signed up, but I was going to work on the investigation."

"The investigation is resolved. Didn't Raphael tell you that? You should definitely go. Xavier is paying for this, and we need to show up. He takes that stuff seriously."

"Okay."

He gestures with his head towards the door. The meeting is over.

I leave and retreat to a stall in the bathroom, which is basically the only private place available because of the open layout of the bullpen. I lock the door and lean against the stall wall.

That was disturbing, especially when he leaned over me. So much for gender sensitivity training. What is going on here? Why did Raphael leave so suddenly? Did Kevin lie about hiring a white hat hacker?

I call Raphael's number. Voicemail. I leave a message, asking him to call me and explain what's going on.

Is this why Raphael said he didn't want to tell me what he'd found? I need to figure out whatever clues he left.

Was Kevin threatening to promote Hank if I continue the investigation?

I'm going to do what is right. My industry reputation is more important than this job, ultimately.

Let him promote Hank. I'm a way better security analyst than Hank. Did Kevin keep me because he thinks I won't investigate and I'll back down easier—that he can bully me? Like he tried to at our meeting this morning? He obviously doesn't realize I used to handle drunk people at my dad's bar.

But it's also going to look terrible on my resume if I am only interim deputy CISO for a short period. It would look like I wasn't competent. I rub my forehead. Have I just been played?

My temple is throbbing.

Sebastian said his boss advised him to socialize so people come to him if they're in a tight spot. I'm in a tight spot. I text him.

> Me: *Raphael left. Can we meet for lunch at StuffIt? 1 p.m.*

Chapter Thirteen

Sebastian

THE SKY IS AN aircraft blue outside my office window, deceptively bright despite the chill outside. Still, Iris's text suggesting lunch has me grinning at my mountain of folders. After introducing Rowena and overhearing Iris tell Ernest they can't date, I managed to stay away for the rest of Rupert's party, but it was hard.

A knock sounds on my door, and Bob sticks his head in.

"Do you have the presentation for the board meeting?" Bob asks. "Colby wants to make some changes. He wants to include more numbers about the tax breaks and other incentives New York City offers for filming. We need to beef up how we're competitive with Albuquerque and, in particular, why the types of movies we make are better filmed here rather than building a city set there."

I pull up the presentation.

"He says we didn't go deep enough," Bob continues. "He thinks Albuquerque will come off as more competitive, especially given all the below-the-line talent that moved there when Popflicks opened its production studio. He wants us to show how the movies set in NYC are doing better than the movies set in small towns."

"During the holiday season?" I ask, thinking of the ever-present Hallmark Channel movies on at my mom's house. Those are definitely not set in New York City.

"In terms of revenue," Bob says.

"We can do smalltown movies in New York State," I say. "There's the New York State film tax credit if you shoot in upstate New York."

"Good. Add that. Here's his markup. I have another call with our outside employment counsel. And I got the term sheet for Raphael's severance agreement, although I still haven't seen the actual agreement."

"Why was Raphael terminated?" I ask. Raphael had been impressive at the senior management meeting.

"Kevin said he thought he was doing something unauthorized, but he can't prove it, so he wants him out."

"Shouldn't we figure that out?" I ask. "What if he took confidential information?"

Bob raises his eyebrow. "Kevin says Raphael is too good to get caught and we'd be wasting money tracking it down while we're in the middle of a fight with Albuquerque. We need to show limited spending. Colby said to let it go."

No way. That's not the proper protocol. Why would Raphael be doing something unauthorized? He gave me a straight-arrow vibe.

"But that's one of the reasons I want you to socialize more with the other people in the company. I can't. I'm too senior," Bob says. "But I think we're out of the loop, and I'm not sure exactly what's going on. I can't protect the company if I don't know."

I flip through the markup. Scratch that—it's not a markup; it's a complete rewrite. Do I cancel lunch with Iris? No. I can get this done. Plus, I want to hear what she has to say about Raphael's departure. I was told to socialize, so socialize I will.

Iris is already at StuffIt, wearing a bright-blue hat. Today's music is pop. A waiter is wiping down the counter in front of me with a little shimmy to his step.

I go to kiss her on the cheek but then remember that I shouldn't do that as her work colleague and end up pulling back. She's kind of turned her cheek so maybe I should? Oh, no. Don't repeat the other night when she thought I rejected her.

I move in to kiss her cheek, but she shifts. Lips. Pink. Aargh. No. Avert. Quickly. I hit her nose.

Her nose.

It's a very cute nose, but still.

I'm usually much more polished.

There's no way to save this. My face heats up.

"Uh, okay," she says. "Maybe we should agree to just say hello in the future?"

"Yes. That sounds like a good idea," I say. "Sorry I had to move this back—and that I'm still late. I'm revising the board presentation. Congratulations on your promotion."

"Interim promotion," she says. "But I'd rather have Raphael here. Do you know what happened?"

"Let's order first and then discuss," I say.

"Good idea," she says. We place our orders at the counter and then retreat to a table in the back. On the turquoise wall is a drawing inspired by the Day of the Dead, lots of dressed dancing skeletons. Is that now an apt comparison to what is going on at Dream?

StuffIt is not exactly private, but it's not crowded at two p.m. The usual lunch crowd has cleared out.

"Do you know what happened?" she asks as we both dig into our burritos.

"Not really," I say. I'm not sure what I can or can't share. "Was it a surprise to you?"

"A complete surprise. We were in the middle of following up on an attack to our system."

"Oh, yes, Bob told me about that, but he said nothing was taken."

"Raphael said *something was* taken, but he didn't tell me what. He said he didn't think he *should* tell me on Friday. So now I'm wondering if that's why he was fired. I have to figure out what was taken."

If I'm supposed to get on-the-ground intelligence, I'm partnering with Iris on this mission.

"Bob told me that Kevin said he thought Raphael was doing something unauthorized," I say.

"No way."

"You can't just dismiss it. Why no way?"

"What's his motive? Why would he tell me he'd found what was taken?"

"To throw you off the scent that it was him?"

"Except that he told me to investigate it."

"Could he have set up that intrusion as a diversion?"

Iris stares at me. "You've got a very devious mind. But looking to see if this intrusion is a diversionary tactic is part of an investigation protocol. In other words, I'm investigating everything, so it doesn't make sense to tell me you found something if you don't want to be caught. Anyway, what motive would he have?"

"I don't know."

"I'm going to set up some honeypots," Iris says.

"Excuse me?" I ask.

"Enticing targets that are fake but look real, so the cybercriminals go after them instead of legitimate assets. And then, as they spend time in the network target, you can assess their capabilities. The reason we knew an attacker was in the system this time was because they tripped one of my traps. I made my trap look like the CEO's files because I figured that the CEO's and the CFO's files are the most valuable targets—other than the movie IP."

Iris gets so passionate when she talks about cybersecurity. She's smart.

"I think Raphael was terminated because he found something while investigating this intrusion. Kevin told me the investigation is resolved, but I plan to keep investigating. He said he's deciding between Hank and me, so he may still plan to get rid of me and move Hank into the position. Apparently, Hank immediately asked for the job. That's such a joke because Hank is a total nepo hire, and as much as we try to teach him, he's lazy." Iris looks completely disgusted.

"I overheard Hank complaining to Kevin about not getting the promotion," I say.

"I still can't believe he thought he was qualified," she says.

"Kevin replied to Hank, '*You* don't want it right now,'" I say. "What do you think that means? It doesn't sound good."

She stares at me. "It doesn't. I don't know." She shakes her head. "Raphael's files were also all deleted. I checked. Deleted by Hank."

"Is that proper protocol?" I ask.

"No. They should have been kept, and I should have been given access to take over his projects."

"Hmm. So proper protocol isn't being followed there either."

"Are you very into proper protocol?" she asks, her head tilted.

She is making fun of me. And boy, do I want to make a definitely *not proper* joke, but this is serious.

"In these circumstances yes," I say. "As the company lawyer."

"I'm going to Raphael's after work," she says. "Kevin has piled a bunch of work on me—probably so I can't spend any more time investigating this hack—so I need to get through that first, and then I'll go. And since Raphael refuses to pick up his calls, I will go to him. Maddie is coming with me."

"I'll come with you too, if that's okay," I say.

"Sure," she says.

"Are you still going to the Big Brothers Big Sisters event this afternoon?" I ask. "I'm meeting my little sibling today."

"I'll probably be late, but I'll definitely stop by," Iris says. "Did you sign up for the ice skating later this week?"

"I'm a terrible ice skater," I say. "I don't think anyone needs to witness me ice skating. I'm much better at skiing."

"You'll make the kids feel better."

"I'm sure the kids skate better than me."

"I'll hold you up. I've been directed to go."

"You definitely can't hold me up," I say, "but I'll come."

Dream's largest conference room is crowded with teenagers and employees grouped in clusters along the one long white conference table. I stop on the threshold. Jazmine approaches me with Aaron in tow.

"I'm so glad you signed up. We need more men as mentors," she says. "I also convinced Aaron—you guys met in the canteen."

I nod hello.

Jazmine waves at us to follow her to a corner where several teenage boys are hanging out.

"Jamal, this is your big sibling, Sebastian. Sebastian is a lawyer," Jazmine says.

Jamal ducks his head in a hello, and I hold out my hand to shake his. Maybe that's too formal. But Jamal shakes it. He's got a good grip.

Jazmine introduces Aaron to his little sibling. "You should each take a get-to-know-you questionnaire and sit at this corner here. I think it will be easier if it's the four of you together." Jazmine gestures to some empty chairs.

We move to the end of the table as directed and take turns asking each other the ice-breaker questions. We bond over playing basketball.

"Maybe we can meet some time to play hoops," I say. "I sometimes play with my friends on Riverside and 76th. We're a bunch of old men compared to you guys, but we're always looking for more players. Just don't hurt us."

"I'd be up for that," Jamal says.

"I also play squash, so I could teach you how to play," I say. "Have you ever played tennis?"

"We tried tennis and badminton in gym, but I like basketball more," Jamal says.

We proceed through the rest of the get-to-know-you questions. It's almost a pity Ernest didn't sign up, because this exercise could suggest a Secret Snowflake gift for him.

Iris enters and sits with her little sibling. Her skin looks flushed, like she's in a rush.

Raphael's departure does not make sense. If the company proves he did something unauthorized, it wouldn't have to pay him severance, which seems like a win when we're looking for cost-cutting options—unless an investigation would cost the amount of his severance. Still, with what Iris said, it sounds like Raphael figured out something Kevin didn't want known. Let's hope we get some answers when we go to Raphael's tonight.

Jazmine claps her hands once and says, "You're welcome to go back to your desks with your siblings to study, but before that, we're looking for volunteers to help decorate the gym for the Alice Walker High School holiday dance. We need a theme. Faith here"—she points to Iris's little sibling—"is leading the project."

Jamal's hand shoots up. "I'll volunteer to help out."

I raise my hand as well.

"Great, you've got Sebastian and Jamal," Jazmine says, "and Nora and I are also happy to help."

"Let's go discuss it with them and see how we can help." Jamal gets up and hurries over to sit next to Faith.

Jamal and I are definitely going to get along.

Chapter Fourteen

Iris

"You got three Secret Snowflake gifts delivered via the mail cart while you were at the Big Sibling meeting," Jin Ae says. "Lucky you!"

I open the first. It's a jar of honey with a red flag taped to it. A shiver snakes through me. Is it a warning—someone knows I'm going to set up honeypots? Not Sebastian, right? Would he have bought a jar of honey this afternoon? Or is it a hint as to what to do? I stick it in my desk drawer gingerly. I don't know. Everyone seems to be occupied—nobody is looking at me to see my reaction.

Why did Kevin say "*You* don't want it right now" to Hank?

The other gift is a calculator. I guess I can always use another calculator.

The third gift is an ergonomic mouse, which is a perfect gift for a gamer.

Raphael said he'd left a trail. Whatever he discovered has to be why he was fired. Otherwise, he would've told me.

I could be fired too if I follow his trail of clues. I chew on my nail.

But I'm more worried about an unknown intruder in our system. I could also lose my job if the intruder steals more company documents and I didn't do something to prevent it.

But I haven't had any time to pursue any investigation because I'm working full out on the migration. And I want to talk to Raphael directly first.

As we walk to Raphael's house in Dyker Heights, Sebastian, Maddie, and I pass by a large building decorated like a gingerbread house, with each of the windows framed in lights. A wreath hangs in the top triangle, a twinkling Christmas tree in the yard.

Dyker Heights is a residential neighborhood in Brooklyn, accessible via one of the last stops on the D subway line. The neighborhood is famous for elaborate Christmas displays, each house creating its own magic. It used to be a mostly Italian neighborhood, but the bubble tea shop with its sign in Chinese characters on the street corner hints that the neighborhood is definitely diversifying.

"You're sure this is where he lives?" Maddie asks.

Raphael lives in a small, brick, two-story house. The windows are completely dark. Plastic reindeer are munching on his lawn, and a Santa Claus stands by the chimney on the roof, but the decorations are very tame compared to the houses on either side. Multicolored lights threaded through the porch eaves blink on and off.

"He invited us out here once for a team dinner last December so we could see the decorations," I say. "I think it was also a gift for his mom so she could get more of a sense of the people in his office. His mom has limited mobility, and Raphael worries she is lonely. But this neighborhood seems pretty friendly. He had the dinner catered from the local diner."

"Well, the holiday lights are on," Sebastian says.

"But the windows are dark and the curtains are drawn," I say.

We walk up the stone pathway to the porch. A few dead leaves lay scattered across the path.

I ring the doorbell. No answer. I press again.

Behind me, Maddie moves away. "Here's an Amazon package, and it looks like it got wet, which means it was delivered Saturday."

I turn around as Sebastian holds up a rolled-up *New York Intelligencer* and the familiar blue plastic bag that covers it when it's raining. "Here's Saturday's newspaper."

"At least he subscribes to the *Intelligencer*," Maddie says.

"So, it looks like he and his mom left on Saturday," I say.

"Hey! Whaddya guys doing?" a muscular guy with a New York accent yells over at us from the yard next door.

The crowd of people on the sidewalk look over at us.

"I came to see Raphael," I yell back. "He's my boss, and I'm worried about him."

Sebastian quickly puts the newspaper back in the blue bag while Maddie hides the package behind a planter. "I don't want anyone to steal it."

The neighbor marches over. "Yeah, so that's why you're picking up the packages. I saw you." He points to Maddie. "Nice try with the mail theft."

"Honestly," I say. "I work with him, and I'm worried about him. How would I know his name?"

"Nice try. Wasn't it on the package?" The neighbor has both hands on his hips and is glaring at us. "Get off the porch and scram. I won't report you this time because it's the holidays, but don't come back. We look out for our own."

The three of us scramble off the porch and scoot past the reindeer.

"Sorry," I say. "I didn't think we'd be facing arrest by checking out Raphael's house." We turn to walk down the sidewalk away from Raphael's house. The guy stands behind us, hands on his hips.

"Still, I think that confirms he left with his mom. Otherwise, the neighbor wouldn't have felt so protective of the house," Maddie says.

"I need to talk to him," I say.

"Me too," Sebastian says. "Maybe he'll send you more clues, though."

"Keep calling him. He might relent and pick up," Maddie says. "I always keep phoning, even if someone doesn't want to talk to me. At some point, they get so annoyed, they answer the phone."

Annoying Raphael is not exactly my goal.

"Speaking of annoying, how are things with your neighbor?" I ask. I explain to Sebastian that Maddie lives next door to an up-and-coming rock star, and their adjoining walls are paper thin.

"He's had some hits on YouTube, but he assured me he won't move out because he's reinvesting everything back into the business," Maddie says.

"Assured?" I ask.

"That was definitely his tone," Maddie says. "I told him I hope his investments include soundproofing."

"Rock stars." I shake my head. "We could look for a place together once I know what's happening with work."

Maddie makes a noncommittal noise. She says she's not interested in Nick, but I worry that she does like him and he's going to break her heart.

"I've never been here," Sebastian says. "Should we at least take a walk around? Maybe we can get some ideas for how to decorate the gym for the high school holiday party."

Maddie winks at me. "Yes, we definitely should."

We walk up 84th Street. Ahead of us, a tourist group speaking in Italian follows a man with a yellow umbrella. I glance back, and I swear someone slips behind a tree. Raphael? Not thin enough.

Koi fish imagery plays over the façade of the first house on 13th Avenue, slipping in and out of brightly colored light strands hung to look like seaweed, giving the impression the fish are playing hide-and-seek. A crowd stands in front of it taking pictures. It is amazing—the whole house is glowing. Sebastian and I share a glance of appreciation.

"Those are the Chinese characters for 'good luck,'" Maddie says.

"We definitely need that," I say.

The next house has a ten-foot Santa Claus statue waving hello from the front porch, and red and white lights cover the trees and the roof. Across the street is a wooden three-story house decorated in red and gold.

I turn around quickly and catch the neighbor behind us.

"Is the neighbor trailing us?" Maddie asks. "Does he think we're casing the area?"

The neighbor points two fingers at his eyes and then at us. Repeatedly.

Is he a crazy person?

"Maybe we should leave," I say.

"Let him follow us," Sebastian says. "We're not doing anything wrong."

"And it took us an hour to get here," Maddie says. "We should see the decorations."

"This is Lucy Spato's house," a tour guide tells his group.

"Who's that?" Sebastian asks.

"She's the one who started this tradition," Maddie says.

"It's amazing," I say. Toy soldiers, angels, and multiple Frosty the Snowmen completely fill in the yard on either side of the path up to her house. A blazing neon green and red Merry Christmas sign glows from the top of her house, surrounded by shooting stars.

"I read up about this," Maddie says. "She wanted to start something free for the neighborhood so people didn't have to go into Manhattan. People have even proposed in front of her house,"

"I'll tell Rupert," Sebastian says.

We pass by more houses decorated to the hilt. It's like the store windows in Manhattan on steroids.

"It feels like we've stepped into a real-life version of Candy Land, the Christmas Edition," I say.

"Where do they store all that stuff in the summer?" Maddie asks. And then we realize that some houses hire professional decorating companies when we see their signs dotting many of the lawns.

"We'll never be able to do anything like this for the school gym," I say. "We don't have the funds, although we definitely could project images over the walls, like the first house with the Koi fish."

"We could always do a winter wonderland theme," Sebastian says. "My mom did that once for her holiday party. I'm sure she still has some decorations in storage she used for that."

"A winter wonderland is a good idea. That's pretty easy and inexpensive to create," I say. "We can cut out paper snowflakes and hang them from the ceiling."

"But maybe not so creative?" Sebastian asks.

"We're not the most creative people of Dream, so we can ask the set design team for ideas," I say. "But Faith said there were no decorations last year, so at least the baseline is low."

"I think the neighbor has given up trailing us," Sebastian says. "Some of these houses are huge."

"And there are so many different styles of architecture," I say. And different materials: brick, wood, clapboard, and stone.

We wander up 83rd street to 10th Avenue and then down 84th Street.

One house is so bright, you can barely see the brick façade behind the multicolored lights. Christmas carols play on outside speakers. The aroma of cooking chestnuts wafts over from a food truck. A re-purposed ice cream truck offers hot chocolates. One house has a large grill set up in their garage, and the smell of frying hamburgers blows over.

I'm only here because of Raphael's departure, but last year when we visited, I thought I should make this an annual holiday tradition and invite all my friends to come with me. But I wouldn't have done that this year, again, because I would have put work first. I really need to make time for my personal life.

The house and trees ahead are covered in green lights. A tour guide holding up a Santa hat on a stick explains that the decorations are inspired by the Emerald City from *The Wizard of Oz*.

As we wander through the neon green wonderland, Sebastian and I smile at each other. Maddie has moved ahead, so it's just the two of us taking it in. His hand brushes by mine. As the tour group barrels by, he pulls me out of the way, his hand lightly gripping my arm. He doesn't release me immediately. We stand there for a moment, inches apart, off to the side, neither one of us looking at the other. Around us little green lights twinkle and glow, as if to say this is a "Go." It's safe.

I move first and catch up to Maddie.

He wants to remain single. And I've got enough going on at work.

Maddie and I reach the next corner first, where Santa, Grinch, Mickey Mouse, and Snow Miser figures occupy a rustic shed. Sebastian seems to be taking his time. Is he having some sort of debate with himself? A little girl bundled up with a green knit hat pushes the button to make the figures talk.

When he finally reaches us, his cheeks are flushed, but that could be the cold. He doesn't look at me and seems to be really taking in the shed.

But then he turns to me and says, "How about a theme of Heat Miser and Snow Miser for the school dance? That would be fun to decorate. Do half the gym in a tropical theme and half in a wintery ice theme."

Was he just thinking of ideas all this time? And here I am wondering if he's debating whether to give in to this attraction.

"That's a great idea," I say. "Let me text Faith and see what she thinks, but maybe they haven't even seen the classic *Santa Claus is Coming to Town*."

"You're making me feel so old. My mom made me watch that," Sebastian says.

"Same," Maddie and I say.

"I can ask Jamal tomorrow when we meet for tutoring. I'm meeting him at the St. Agnes library uptown," Sebastian says.

"I'm impressed," I say.

"He really wants to give a better report card to his mom for Christmas," Sebastian says. "We went over math problems today. He has a test on Friday."

I text Faith about Sebastian's idea.

> Faith: *Yes! Can we meet after school tomorrow and get decorations?*

> Me: *How about we meet at Banter & Books? We can do some math tutoring first.*

> Faith: *Really?*

> Faith: *Way to be a killjoy.*

> Faith: *Jamal says he is studying with Sebastian, so maybe we do need to step it up.*

Sebastian asks Maddie what she does. I watch them chatting.

Today was crazy.

No Raphael.

Huge promotion.

I'm the Deputy CISO of Dream. It's a dream come true, but it doesn't feel like one. What happened to Raphael? And Kevin's behavior was disturbing. It wasn't a positive start.

Tomorrow, I need to get into the office early and do more investigating. As part of our security protocol, our files are backed up to another facility in case of a ransomware attack, and I checked—they still have Raphael's files. I'll look through those tomorrow.

The next house is covered in American flags and has a huge Statue of Liberty. Speakers blare Alicia's Key's "New York" anthem, but as that song finishes, Patrick's New York song comes on.

I wince. This song is inescapable, a constant reminder that I blinded myself to Patrick's faults and thought he really loved me.

Maddie's arm suddenly slips through mine, and she pulls me along.

"C'mon, I hear the next block also has good decorations," she says. Maybe I don't have to worry that she's falling for her rock star neighbor.

MADDIE AND I EXIT the subway together at Grand Street. The wind whips my hair in my face. It's so cold it's taking my breath away. The temperature has definitely dropped since we first entered the subway. We walk past the shuttered stores; signs in Chinese adorn the storefronts.

"What's going on with Sebastian?" Maddie asks.

"He wants to stay single," I say.

"He's not acting like he wants to stay single," she says.

"He came out to Dyker Heights because he also thinks Raphael's termination is suspicious—especially because Kevin said Raphael did something unauthorized, though Kevin can't—or won't—prove it."

"Kevin said that?" Maddie asks.

"That's what Sebastian said," I say.

Maddie shudders. "That Kevin is such a snake. Making false in-sinuations without any facts. Maybe you should get out of there. I don't trust him. Especially how you described the way he used his body to try to intimidate you."

"But I'm Deputy CISO," I say.

"You should use that title to look for a job with a better boss. Especially now that Raphael is gone," Maddie says.

"It's not like Deputy CISO jobs are out there for the picking," I say wryly. "And it's not like I even have time. I'm already trying to investigate this hack in my free time because company time is consumed with the migration."

"I wish I could help," Maddie says.

"You did help today, by coming out with me to Dyker Heights."

Maddie slips her arm through mine. "I can't decide if it was good I came along or not. I'm worried you're falling for Sebastian because he's safe and he won't reciprocate your feelings. But I'm not sure he's so safe. The way he looks at you...and when the two of you were making cookies at Lily's, it was a miracle you needed to use the oven to heat up the cookies. I worry you'll get your heart broken if he isn't interested in a serious long-term relationship."

We stop in front of Maddie's apartment building. The light is on in her neighbor's apartment, and faint strains of Christmas music can be heard through his window.

"Nick is trying to come up with a Christmas song. He's been doing some Christmas song covers, but he also wants to write his own," Maddie says.

"Well, it can't be too bad to listen to Christmas music right now," I say.

"If Sebastian said he was interested in a relationship right now, what would you say?" Maddie asks.

So much for the brief reprieve.

"I don't know," I say, facing her. "I admit I'm attracted to him. And at Dahlia's party, when I was tipsy, I leaned in to kiss him—"

"You did?"

I sigh. "I did. And he admitted he leaned it to kiss me. We both acknowledge the attraction. But we're also adult enough to know that we can't act on it. I don't do flings well. I *can't* go through another breakup like Patrick. Especially with what's going on at work. And we work together. Our friends are getting married." I shake my head. "You don't have to worry. We're not going to date."

Chapter Fifteen

Sebastian

COLORFUL COUNTRY FLAGS WAVE from the tall poles surrounding the Rockefeller Center ice rink. "All I Want for Christmas" and the sharp slish-slash of skates slicing through the ice fills the air. The majestic Rockefeller Christmas tree is always an impressive sight. I never called Melody to see the tree lighting this year. That used to be our thing. Among others. Not that she called me either. It's good. I'm moving on.

Iris is already out on the ice, and she's grinning at her little sibling. The more time we spend together, the more I'm attracted to her. When I pulled her out of the way of that guy about to poke her in the face with his umbrella, I didn't want to let her go. Rupert and Lily. Zeke and Tessa. Four very good reasons why we are off-limits for each other.

Jamal already has his skates on. I lace up mine and wobble over to the area where our group is gathering. I gingerly step onto the ice as Jamal rushes on with all his friends. He's definitely a better skater than me. To be honest, though, his technique seems to be to run on the ice. Definitely more fearless.

I wasn't lying when I said I'm not a good ice skater. I want to join the one kid clinging to the side. Jazmine skates over to reassure her.

I sort of glide around in a circle, keeping my eye on Jamal. He's having a great time with his friends. We've clearly done whatever bonding we're going to do for now.

Ahead of me, a woman jerks backwards and spin-wheels her arms. I give her wide berth. I barely have my own balance and definitely don't want to be taken down.

Ice skating may have been a mistake. I look pathetic—more walking than gliding—but I'm trying.

Iris skates up to me and slides her arm through mine. "Are you okay?"

"I'm not sure humiliating myself is giving my little sibling the best impression of me."

"Of course it is," Iris says, her warm body pressing against mine. Maybe ice skating isn't so bad after all. "It shows that you're willing to do a lot to hang out with him and that you also have enough confidence to try something new, even if it means failing at first."

"Does it show all that?"

"Subconsciously." She grins.

I slip on the ice slightly, and Iris grabs me.

"I don't want to take you down with me," I say. "I don't think you should hold me."

"I'm stronger than I look," she says.

"I think that's true, but I'm not sure you believe it," I say.
She blinks.

It's pretty clear that Iris is still recovering from being cheated on. When that song came on yesterday, she noticeably froze. Is she afraid to date again—except with someone like Ernest? She was being very friendly towards him during the cookie-making session. But at least she told him she doesn't date coworkers.

Like me.

But this is good because we can get to know each other as friends and colleagues, without stepping immediately into a relationship that may fail. The way my father got to know my mother.

"I guess I can lean on you," I say, pulling her closer.

She manages to hold my weight.

"I think you're single because you're a flirt," she says.

"I don't flirt with just anyone," I say. "But you're a lot of fun to flirt with. And I know you're not looking for a relationship right now, so you're safe."

"Exactly." She nods.

Confirmed.

Not that that approach worked with Melody. Our best friendship didn't turn out to be a firm foundation.

The first lines of "Last Christmas" by Wham play, filling the resulting silence between us. The air is crisp, and everything looks so bright under the lights. My breath forms a cloud in the air. Someone dressed in an ice hockey jersey does a quick stop in front of us, slashing through the ice.

A few snowdrops fall. Iris sticks out her tongue to catch them.

"First snow," she says. "Perfect."

She's glowing. *Maybe not that safe.* I need to keep this all business.

"I looked through our files, and I found a partially executed white hacking agreement," I say. "Kevin signed it. But it doesn't have the assignment attached."

"I found what the hacker went after." She looks around. "It was the board presentations. The board presentation of the New Mexico CEO and Xavier's board presentation."

I stop short. Iris keeps going. She almost pulls me over, but we grab each other in time. Now we're standing in the middle of the ice, holding on to and staring at each other. Other skaters flow around us.

"Sorry," she says.

"You can't tell me stuff like that when I'm ice skating." I wobble.

"I can't tell you via email, either," she says. "And I don't want to tell you where anyone can overhear me."

"Ooh. What are you telling each other?" Jazmine skates up. "You guys look so cute together. Is there an office romance brewing?"

"No." Iris shakes her head. "I'm asking him legal advice on the asset segregation strategy."

Jazmine's whole face falls. "What am I going to do with you? There's holiday music playing, it's snowing, everything is twinkling, you're skating under the Rockefeller tree, and you're asking him legal advice? She's obsessed with her job." Jazmine puts her hands on her hips. "I'll rescue you, Sebastian."

"What about Aaron?" Iris asks.

"I need to make Aaron jealous." Jazmine grabs my hand and pulls me. I shrug sheepishly at Iris and skate slowly off with Jazmine. For my own reasons. I want to find out more about Iris. Jazmine is a very good ice skater. That doesn't surprise me.

"Aaron is definitely looking over," I say. "But you shouldn't tease him like that."

"He is?" Jazmine grins. "That was just an excuse to talk to you about Iris. Iris is a very good friend. I want to ask you about your intentions."

"My intentions?" I falter on the ice, the front of my skate catching on an ice chunk. "We really were discussing work."

"Iris was really asking for legal advice just now?"

"I started discussing business first," I say.

"I'm disappointed in you, Sebastian," she says.

"But you just questioned my intentions," I say.

"Well, I'd hoped you *had* intentions," she says grumpily.

"Shouldn't I keep it to business? Isn't she interested in Ernest?" I ask.

Jazmine's head whips around to face me. "You know that?"

Well, that confirms my suspicion. I can't say I'm happy about it.

"I suspected it," I say.

"She's only asking you questions about Ernest because she's the secret snowflake for him," Jazmine says.

"I don't think that's the sole reason," I say.

"Maybe she thinks he's good boyfriend material, but Aaron doesn't like him, so I don't think so."

"Aaron doesn't like him?" I ask.

"Aaron says that Ernest is too subservient to management," she says.

Okay, so maybe Bob was right and I should socialize more if I can get this kind of on-the-ground intelligence.

"In what way?" I ask.

"I don't know," she says. "I shouldn't have said anything. Don't tell Aaron I said anything."

"I won't. But I may indirectly follow up with him in case there's something I should know. You should skate with him, though, not with me, because he looks lonely over there. And I should hang out with my little sibling."

I catch up to Jamal, who introduces his group of friends.

"Do you want to take a break and get some hot chocolate?" I ask. "We can talk."

"You may not be good on the ice, but you got two of the prettiest women at the company to skate with you," he says. "Not bad, bro."

"I can't say it was intentional. I'm not that clever. But…"

"I think you're definitely milking it," he says.

"Just a little." I grin. "And not to set a bad example. I thought I wasn't that obvious."

We sit down with hot chocolate. Iris, Aaron, and Jazmine join us with their siblings.

"Jazmine and I are going to go shopping for her secret snowflake this weekend," Nora says.

"After we look at your homework." Jazmine explains what the Secret Snowflake program is. We all admit that we've signed up.

"Do you know who your Secret Snowflake is?" Faith asks Iris.

She shakes her head. "I've received so many gifts that I think I must have more than one."

"We do secret snowflakes too, but we just exchange a gift on a certain day, so it's not really a secret," Jamal says.

"And it usually ends up being candy," says Faith.

"Which I give to my mom," Jamal says.

"What your mom would really like is for you to get top honors in math," Faith says.

"So would yours," says Jamal.

"True. And your mom would like you to get a summer job or internship," Faith says.

"What do you like to do?" Iris asks Jamal.

"Play computer games," says Faith, answering for him.

"You like to play them too," Jamal says.

Are they dating?

"You guys are close?" I ask.

"We're neighbors," Faith says.

"We'll get you there in math," I say. "We can keep meeting after school via Zoom to go over your homework."

"Me too," Iris says.

"Our internet is not always that reliable."

"We can also have a phone call," Iris says. "What's your textbook called? Maybe we can find a used version on the internet."

"And we should research possible summer jobs or internships now. The applications probably open up in January," I say. "Should I get another round of hot chocolates?"

"I'll come with you," Jamal says.

Jamal punches me playfully as we leave to buy more hot chocolates. The price is outrageous.

"Way to play wingman," he says. "I just might get honors this year if I'm spending all my evenings with Faith."

"Have you asked her out?" I pick up the tray with hot chocolates and turn to carry it back to the table.

"No." He shakes his head. "She's made clear she's all about studying right now. No time for guys. I'm just lucky to have grown up with her and be her neighbor. But maybe if I get top grades, I can prove to her that I'm good enough."

BOTH IRIS AND I elect to return to the office. Jazmine raises an eyebrow.

"How are you getting home?" Aaron asks Jazmine. "Maybe we can take the subway together. I'm uptown."

"I'm uptown too," Jazmine says.

"I'm downtown. Maybe I should go back to the office too." Ernest shakes his head. "But I promised Mother I'd be home early tonight."

"Is your mother not feeling well?" Jazmine asks.

"No. Mother is fine. She just made her beef stew for me, and I promised I'd be home in time to eat it."

Ernest may give the nice guy vibe, but he seems to be a package deal with his mother.

We all say our good-byes, and Iris and I walk off. Or try to. We immediately get stuck in a crowd that's not going anywhere. We stand there, waiting, taking a step here and there, as the person in front of us inches forward.

I hook my arm through Iris's. "I don't want to lose you in this crowd."

She laughs. "Like you could."

But Iris doesn't pull her arm away. And I'm happy to be back in my shoes on flat ground. I feel so mobile and free—except for being utterly hemmed in by the crowd.

We shuffle along, following the person in front of us, surrounded on all sides by people. We finally pass by the side doors of Radio City Music Hall. The smell of buttered popcorn is strong. Next to us is an Italian family chattering away. They're probably figuring out directions, but it sounds like they're reciting poetry.

"There," Iris says. "It's moving over there. Let's follow them." We scoot behind a line of pedestrians advancing down the pavement. Iris shivers and sticks her hands into her pockets.

"Can you show me what you found?" I ask.

"Yes," Iris says. "Also, I received another Secret Snowflake gift today—a very dog-eared copy of *Zero Trust Networks*, which I swear I've seen on Raphael's shelves. Raphael must be my Secret Snowflake. I asked his assistant if she was sending me his gifts, but she said no."

"Did you think she was going to tell you if she was?"

Iris pouts. "So many secrets."

"Christmas is kind of a time for secrets—the whole Santa Claus thing, and parents trying to keeps gifts hidden from their children—but there's a joyful revelation at the end," I say.

Iris glances at me. "I hope it's joyful in this case. I feel so guilty about getting this promotion because of Raphael leaving." Her face is clouded by concern and doubt.

"Raphael is a grown-up. He made a decision to leave, and he received a very sizable severance package."

"Did he?"

"I shouldn't have told you that." I shake my head. I'm usually very good at keeping company matters confidential. Iris just seems to be able to undermine my defenses.

"So did you discover where your parents hid your presents?" she asks.

"Yes, in a bathroom closet, high up. And my mom sometimes hid them under the bed. I bet you found where your parents hid yours."

"They hid them in the basement. They really didn't do a very good job. I hide all my presents in an extra laundry bag because my siblings will definitely look if they come over. Believe me, nobody goes looking in the dirty laundry."

"Clever," I say.

"Except that the true meaning of Christmas—and any holiday, really—is not a secret," Iris says slowly. "It's about giving and creating community. It's about shining light when the season is at its darkest."

She looks up at me, and her eyes brim with tears. I want to kiss them away.

I pull her closer to me. My usual flippant response isn't the right answer here. "We'll figure out what's going on."

Back at Dream, we meet in my office since Iris's desk has no privacy. Iris places her laptop on my desk and scoots her chair around so we're sitting next to each other. She's wearing this soft, fluffy pink sweater that looks like an invitation to touch. I turn away and sign into my computer.

"How did you find out what was stolen?" I ask.

"Raphael put them in his investigation files. We keep a backup of all our files offsite in case of a ransomware attack. Raphael's backup files were not deleted, and I found the two presentations in his investigation files in a folder called Zero Trust. Raphael said I had to follow the clues. I think his sending me that book was the first clue."

"Wow, that's clever. Doesn't Kevin know about the backup?"

"He definitely knows we have a backup, but he must've assigned the deletion to Hank. According to the version history, Hank deleted Raphael's files. Like I said, Hank was hired as a favor, and he's not the most competent guy."

"And isn't Kevin a good friend of Colby's from college?"

"I didn't know that," she says.

"Bob mentioned it," I say.

"Who would want to steal the board presentations?" Iris asks. "Rivals? The competing CEOs? Is that legal?"

"Not without some official company authorization. The work product is the property of the company, but the CEO is not the company. Also, don't you agree that Kevin must be involved because there's that partially executed agreement authorizing white hat hacking? Can I see the presentations?"

"Here are the documents. I copied them into another file on premise." She hands me the documents.

I read aloud the file name where she re-saved the board presentations on our system. "Backup for Training on Interacting with Colleagues—Think Courtesy."

"Nobody is going to want to look at that," she says.

"That's for sure."

"Here's the New York presentation," Iris says.

I flip through it. "That's not our presentation."

"What do you mean?"

"I've never seen that before. And I've been working on our presentation." I pull up our presentation on my monitor. "Look. There's nothing similar except the title page."

"So, it's a fake presentation?" Iris asks. "They must have told the hacker to steal both presentations so it looked more legitimate to the white hat hacker. Then it would look like a corporate-approved exercise to assess both CEO's vulnerability. But they planted a false New York presentation for the hacker to steal so that the real one wouldn't get out. And that means it's New York who wanted the presentations."

We stare at each other. This is so much worse than what I expected.

I click on the folder labeled "No Micromanagement" in Iris's files. "N and M for New Mexico?"

She nods.

I read through it.

"These are basically the slides New Mexico gave at the board meeting. And I think someone here definitely saw this Albuquerque presentation before we gave ours because I can see why we had to buttress certain points they told me to improve before the meeting."

"So, it seems that the Albuquerque presentation was the target of the attack, and a senior executive here had to be involved because that person saw this New Mexico presentation and then had the New York slide deck changed to make it better than New Mexico's," Iris says. "Kevin signed that agreement, but he must have acted at Colby or Xavier's direction."

We look at each other for a second before speaking.

"This is not good," says Iris.

"This is bad," I say at the same time.

"Did you tell Kevin yet?" I ask.

"No. I don't trust him anymore. But he insisted that I tell him anything I find. But if he's the one who authorized this…"

"We could tell the board," I say.

"The board. I don't feel I have enough to tell the board."

"Two CEO presentations were exfiltrated, and we have a partially executed white hat hacking agreement."

"Which Kevin could just say was never actually implemented. And if I go above Kevin's head, I'm definitely going to lose my job. Maybe not immediately because I'll be protected as a whistleblower under the no retaliation policy. But eventually, Kevin will figure out a reason to fire me. If I could figure out the identity of the hacker, we could ask that person what they hacked and who authorized it. And then we'd have enough to inform the board."

"Could Raphael be the hacker?"

"What's Raphael's motive?"

"Remember Bob said he did something unauthorized."

She shakes her head. "Raphael knew about the traps, so he wouldn't have tripped them. And given our investigation to date, we could have gotten that PowerPoint via either the CEO or the assistant with no trace. They sent the presentation to their personal emails so they could work on them at home." Iris bites her nail. "I could tell Kevin. If I'm thrown out tomorrow, we'll know why Raphael was thrown out."

"But L'Etoile wants another presentation—in two days," I say.

"On what? Didn't you cover everything in the last presentation?"

"This is to showcase our new movie ideas, so Bob said our role is limited and it's mostly up to creative. A few updated budget numbers will need to be included, but that's about it."

"If Colby, Xavier, and Kevin hired the hacker the first time, won't they be tempted to steal New Mexico's draft presentation again?"

"I think so. We have to tell the board," Sebastian says.

"Kevin is meeting with Colby tomorrow at nine a.m. in the conference room. I had to give him updated budget numbers today for that meeting before I left. We should listen in," Iris says. "If that meeting is completely innocuous, I'll tell Kevin. If it's not, I'll tell the board."

"We can't listen in," Sebastian says. "If they're discussing some sort of hacking, wouldn't they meet in their offices?"

"You'd think. But he definitely told his assistant to reserve the conference room. It's the one with the walk-in supply closet. We can hide in there. Are you in?"

"I'm in. But I'm not sure it's a good idea."

Chapter Sixteen

Iris

THE CONFERENCE ROOM HAS a slight whiff of Meyer's geranium cleaning spray from last night's housekeeping visit. The sharp morning sun is just catching the aluminum backs of the conference chairs.

"Make sure you put any supplies that they might need out on the table," I say. "I definitely don't want them to find us."

Sebastian sets out a pile of notepads as I add more pencils and pens to the leather cups on the table.

"And what are we going to tell them if they do?" Sebastian asks.

"That we're dating, having a tryst in the closet, and we were too embarrassed to come out and get caught. That's if they catch us. Otherwise, if they seem to be coming towards the closet, I will exit and tell Kevin what I found and say I was in the room and ran into the closet because I wasn't ready to face him yet with my suspicions."

It's 8:50.

Go time.

We walk into the closet. It seemed a lot more spacious when we weren't inside it together.

"Maybe we should move this easel closer to the wall." I brush against Sebastian as I move it closer.

"It'll be worse if it falls and makes a noise," he says.

"Where's it going to fall?" I ask. "There's no space."

I'm standing in the front, and Sebastian is behind me. He's so warm. It's like heat is radiating off him. I'd fan myself, but that's hardly going to decrease the temperature in here. I unbutton my sweater.

We shift so that we're facing each other, Sebastian closer to the door opening.

"We should switch so I'm closer," I say.

"I'll go out first," Sebastian says. "I'll tell them I came in here for a legal pad. You stay here."

"And you didn't come out?"

"Because I was suspicious after finding the hacking agreement that the cybersecurity team didn't know about." He stares at me as if daring me to force him to move. Somehow, I don't think wrestling for the position closest to the door is a smart idea in this tight space.

The conference room door handle clicks.

"Turn off the light. I hear them."

I switch off the light. Our breathing sounds very loud.

My eyes adjust to the darkness, and Sebastian puts his finger to his lips. My heart races. It's not his proximity. It can't be. It's the fact that I'm spying on senior management. He's so close. That broad chest and those shoulders. And he's tall.

"Do you think France is still deciding between the two locations?" Kevin asks.

"Of course they are," Colby says. "Why else would they want another presentation?"

"But it's movie content. There's nothing we can do. It's up to Xavier," Kevin says.

"They want to know if we have any good ideas before they close us down," Colby says. "Maybe they will even take our ideas and shut us down anyway."

"Our presentation was clearly better than New Mexico's."

"And we need to make sure this one is also better. She needs to get their draft," Colby says.

"We can't. She's not going to want to do it again. She was suspicious the first time. I think she talked to Raphael. And the site is mined with traps and honeypots. The cybersecurity team is watching twenty-four-seven."

"Can't is not an acceptable answer. Figure out a way," Colby says. "Find some other urgent project for cybersecurity to work on. You keep telling me we're short on resources, so tell them this isn't the priority. I thought she was one of the best white hat hackers. She should be able to get around a few traps."

Kevin mutters something I can't hear. I move closer to the door, closer to Sebastian. My body brushes up against his.

"Stop moving," Sebastian says in a low, deep, strangled voice.

"Sorry," I whisper.

Silence on the other side. I tense. Sebastian's body tightens next to mine. Did they hear us? Did I mess it up?

"What about replacing her with that guy Hank?" Colby asks.

"I'll figure something out."

"You do that," Colby says.

"Hi. I thought *we* had the conference room for 9:30. Should we find another room?" It's Jazmine.

"We're leaving," Kevin says.

"How's everything going?" Colby asks. "Great work the other day on finding that hire."

"Thank you. I didn't realize you knew about that."

"I pride myself on knowing what's going on in my company. Who are the stars, who are the shirkers. In fact, I just learned a Swedish word for it: *maskning,* which means foot dragging or working very slowly. I know who is doing what at Dream."

My eyes widen. Does Colby know we're in the closet? I glance up at Sebastian.

The door clangs shut. Hopefully Colby and Kevin left.

My chest touches his. I pull back quickly, standing up straight, the shelves hard in my back. My head hits some pencil boxes, and Sebastian quickly reaches out to hold them in place. His arm is by my head. I swallow. He's so close. His breath brushes against my cheek. And I'm trying to press back and basically not breathe so I don't touch him, but it's like my body won't listen to me and keeps leaning forward. Sebastian's body is equally rigid.

His face looks pained.

"Are you and Aaron dating?" a woman's voice asks. She sounds familiar, but I can't place the voice.

"He asked me out yesterday after the ice skating event," Jazmine says. "He's so sweet. I swear, he moved closer to me yesterday when we were drinking hot chocolate. And then we took the subway home together. And it was so crowded that we got squished together." Jazmine giggles. "He had his arm by my head against the metal door, trying to stop his body from being pressed into mine."

I stare up at Sebastian. He pulls his arm back. I look down at the carpeted floor.

Jazmine sighs. "He's such a gentleman. He even got off the sub-way to walk me home, and then he asked me out."

"You're so lucky. I can't find any good guys. I had a date the other day. I thought it went well, and then he called me and told me he wanted to remain single. Why did he go out on the date in the first place, then?"

I look at Sebastian and tilt my head.

Sebastian shakes his head.

The initial personal chitchat over, they get down to the serious business of their meeting.

Sebastian tilts his head back and swallows. And oh, his Adam's apple.

This closet is way, way too small. And we're way too close. And I'm afraid to move and make a noise.

Our glances meet again, and he takes a deep breath. I can smell the peppermint of his toothpaste. His gaze travels over my face, and it's almost as if he's touching me with it. My whole body is flickering, my senses are buzzing. *Must* squash down these feelings of desire.

"Great. That's all settled," Jazmine says.

There's a slight tap as if they've picked up their laptops. And then the door creaks as it opens and clicks shut.

"We've got to go before someone else comes." I reach to open the door.

"I can't leave yet," Sebastian says, his voice low and tight. "You go."

Sebastian is attracted to me.

Or he is just a guy in a tight space with a woman.

I open the door just a bit and slip through the space, closing the door behind me.

And out steps Xavier from the opposite door—the door that leads into his office.

"Eavesdropping?" he asks.

Chapter Seventeen

Sebastian

THE SOUND OF XAVIER'S voice quickly cools any desire. I step out. Iris looks shell-shocked.

How much did he hear? Do we proceed with our cover story? Does Iris want me to say that?

"I heard you guys when you entered. I was waiting for Colby and Kevin," Xavier says.

No cover story.

"Why are you eavesdropping?" he asks.

"Because we think Kevin hired a hacker to obtain New Mexico's board presentation so he could give it to Colby—and maybe you—so you'd have an inside knowledge on how to make the New York presentation better," Iris says.

Xavier nods. "I wasn't in on it, but I definitely suspected something when our presentation changed so much. It was so much better than New Mexico's in ways it wouldn't have been without those last-minute changes."

"That also raised my suspicions. The changes were just so on point," I say.

"I also know my brother. He always cheated at Monopoly. But even so, I didn't expect this. And I don't expect you to believe me when I tell you I wasn't involved. But I'll prove it by my follow-up actions. My brother and Kevin will have to go. I will tell the Board." He slumps down into a chair. "I wish he'd trusted me. L'Etoile is not going to shut us down—our ideas are just too good—but now I don't know."

He looks at me. "Why are you involved?" And then he turns to Iris. "Did you think to involve Legal? You two aren't really dating?"

"No," Iris says quickly. Way too quickly.

"Iris and I are friends, and Legal was informed of the unauthorized hacker. And then I looked through our files and found a partially executed hacker agreement." We explain the rest of what we found.

"Thank you for your hard work and your honesty," Xavier says. "I'll schedule a meeting with the board. You can tell them what you've told me. Do you think Bob is involved?"

"Not that I'm aware of," I say.

"I'll talk to him, then," Xavier says. "We'll figure out if there's any way to save the company while admitting to this."

The door to the conference room opens, and Colby enters. I take a step back.

"I thought you were in LA," Colby says to Xavier.

"I flew back early. Did you hire a hacker to infiltrate the system and steal New Mexico's presentation?"

Colby juts out his chin and folds his arms. "Yes. The company wasn't going to shut down on my watch, not before the holidays."

"They're not going to shut down the company. They didn't buy us to close us down," Xavier says.

"Don't be so naïve. They bought us for the IP. They don't need us," Colby says.

"They need me. They need the creative minds behind the IP. That's the value of the company," Xavier says. "They want more content, not just the movies we've already created."

Colby waves at Iris and me. "What are these two doing here?"

"They figured it out too," Xavier says.

Colby frowns at us. "I'll come clean to the board and step down, if you think they won't close the company."

That's quick. And not like Colby. He must have something up his sleeve.

"I can't promise that now," Xavier says.

"But they'll still have you. Not so convinced of your position now?" He gestures again towards us. "We can show the internal controls worked."

"Who else knows?" Xavier asks.

"Let's discuss that privately," Colby says.

"Fair enough." Xavier turns to us. "Perhaps you can leave us now? Thank you for your commitment to the company."

Iris and I walk out. I run my hand through my hair. *That was crazy.*

"At least Xavier wasn't involved," Iris says. "Maybe the company can be saved."

"Let's hope," I say. We part outside the Cybersecurity bullpen.

I return to my office but then decide I'm going to walk around the block to clear my head.

Colby hired the hacker. That's next-level insanity.

It snowed a bit this morning, but the sidewalks have already been cleared. My shoes crunch in the sand scattered to melt the snow. Brown branches outlined in white arch over the street.

I'm so attracted to Iris.

I don't want to be friends.

I don't think I can just be friends.

Maybe this is what Melody was talking about? That we were friends for too long and the passion just wasn't there.

The passion is definitely there with Iris. It was hard not to kiss her in the closet. And she acknowledged that she's attracted to me. I just need to persuade her that we should try dating.

Chapter Eighteen

Iris

I TEXT SEBASTIAN THAT I hope to see him at the Big Sibling event. Both of us have been in meetings nonstop with Bob preparing the board presentations since yesterday morning's shocking revelation, but the board session went relatively well. Xavier briefed L'Etoile, so they didn't have many questions for Sebastian or me. Except one person asked me if *I* had ever been asked to retrieve the New Mexico CEO's presentation by Kevin. I said no.

Dream combined the book-wrapping session with the Big Brother Big Sister event to make handcrafted items as Secret Snowflake gifts. Company morale is so low that Amelia and Jazmine couldn't get many sign-ups. Amelia couldn't even come to this because she's busy with crafting a memo to all employees that the company is not about to shut down. But Jazmine admits privately that they won't *know* if the company is fine until L'Etoile makes its final decision, so Amelia is working with outside employment counsel to figure out what to say.

Jazmine also had no information on Raphael's departure—Amelia handled all that.

It's mostly big siblings and little siblings in the conference room, which remains decorated as it was for the Secret Snowflake event. Sebastian enters and heads straight for the seat next to me.

Jazmine explains the available activities: wrapping books, making ornaments, or creating a popsicle stick "why I love you" gift for your parents. She then walks us through the crafting instructions. Most of the little siblings want to do craft projects, so Sebastian and I wrap books.

It feels good to do something relaxing and mindless like this after the intensity of the past twenty-four hours.

Sebastian wraps *Seoulmates*, a friends-to-lovers YA book.

"I guess that's your trope," I say.

"Friends-to-lovers?" Sebastian asks.

I nod.

"I thought it was," he says. "I really thought a strong friendship was the key to the perfect relationship."

"And now you don't?"

"No, you still need that." His eyes darken as his glance seems to memorize my face. "But maybe I was downplaying the passion part."

I swallow. Why does it feel like we're back in the closet?

He tips his head towards the book I'm wrapping, which is *Once Upon a K-Prom*. "Did you pick the one where she dates a K-pop rock star on purpose?"

"No. It was just in the pile I picked up."

He raises his eyebrows and looks down. He can't really think I'm still mourning Patrick.

"I definitely don't recommend dating a rock star," I say. "I can't speak for a K-pop star. I think part of the reason my relationship with Patrick faltered is because I didn't want my emotions shared in his songs, so then I didn't feel like I could tell him everything I was thinking in case he then shared my inner thoughts with the world. Maybe not consciously, but subconsciously. And he could feel that. He complained that I didn't share everything with him."

"Do you think you're ready to date again now?" Sebastian asks. "Or is something holding you back?"

"I'm not sure." I bite my lip. "But I do know what's holding me back—the fear of being betrayed again."

He nods, his eyes warm pools of understanding and care.

"Maybe friends-to-lovers is the right trope for you too," he says.

I tilt my head. It's as if he knows my plan to thoroughly vet any prospects. I pick up more books from the pile. It's two that I bought: *Corduroy* plus *My Outback Rider* by Giulia Skye, while Sebastian wraps a cozy mystery called *Mutts, Murder and Mayhem*.

"I'm glad you can come to my parents' holiday party this Saturday," Sebastian says. "I hope you will save me a dance."

"I'm looking forward to it. Lily and Tessa said they'll be there too," I say.

Nora passes by and hangs her homemade ornament on the tree. "I'm Muslim so I don't celebrate Christmas, but it's still fun to make ornaments. Jazmine said I could hang it on this tree."

I glance at Jazmine. Isn't Amelia going to freak out?

Jazmine grins at me. "It looks better now. It's not so perfect. Now it's got a touch of homemade love."

Is Sebastian searching for a perfect love?

I shouldn't care, but I do. Now that the hacking mystery is cleared up, I can't help it. *I like Sebastian.* But am I ready to date him? If he is even interested. But we're friends, right? So was he trying to suggest something? He has to feel this attraction.

A woozy feeling fills my stomach, like when you're standing on a beach on firm sand, but then a wave washes over your feet, and suddenly the firm surface erodes out from under you. It's either anxiety or anticipation.

Chapter Nineteen

Sebastian

Tonight is the night of my mom's annual holiday party. I pace along the dark-red-painted hallway with wood paneling in my parents' apartment, checking the entrance. I should have volunteered to be the coat checker for the first shift. The candles flicker in their bronze sconces. For just this event, my mom insists on real candles.

I call my sister Annabelle because it feels weird that she's not here. Let's see if she picks up. My calls seem to be directed to voicemail purgatory. I lean against the wainscotting, still keeping an eye on arrivals.

"Hello." Her voice sounds tired. Wary.

"I miss you," I say simply.

"Ugh. You're so unfair," she says. "How's Dad doing?"

"Mom says he's doing much better," I say.

"Really?" she asks.

"Really. He's holding forth in the library right now."

"Because I really think I have to tell Neville that his son needs to shape up. But if it's going to cause stress for Dad..."

"You should tell Neville," I say. "Dad can handle it. And it's not fair for you to shoulder it all."

"Yes, you were supposed to handle this with me," she says, but it's lacking the heat that was there before.

"It doesn't excite me the way it does you," I say.

"I know. Okay," she says. "Say hello to Rupert and Rowena for me. Are we all going out for New Year's? I'm looking forward to that."

"Me too," I say, my voice deep, so relieved that our relationship seems to be back on track.

"I have to go to bed. Early day tomorrow," she says.

Someone with glossy brown hair just arrived. It's Iris.

"I have to go too." I hang up.

Iris looks stunning in a midnight-blue dress that swirls around her body as she hands her coat to the attendant hired for the occasion.

She meets my glance. My breath hitches. I can't take my eyes off her—and I can't get to her side quickly enough.

"I'm glad you could make it," I say. "You look beautiful."

She blinks, and a faint blush stains her cheeks.

"Thank you," she says. "You clean up rather nicely yourself."

"I haven't worn a tux since last year's party," I say.

"I bought this dress for college formals. I'm glad it still fits," she says. "But I think I've been losing weight with the stress of what's going on with Dream."

"Shh," I say reflexively.

"Sorry," she says.

"I don't want my father to know. Can I get you a drink?" I put my hand in the small of her back. Her skin is warm to the touch. The dress is backless. I didn't realize. I should withdraw my hand, but I don't want to.

Iris doesn't seem to be objecting.

I can feel the way her spine dips in. I'd like to trace her spine up to—okay. This is not good.

I need to take it slow.

Iris said she's not sure she's ready to date yet.

I need to show her she can trust me.

I pull my hand back before it gets a mind of its own.

"My parents' friends are mostly in the library," I say as we pass by the open doors, revealing a room filled with well-dressed gray-haired New Yorkers, and enter the living room. A quartet plays Bach's "Air on the G String" in the corner next to a Christmas tree decorated in green and red. The violin chords rise up in hope. "We cleared all the furniture to the side to allow for dancing later. There's a bar in the library and another in the dining room. And plenty of appetizers."

"This apartment is huge," Iris says.

"That's why my father wants me to go into finance," I say. "But he also bought this a long time ago. What can I get you at the bar?"

"A white wine is good," she says.

Smiling at each other, we stand there, making no move to join the line at the bar.

An older woman's voice interrupts us. "Hello."

Mrs. Potik *would* be the first to approach us.

"I was so surprised when your mom told me," Mrs. Potik says. "You said 'my wife' so convincingly, Sebastian."

"Who'd you call your wife?" Melody asks.

Melody too? I just want Iris to myself for a second, but fine. This is good.

"Iris. This is Melody. Melody, Iris," I say. "We pretended to be fake married as an extracurricular company-related activity." That's sort of true because it was for the Secret Snowflake gift exchange. And hopefully Melody won't ask any questions.

Melody's brow furrows. She is clearly trying to figure out how being fake married could *ever* be an extra-curricular work activity. Rightly so.

"I had no idea that so much research went into movie companies creating fake dating or contract marriage plots," Mrs. Potik says. "What kind of questions did they ask on the survey afterwards?"

I am lost. Iris smirks. I'm never going to hear the end of this. I should have been the one studying up.

Iris says, "Did we feel like a couple because we were fake married? Did we think a contract marriage could lead to deeper feelings? What situations threw us?"

Not bad. Has Iris actually given thought to fake dating?

"And what did you answer?" Mrs. Potik turns to me.

"I answered yes, yes, and meeting someone we knew, like you, Mrs. Potik, definitely threw us." That's all true. I liked calling Iris "my wife."

"Are you a screenwriter?" Melody asks Iris.

"No," Iris says. "I'm in cybersecurity, but Sebastian and I met through friends, so we agreed to pair up for this."

"Iris is friends with Lily, Rupert's girlfriend," I say.

"Oh, Rupert. I haven't seen him in ages. And I haven't even met Lily." A shadow passes over Melody's face.

We used to hang out all the time together, but that changed when Melody started dating Wim. I'd call her to invite her to a dinner, but she'd say she and Wim already had plans. And honestly, I don't like Wim. Not just because he's Melody's fiancé. He's not fun. It makes me sad that Melody will marry him. Even if she doesn't want me, she should marry someone fun and warm—someone who fits in with our friend group.

"Rupert and Lily should be here soon," Iris says.

"Did you take the survey separately?" Mrs. Potik asked. She's not going to let this go, is she?

"Yes. I had the same answers as Sebastian, though," Iris says. "It was pretty fascinating. One of my close friends writes romantic comedies. We once spent a night debating whether fake dating would actually work."

How did Iris know what I was thinking?

"You really looked pregnant," Mrs. Potik says.

"You pretended you were pregnant?" Melody asks, her voice rising.

"It made sense to add that into our fake marriage charade," Iris says.

And now my mom joins this awkward conversation.

"I'm so sorry I didn't get a chance to meet you earlier. Hosting duties. But I've been wanting to get to know you." My mom smiles at Iris.

"Sebastian told me you insisted I come," Iris says.

"Did I insist?" my mom asks. *As if she didn't.* "But I'm not the one who kept checking the entrance to see if you'd arrived yet."

Thanks, Mom. Way to out your son. My mom is definitely fanning the fire here. Of course, she's never forgiven Melody for dumping me.

"I did want you to come," I say evenly.

"Do you waltz?" my mom asks Iris.

"I love to waltz. My dad taught me. He thinks it's the best dance ever. I heard from Sebastian that you forced him to learn to dance."

"He certainly didn't go willingly, but I think he's happy he learned now."

"It has its uses," I say.

"Does your fiancé now waltz?" my mom asks Melody.

"I don't think he's had time to learn since last year," Melody says. A server offers glasses of wine from a tray. We all take one. The lights in the sconces flicker against the deep-green wallpapered background.

"Where is Wim?" I ask, realizing I have yet to see him.

"He asked if he could use the study for a call," Mom says. "And then I saw him hanging out in the library talking to your dad."

"He's closing a deal in Asia," Melody says. "Work has been hectic for him lately."

Wim is in finance—what my father wishes I were doing. When Melody first told me what he did, it hurt. It felt like a betrayal. Would she have fallen for me if I'd been a private equity manager? Was that what she was looking for? Was it because I decided not to join my father at his firm? Was Rowena right about that? Wim definitely radiates that high-powered, high-stress, "time is money" attitude. But Melody wasn't about all that. Or so I'd thought.

"Mrs. Potik, you mentioned you have a green thumb. I want your advice on my orchid." My mom winks at me as she walks away with Mrs. Potik, guiding her towards a bare orchid on the windowsill that someone gave her as a gift. She's never been able to get it to flower again.

"There you are." Rupert claps me on the back. "Melody. Haven't seen you in ages. All good?"

One of the reasons Rupert and I are such good friends is because we like each other for the person underneath.

"All good," Melody says.

"This is Lily. I don't think you've met." Rupert puts his arm around Lily and pulls her close. "Melody went to college with Sebastian and me. She also loves reading and Wilhemina Chrissy."

"Nice to meet you," Lily says. "Have you read her latest?"

"The minute it came out," Melody says. "That twist at the end—mind-blowing."

"I never see the twist coming," Lily says. "And this time, I really thought I'd guessed it. And Rupert and I were reading it at the same time, so we were discussing it. We both thought we had it figured out."

"Melody," a deep voice says.

Wim.

"Can we go?" Wim reaches for her hand. "I'm sorry. Hey, Rupert. I just flew in from Tokyo, and I'm beat." He pulls her to his side, slightly away from our crowd, and says in a low voice but one that we can all still hear, "I've missed you, and I just want to be with you."

I'd believe that more if Mom hadn't said he just spent the last half hour shmoozing with my dad and his finance buddies.

"Sure," Melody says. "It was great to see you all. But I think we'll head home now."

"No waltzing?" Rupert asks. "But you like waltzing, Melody."

"I meant to take waltzing lessons after last year," Wim says, "but there was never time."

I waltzed with Melody last year. Wim probably wants to avoid a repeat of that. Fair enough.

"Sebastian insisted we take dancing lessons in college," Rupert says, "so Melody and I signed up together because there was a discount for couples, but then—"

"The instructor separated us because he thought we were a real couple. He said couples have too many fights when they're learning to dance together," Melody interjects. "We could never convince him that we weren't really a couple."

Wim stares at Rupert as if suddenly wondering if they ever were a couple and then says, "But that's why you won't teach me the waltz."

"Exactly," Melody says. "He was adamant about it. I figure he knew what he was talking about."

"I'll walk you out," I say.

"It's okay. You're with your friends," Wim says. "We'll say thank you to your mom and see ourselves out. I'm sorry I'm stealing Melody away and that I didn't get a chance to catch up with you all. We should plan to have a party soon and get together."

I've yet to see this party materialize in eighteen months.

Melody smiles apologetically as she leaves. Personally, I think he should have gone home to sleep and left Melody to hang out with her friends. But maybe they are really going to spend some quality time together.

The waitstaff offers a tray of quiche appetizers. We all take one. Zeke and Tessa arrive, and we all stand in a group, joking and devouring the finger food. I feel lucky to have this group of friends—and that I like all of my friends' girlfriends.

And Iris. I turn to Iris and smile at her.

"Shall we get drinks?" I ask. She nods, and we move away to join the line at the bar. There's quite a cluster, so we stand off to the side by the wall to wait.

Iris takes a step closer. "There was a guy I liked once in college, but I wasn't his type. He asked out this other woman who was very nice but never seemed to have her own opinion. I felt a lot better about his rejection afterwards." Iris waves her hand. "So, what I guess I'm trying to say is that I think Melody has a different type than you. You and Wim are completely different."

"How so?" I agree, but I want to know how Iris views Wim.

"I thought he was kind of a jerk. It could be that he was jetlagged, but there was no need for Melody to leave the party early. Is the only time for them to be together now—when she's hanging out with friends she clearly hasn't seen in a while? And he seemed kind of threatened by you. I just think you'd be completely different and suck it up and hang out with her friends even if you were jetlagged."

Iris's green eyes blaze. It's adorable that she's defending me. And getting so worked up about this.

"Are you saying I fall into the 'too *nice guy*' bucket?" I ask.

She nods very earnestly.

"That might be the worst thing of all. Do you think of me as a nice guy?"

"Of course," Iris says.

I pretend-crumple against the wall.

"I admit, at first, I thought you were a bit of a flirt and not to be trusted."

"But now I'm nice—as in boring and tame?"

"No. As in..." Her gaze searches my face. "Someone I'd trust."

"Thank you." That's a high compliment coming from Iris. "That means a lot to me."

A waiter passes and offers more appetizers. We each take a chicken satay stick and a napkin.

"Maybe you're right that Melody thought I was too much of a nice guy. One of our last fights before we broke up was because I was upset she took the hotel bathrobe. She complained that I was such a straight arrow, that we can't all be born with a silver spoon in our mouth. That hurt. But I said—what if the staff gets blamed? And it wasn't like she couldn't afford to buy it. It was an ugly fight, and we broke up soon after."

How did I ever think Melody and I were meant to be? It's so obvious now, with Iris, how it should be. Iris sees me so clearly.

"I definitely prefer the nice guy," she says. "What attracted me to Patrick was his consideration and, to some degree, how open he was about his feelings. At least, I usually knew where I stood with him."

My phone beeps.

Melody: *I'm glad you've found someone.*

My finger hovers over a reply. Do I write, *We're not dating?* Or save my pride and let her believe I've found someone? Because maybe I have.

Me: *Me too.*

The opening notes of *The Blue Danube* waltz fill the room as the violins call out to the responding cello.

I turn to Iris and hold out my hand. "May I have this dance?" Maybe it was best that Melody did leave.

Chapter Twenty

Iris

"I'd be delighted." I take Sebastian's hand. His grip is warm and sure, and his lips have curved up in a smile.

If Melody had stayed, would he have danced the first dance with me? He didn't look that upset, though, when Melody left.

We walk into the living room, where other couples are already swirling around the room. He pulls me into his arms, and I rest my hand on his shoulder, my arm on his.

And we're off, sweeping across the floor. As he guides me around the floor, around the other couples, I feel like I'm flying.

I grin at him, and he smiles back at me.

My dress swirls out as we twirl around the room, the hope and yearning of the violin chords filling my veins. Sebastian holds my hand firmly, and the warmth of his hand on my bare back is making my heart take flight. He smells of Ivory soap, and my mind skitters back to that desire to melt into his arms when we met. My dress flows between his legs as we dip to the music and turn again.

I step between his legs as we do the outside spin and our hips brush each other, our stomachs pressing against each other as we finish the turn. Shivery tembers of fire light up inside me as my body brushes against his and then retreats in time to the music.

His hand splayed against my back presses firmly as he leads us around the room. Now it's the deeper tones of the cellos calling out to the violins, seeking a response.

To avoid colliding into another couple, he pulls me tighter against him. My body arches against the hard wall of his chest, and I glance up at him. I can't look away. His eyes darken. The air feels heavier. My heartbeat zips. I miss a step. Sebastian catches me, and we're back on track. He holds my gaze as we swoop and spin again together.

Our bodies are communicating what we don't yet want to say in words: *I like you.*

"What are you thinking?" he whispers, his head close to mine.

Not something I can share with you…yet.

"I love the waltz," I say.

"I like dancing with you," Sebastian says. "You've clearly danced it a lot. I'm looking forward to waltzing with you in your parents' bar. How come it wasn't part of your sister's party?"

"My sister was worried she'd get nauseated with all the spinning," I say. "She doesn't like it as much as me."

Lily and Rupert pass us, completely engrossed in each other. I smile fondly at them.

The music stops. We pull apart, but Sebastian still holds my hand. He releases it, reluctantly—I think—to clap.

His parents come over, and Sebastian introduces me to his dad, who looks like an older version of Sebastian.

"Iris works at the same company as Sebastian," his mom says.

"That's how your mom and I met," Sebastian's dad says.

"I think it's a different time now, though," his mom says.

"That's for sure. Now that's all frowned upon, but back in the day, it seemed a good way to meet someone because you really got to know them before you dated them." His dad smiles at his mom. "Not that I wasn't attracted to you the minute I saw you. But it was when I realized you were whip-smart too—that's when I was really hooked. And she said no at first."

"Why'd you say no?" I ask.

"He seemed like a workaholic and not much fun," she says dryly.

"That was fair enough," he says. "I *am* a workaholic, but Jen reminds me what's really important in life. Sebastian here is too much of a workaholic like me, unfortunately."

"You think I'm a workaholic?" Sebastian asks.

"I think you have to work way too hard as a lawyer to earn money as opposed to what you could earn in finance for the same effort and intellect," his father says.

"Not here." His mom frowns at his dad.

"I think you have to work hard at any job to learn everything you need to learn, and if so, it's best that you love it," I say.

Sebastian tips his head at me while his mom pokes his dad.

"Well said," she says.

"What do you do?" Sebastian's dad asks.

"I work in cybersecurity," I say.

"That's impressive," his dad says. "A very up-and-coming field. Essential, really, nowadays."

"Where'd you grow up, Iris?" his mom asks.

"In New York City."

"Really? Are your parents still living here?"

"Yes, they love New York. They own a bar/music club on the Lower East Side." I'm not sure Sebastian's parents will approve of my family, given this Upper East Side apartment and the fact that his father is some hot shot in finance. I might as well state it up-front, because dancing with Sebastian is definitely making my heart flutter. I need to nip these feelings in the bud if this is some weird nineteenth-century situation where they will oppose our dating.

And indeed, his mom glances at his dad, only I can't tell what the look means.

"Sebastian mentioned that you have a sister? And she's pregnant?"

I guess I'm still worth being interviewed.

"I'm one of four," I say.

"That's wonderful." His mom grins.

Sebastian shakes his head slightly at his mom. She frowns, opens her mouth, and then closes it. She clearly wants to ask something.

"Your parents must be thrilled to be expecting a grandchild," she finally says.

"It will be their fourth, but they are excited," I say. "My mom is busy knitting a blanket."

"Four already. They're so lucky," his mom says.

"Okay, Mom," Sebastian says. "Aren't you busy enough with Pepper?" He turns to me. "That's our dog. Annabelle, my sister, always wanted to name a dog Pepper when she was a kid, so that's what we named our puppy."

"Yes, it sounds like Iris is concentrating on her career right now," his father says, "as she should be."

"I don't need grandchildren immediately," his mom says, "but if Sebastian keeps telling everyone he wants to remain single forever, then I'm worried I'll never get any grandchildren."

"You heard?" Sebastian asks.

"As if I wouldn't hear that you extolled the benefits of being single to Mary's daughter. It was embarrassing," his mom says. "Something about 'it's great to be single because nobody eats your last banana'? What is that?"

"She said she was about to move to Hong Kong and didn't want to start a relationship," Sebastian says, clearly caught flat-footed.

"She might have said that, but that's not what she meant. Obviously, she wouldn't have gone out on the date if she wasn't looking for a relationship. And she's only going to Hong Kong for a year. You can fly over every once in a while or Zoom or WhatsApp. But really? *Nobody eats your last banana*? I'm going to come over to your house every morning and eat your last banana. Be forewarned."

I try to keep a straight face. His mom catches my glance and starts laughing too. His dad joins in.

She shakes her head. "I seriously thought I brought him up better. I hope he hasn't given you the banana excuse too."

"You *should* steal his last banana," I say.

"I should, shouldn't I?" she asks.

The quartet begins to play another waltz. Sebastian laces his fingers through mine and pulls me closer to him.

"Will you excuse us so I can dance this waltz with Iris and try to go back to impressing her?" Sebastian asks and then turns to me. "Do you even want to still dance with me now that you've met my parents?"

"I still do," I say.

"You two looked wonderful dancing together. Maybe you want some fresh air." His mom says, "Don't forget they've set up little heaters on the roof, Sebastian. You should show Iris up there. It has a very nice view."

Sebastian blushes, and his mom laughs.

"I'm embarrassing you, aren't I?" she asks. "Okay, I'll leave you alone." She walks a few feet away and then turns. "Don't worry about clean-up."

As his mom leaves, Sebastian says, "She's not very subtle at matchmaking."

He pulls me into his arms, holding me closer than before.

He nods to the beat, and then we're off.

He smiles wryly at me. "I guess the bananas are not a worthy substitute for a relationship."

"I guess not," I say, but my voice comes out breathy. The way he's looking at me and holding me... I'm having a hard time breathing. My heart is racing—he must hear it, feel it, in the pulse of my wrist where his thumb grazes. But he, too, seems affected, his eyes staring into mine.

We nearly bump into another couple, and we apologize and turn back to each other, smiling, even laughing a little.

As our glances meet, it's as if there's nobody else here. It's just the two of us. His blue eyes, dark and intense, the dimmed lighting of the crystal chandelier flickering over his chiseled cheekbones, his full lips, his breath, smelling of red wine, caressing my cheek. His back arm holds me close against him, and he sweeps us around. I don't look away, and I just follow him in time to the music, my feet flying. I'm not even sure they're touching the floor. His arm holds me securely and firmly. Our bodies move in perfect synchrony. The deep notes of the cello linger, the expressive tenor tones weaving in and out. A faint whiff of cinnamon mixes in with the scent of holly as we sweep by the tree in the corner.

And I don't want to fight these feelings anymore. I want to be swept away. I want to let myself fall in love. I want to trust Sebastian.

The music ends, and the quartet lead thanks everyone. They bow. Everybody is clapping. It's over. The hour passed so quickly, I didn't even realize.

"Do you want to come back to my apartment for a drink?" Sebastian asks.

As if there aren't drinks here.

"Yes," I say. "I should say thank you to your parents, and then I should use the bathroom."

"You can write my parents a card, and let's go to the bathroom near my old bedroom. That should be empty."

He pulls me down the hallway. I can see his parents saying good-bye to guests in the dining room. Did Lily and Rupert leave?

"I can't write your parents a note," I say.

"Yes, you can," Sebastian says, his voice gruff. "I'll explain that you wanted to say good-bye and I pulled you away. My mom loves getting handwritten mail."

He stops in front of a white door. "Here. I'll meet you in my bedroom over there." He points to another door. "I definitely don't want another cross-examination from my mom."

"You can give her a banana in a baby sling." I open the bathroom door.

He puts his hands on either side of the door frame and leans in. "I didn't know you had such an evil streak, Iris. That's very tempting."

I'm tempted to kiss him. He's inches away.

"Only as long as your mom has a good sense of humor," I say.

"She does." He backs up to let the door close.

I stare in the mirror. Am I really going to his apartment? Am I ready to start another relationship? And with a work colleague? And the best friend of Rupert? And Zeke? Do I really have to call my parents and tell them I won't be home tonight?

I OPEN UP THE door to his room. The walls are painted blue, with a single bed in the corner and a desk by the window. He's leaning against his desk, outlined by soft lamp light.

I step in and close the door. The click sounds loud in the silence. He watches me.

"What secrets will this reveal about you?" I ask.

"Are we about to reveal secrets?" He grins and takes a step closer.

I back up.

Am I ready?

I pick up a trophy that stands on a bookcase. "Squash. And you read books." I pick up another trophy. "Debate."

"Makes sense, for a lawyer." He stands there, watching me.

I think he can tell I'm nervous. But it's also excitement. I can't believe this man might be mine. And the fact that he's waiting—that he's letting me call the shots...

I swallow and take a step forward.

I put my hand on his chest. His heart is beating fast. My heart skitters.

He reaches up and caresses my face as he whispers, "May I?"

I swallow and nod.

He smooths a tendril of hair behind my ear, his fingers fanning out and then caressing the skin behind my ear and down my neck. My skin feels heated where his fingers skim. I can't take my eyes off him. I don't dare breathe.

"I've wanted to do that all night," he says. "You're so beautiful."

He rests his hand on my shoulder and traces my collarbone. I tilt my neck, and he slides his hand back under my hair. He steps closer, backing me up against the wall.

"Can I kiss you?" he asks. "I wanted to wait, but I don't think I can." Outside, the muted sound of good-byes dims as party revelers leave.

"Yes," I say, and I reach up to pull his head down. His lips are firm. He pulls me against him. His hair is soft. His other hand cups my face. Our lips slant as we explore each other. He tastes of red wine. Shivers are cascading through me as he holds me tightly. His fingers skate over the heated skin of my bare back, teasing. He growls, and I feel that guttural sound deep in my stomach. He presses little kisses down my neck, down to my collarbone. He looks up, and I think he trembles, need and desire etched into his face.

"I'm so into you," he says. His Adam's apple bobs as he swallows. He closes his eyes and then opens them. He groans. "I really was very happy being single."

I hold his face in my hands. "Let's be happy being together."

"Let's," he says. He sweeps me up and carries me over to the bed, stopping to lock the door on the way over.

"Just a few more minutes kissing, and then let's go to my apartment." He lays me down on the bed and scoots in next to me. "Maybe we should always sleep in a single bed."

"Not if you want to get any sleep," I say. "I'm a restless sleeper."

"I'm not planning on a lot of sleep tonight." He pulls me close to him, so I'm lying half on top of him. His heart is beating so fast as he caresses my back.

"Mmm." I arch against him. His lips claim mine again. All I want is Sebastian and his teasing, tender touch.

Chapter Twenty-One

Sebastian

IRIS IS SLEEPING SOUNDLY still, her dark hair spread across my pillow.

Her eyelashes are so dark against her pale skin. Her lips are still full from all the kissing last night.

I'm falling way too quickly.

This is probably a weakness of my happily single plan—that I'm way too vulnerable now because I've been solitary for so long. I should be less vulnerable, though, because I'm fine on my own.

But I'm even better with Iris. Last night was everything.

Sneaking out of my parents' house and back to mine, I felt like a randy teenager again. But one who was very happy I was not and had my own apartment.

I want to smooth back Iris's hair from her face again and kiss her awake and start all over again now that I know what makes her arch her back in delight.

But she looks so cute sleeping.

I pull the cover up over her bare shoulder.

Iris opens her eyes, and I kiss her firmly on the lips.

"Morning," I say.

"Hmm." She stretches. "Morning."

I run my fingers through her hair. It's so soft.

"I have to run to the bathroom, but hold that thought," she says. She grabs a T-shirt from the floor.

She comes back, looking like a cat that ate the cream. "Do you know what I remembered?"

"What?" I ask.

"That you still haven't told me what you were thinking when you hoisted me through the window. And now we're not just colleagues...and we're more than friends," she says.

"Definitely more than friends," I say. "But I don't think I should tell you. Right now, you have a good opinion of me."

She bites her lip. "We'll see. I think I have my ways of getting it out of you."

She crawls back into the bed and straddles me.

"I'm definitely intrigued," I say.

And then she tickles me. I squirm, weakening, but tighten my abs.

"Surrender?" she asks.

"Not on your life." We wrestle, and she ends up below me, her cheeks flushed, and I can't help kissing her again. When we come back up for air, I tenderly brush her hair out of her face. She's so gorgeous.

"You're not going to tell me?" she pouts, and she traces a heart across my chest.

"Seduction." I groan. "They gave me thoughts of seduction."

"I thought you didn't like them," she says.

"I liked them way too much. I was very happy to see another pair last night." In purple.

She giggles. "Keep kissing me, and maybe you'll meet the rest of the bunch."

"I hope so." I stare into her green eyes, so full of vitality, mischief, and intelligence. She pulls down my head to kiss me again, and the world dissolves to just the two of us, communicating our feelings—by touch, by sensation, shiver by shiver.

WE FINALLY GET UP because we're hungry. Iris picks out some sweatpants and a very oversized sweatshirt. She looks adorable in my clothes. I make oatmeal with sliced bananas and strawberries as the topping while Iris brews some coffee.

"Your place is really nice," Iris says. "I barely saw it last night."

I kiss her on the lips lightly. "That's because we had more important things to do than look at my apartment."

"But why do you have no Christmas decorations at all?"

"Because I'm a guy?"

"Seriously? My brother has Christmas decorations."

"Because I've been so busy at the office?"

"You should get something, even some pine boughs from Trader Joe's."

"Maybe we can do that together," I say.

"You didn't want to live on the Upper East Side?" Iris asks.

"And have my mom stopping by all the time? Definitely not," I say.

Iris hides her face in her hands. "I can't believe we sent that photo to your mom last night."

I laugh. We sent my mom a picture of us both holding a banana as a telephone with my apartment as a backdrop. Iris insisted on saying thank you, and I told her this would make my mom's night, even more than a handwritten note.

I was way too...happy last night. Because that's a pretty cringey thing to do. I wince. But at least it prevented my mom from showing up to steal my bananas this morning.

"I'm not sure I would've necessarily picked the Upper West Side, but I love it now that I'm here. I love having the two parks so close. And then we've got Fairway, Citarella, and Zabar's. And so many bakeries. I have no idea who is supporting all these bakeries. I moved in here because Rupert convinced his uncle and grandfather to include squash courts when they developed the building and Rupert promised to play with me. And they gave me a friend-of-the-family sale price."

We sit at my round dining table as I serve us breakfast.

"Lucky you," Iris says. "This oatmeal with bananas is yummy. But I still promise not to steal your last banana."

"I'll buy two bananas for us. Do you still want to live downtown?" I ask.

"I thought I did, when I was dating Patrick. We were planning to buy my neighbor's apartment when she was ready to sell. I was saving up for that." Iris looks down. "But I've slept over at Tessa's a lot, and this neighborhood also feels like home. Plus, I also like the parks close by. I don't know." She sips her coffee. "Your parents are pretty cool. Where was Pepper?"

"Our neighbor took her. She's a puppy, so all those people would have been too much for her. Plus, our neighbor's daughter loves dogs. I can understand that you think my mom is cool—because she is—but even my dad?"

"I like that he's still so in love with your mom," she says.

I nod.

"Why is he pressuring you to leave law?" she asks.

I sigh. "He just thinks that the payoff is better in finance. And that the hours can be better when you get more senior. He has some good points, but I like practicing law."

"I'm sure he'll come around," she says.

My phone beeps, and I read the text. "Melody. Weird. She wrote that she feels bad that she left early last night and wants to know if I want to get together today."

"She's totally fishing to see if we ended up together," Iris says.

I grin. "Well, we did. So, I definitely can't meet up today." I text back that I'm spending the day with Iris.

There's no reply.

I finish my oatmeal. "What should we do today?"

She looks out the window. The sky is a bright blue.

"We could go for a bike ride. We could go down Riverside Park, and I can take you to some of my favorite restaurants on the Lower East Side. I was planning to do some Christmas shopping today. I thought I'd give Ernest some coffee beans from Porto in Essex Market. He seems to drink a lot of coffee. And I'll get some for Jazmine to give Aaron because he also drinks coffee. And you could show me some of your favorite places on the Upper West Side."

"I'm all for that," I say.

Chapter Twenty-Two

Iris

I CALL TESSA AND ask if I can borrow her bicycle and helmet.

"Are you at Sebastian's?" she squeals.

"Shh," I say.

"Yes! You're dating! This is great," Tessa says. "And yes, definitely you can borrow my bicycle and helmet."

I turn to Sebastian. "Tessa just told everybody there."

"I'm happy for everybody to know it," Sebastian says.

I say goodbye and hang up. "But I'm not sure we should be public at work."

"Why not?" Sebastian nuzzles my neck.

I get distracted, kissing him back, but eventually recall my surroundings.

"You know, my boss is kind of a jerk, and what with Raphael's firing and everything going on, I just don't want to deal with any negative comments about us dating. I'd rather keep it to ourselves for now."

"That makes sense," Sebastian says. "But we should tell Lily and Rupert. I don't want them to be the last to find out."

"We should have invited them over for breakfast," I say.

"If they're up." Sebastian pulls me into his arms. "Anyway, I wanted you to myself for this morning."

"It's 11:30," I say. "And her dad is visiting. I'm sure they're up."

I call Lily as Sebastian calls Rupert.

"I'm so happy!" Lily says. "This is perfect. We're about to walk over to my apartment because my dad is staying there. Let's meet up."

"We're about to walk over to Tessa and Zeke's to pick up a helmet," I say. "And Sebastian says we have to stop by Levain Bakery."

"Oh. That's a good idea. We'll go with you. My dad loves their cookies, and we should pick up some things from Fairway," Lily says. "We can meet in the lobby."

THE FOUR OF US stop in front of the Levain Bakery on 74th Street. It's a small space, a set of steps leading down to the glass-fronted store with its name in bright-blue script on the front window. Above it is a waxing place. There's no line out the door yet, but the inside looks crowded.

Sebastian and Rupert stay outside holding Sebastian's bicycle while Lily and I go inside. About six people are smooshed into the space in front of the counter, and with us, no more can fit inside. We find our place in the line, next to a wooden shelf counter that intersects the window.

Outside, Rupert is clapping Sebastian on the back, and Sebastian is blushing. I smile.

Lily nudges me with her shoulder.

"I'm so happy for you," Lily says. "I was wondering last night when you guys disappeared so quickly off the dance floor. I thought you two would hit it off. I'm counting this as a matchmaking win for me."

I blush. "Last night was pretty magical."

Lily grins. "Sebastian also looks really happy. I wasn't expecting him to look quite so delighted to not be single. This couldn't have all just happened last night?"

"There's been an ongoing flirtation for a few weeks—because we see each other at the office."

"That's good. What did you think of Melody? She's cool, right? I just don't understand how she could choose Wim over Sebastian."

"That's exactly it," I say. "What if she realizes her fiancé is a jerk and decides she wants Sebastian back? Won't Sebastian return to her? He's been in love with her for years."

"I don't think he's that kind of guy," Lily says.

"Well, I don't want him to stay with me out of some misplaced loyalty either. That's even worse."

We move a few spaces up and stand by the glass counter. Behind the counter, bakers in blue smocks are sliding large trays of cookies into tall metal racks on wheels. Another baker is measuring scoops of cookie dough to put on a sheet pan.

"He must be over her. He looks at you like he really likes you," Lily says. "I don't think he's still in love with her."

We give our orders to the server. Mine is always chocolate chip walnut, but Lily also orders a chocolate-chocolate chip for her dad.

"Does your dad like Rupert?" I ask.

"He loves him," Lily says. "Their first meeting went really well, and tonight our families are getting together. I think my dad will really like his family too. I think he was worried they wouldn't be very down-to-earth, but his parents are. And his grandfather is a treat, even if we don't always agree."

As we jog up the steps, Tessa and Zeke arrive with the bicycle and helmet for me. Since they were on their way out, they figured they would bring it over.

"We need a girls' night with ice cream to celebrate," Tessa says to me.

"Yes," I say.

THE HUDSON RIVER IS a dark blue today. Sebastian and I cycle single file on the bike path under the steel columns that hold the highway above us and then down the Hudson Greenway. The breeze is cold, but I warm up quickly as I pedal. Sebastian suggests I stay behind him so he shields me from the wind off the Hudson.

Wooden posts stand in the water, the remains of what used to be a pier—now perfect perches for seagulls.

Sebastian looks back and smiles at me.

Piers with parks pop up every once in a while. We pass a Department of Sanitation outpost with sand outside and then Little Island and some more developed piers. When the road widens, we bike side by side. It feels good to be outside, enjoying the view of the water and the fresh air.

And it feels good to be with Sebastian. I want to pinch myself—to assure myself that this is real and that last night really happened. And now we're spending the day together. It feels both too easy and too exhilarating—like I want to just sit in my room, grab my pillow, and jump up and down that this is happening—but a small frisson of fear wavers underneath. Am I falling too fast? Does he really feel the same way? Did we just decide to do a "fling" but not say that openly? What if Melody does realize her mistake?

I *can't* go through that kind of heartache again.

Farther south, we encounter a pier I think is new. It seems like I should have seen it before, but there's been so much development along this trail that maybe I missed it. But it's all improvements, so it's good to embrace the new, even if it means feeling like parts of New York City which should be familiar are not.

I have to trust Sebastian.

I don't even think it's possible for me to hold back my feelings. They're overflowing like the Hudson at high tide during a severe rainstorm.

We turn left at Clarkson Street, cross the West Side Highway at the intersection, and ride down a cobble-stoned street away from the river and into the West Village. We follow the green bike lane of Bleeker Street as it meanders through the narrow streets, curving every once in a while. Small colorful shops with picturesque fronts dot the street.

We pass by the NYU campus buildings, their purple flags waving in the air, clearly proclaiming school pride. Chinatown is next. Then Bleeker Street ends abruptly at Bowery, an open and wide two-way thoroughfare. We stop in front of a colorful mural of Blondie, part of a street art project, covering the entire front of a building. There's her iconic pose in a white dress, her arms akimbo, in front of the guys all dressed in black suits. We dismount and walk our bicycles down to East Houston then turn to stroll a few blocks over to Katz's Delicatessen. A line of people waiting to eat winds down the street.

"We can leave the bikes at my parents' house," I say. "But then they'll probably invite us in for lunch. Maybe we should go straight to the Essex Market. We can take turns going inside so one of us can watch the bikes. Are there any gifts you need to get?"

"I'll take a quick look, but I usually get my family books, chocolate, and warm socks. It's easy and usually well-received," Sebastian says. "But I'd definitely like to check it out because I didn't even know this existed. I'm not that familiar with the Lower East Side, other than coming here for dinner or to go to a bar."

"Okay, you go first, and then I'll run in and grab us some food and the coffee beans," I say. "I actually bought my parents their gifts during the company retreat in France."

"Sounds good," Sebastian says.

Essex Market is now on the corner of Delancey and Essex and has become a very upscale establishment. Sebastian goes in first, and I watch the passersby. Two young men dressed in sweats head for the gym across the street, their duffel bags slung over their shoulders. A woman in heels hurries by, a coffee in her hand. Another person walks by with an enormous button as a necklace.

Sebastian comes out with a bag of coffee. "I thought I might as well buy some for my parents."

I run in and buy two bags of coffee beans at Porto Mark Importing Company. Then I pick up two cheeseburger empanadas and Khao main gai at Eat Gai.

Sebastian is outside, studying his phone, the bikes leaning against a wall plastered with concert posters. He looks up, and a huge smile envelops his face. As I near, he kisses me on the lips hello.

"We can go to Sara Roosevelt Park and sit there," I say. "There's also a dumpling place we should stop by. They have the best dumplings—and the cheapest. Maddie found it."

"I'll follow you," he says.

I place the bags of coffee and two dishes in my basket, and we bike down to King Dumpling, a very small place on the corner of Hestor. Graffiti covers the building. A huge menu hangs in one glass window. I run inside to order six dumplings for $2, and then we walk our bicycles over to the park. We find a bench and sit. Sebastian lets out an *mmm* as he eats the first dumpling.

"This is an amazing find."

"Right?"

"Shouldn't we stop by your parents'?" Sebastian asks. "I feel like I should introduce myself more formally or something—that you're not just sneaking off in the night to be with me."

"That your intentions are honorable?" I ask, almost holding my breath.

Sebastian smiles wryly. "Yes."

I release my breath.

He glances at me, tilting his head.

"Were you worried about that?" he asks.

How can he read me so well?

A shadow briefly passes over his face. "This isn't a fling for you, right?"

"No." I reach out to hold his hand. "Definitely not. But you mentioned flings, and then last night happened so quickly that I just got worried. I'm probably a little overly sensitive because of what happened with Patrick."

"You don't have to explain yourself. You're right that we didn't talk much last night. But I really do like you, and I wouldn't have kissed you last night if I wasn't serious."

"Do you think you're over Melody?" I might as well address what concerns me.

He pauses. "Yes. I'm not in love with her anymore. I still care for her as a friend, but not as a potential partner."

There was a definite pause. But the warmth in his gaze makes me want to believe him.

"Are you over Patrick?"

"Definitely," I say. Without a pause. "And not just because he cheated, although that does have a way of killing any remaining feelings. But even before that, we'd been having so many issues. He begrudged me the hours I worked for my job. So why do you think you're not in love with Melody anymore?"

He frowns.

What am I doing? This is the worst conversation to be having the day after. I'm looking like some insecure needy woman. And I'm not. But I also don't want to be the consolation prize.

"Because just a week ago, you said you still had feelings," I say.

Shouldn't I have asked these questions before last night? I was just so caught up in the magic last night that I didn't stop to think.

"I *thought* I still had feelings—that was my default for so long, but I've probably been over Melody for a while. I *realized* I was over her this week—because of you. I wanted to be alone with you. And not with Melody. And that's never happened before. And even before that, I haven't even called Melody to do any of our usual holiday activities, like seeing the Rockefeller tree lighting."

He releases my hand and takes my face into his hands. "But I know why I like you. I like the fact that you stand up for what you believe in. I like that you're willing to take risks and think outside the box. I like your loyalty to your friends. You're smart. You make me laugh. And boy, do I want to kiss you. I've been fighting that ever since I saw your underwear. Although you do look cute in my boxers."

His hands are so warm on my face.

"Maybe we should take a trip to Ikea and buy a set of Ikea drawers for your clothes in my apartment. You could move in," Sebastian says, and the way he looks at me, I know I don't have to worry about Melody.

And I want to say yes.

But I'm still scared.

I moved into Patrick's apartment, and I resolved not to do that again.

"I'm moving too fast."

"Maybe," I say. "It's just I thought I'd get my own apartment this time." He nods, but I fear he's thinking that my intentions aren't serious.

I reach out to him and grab his hand. He turns to look at me.

"But then I didn't expect to fall so hard for you," I say. "I'm sorry. My head is still catching up to my heart."

His eyes are intent on mine, his expression open and sincere. "I'm not going to cheat on you, so you don't have to worry about that."

"I'm worried you'll break my heart," I say.

"But that means you really like me."

"Are you being a lawyer again?"

"It's only fair because I think you found the hole in my defenses. I'm probably the one who's going to get my heart broken, not you. When you steal away with it."

"My intentions are honorable too," I say.

I shiver at the way he's looking at me.

"You're cold. I didn't think." Sebastian slips off his scarf and wraps it around my neck. It smells of him and is so warm.

"Thank you."

He grins crookedly and pulls the edges of my collar towards him, shifting me closer.

"But I know another way to warm you up."

Chapter Twenty-Three

Iris

> Sebastian: *I miss you. Can we visit the supply closet again? C is in France.*

> Me: *C was supposed to be away last week and he wasn't. We can't trust that.*

NONE OF THE SENIOR management team are here. The office has a very eerie feel—like this is the precursor to our being shut down. Even Hank is head down, working. Then I pass by his desk and see his screen. It turns out he's sending out resumes.

He looks up and says in an unapologetic tone, "You should be doing the same."

I probably should. But I don't want to let go of the bubbly feeling of happiness I have from this past weekend yet. And I had such high hopes for Dream.

"HOW WAS YOUR WEEKEND?" Jazmine asks as we enter the conference room to plan the high school winter dance.

Wonderful. Like a dream.

But I can't say that. I want to tell Jazmine, but I also don't want the word to get out.

"It was good. I picked up some Porto coffee beans from Essex Market, as you requested." I hand her the package.

The teenagers pile into the conference room, and the space comes alive.

Sebastian arrives. I can't help but steal a glance at him, and he winks at me. It must be so obvious that we're together

I turn away abruptly and then hope that didn't hurt his feelings.

Sebastian looks happy as he jokes around with Jamal. I like that he's so committed to the Big Brothers Big Sisters program. When I asked Patrick to do a free concert for the community garden, he grumbled and promptly scheduled a paying concert for that date. It's good we broke up. Maybe I should have broken up with him earlier instead of holding on for so long.

Jamal immediately sits next to Faith, so Sebastian takes a seat next to me. His hand brushes my thigh, but I definitely don't look over. No way am I going to encourage him. Especially when Jazmine and Nora join us.

The first hour is for studying, so we all work on math. We bought some tenth-grade math books online after Lily also asked a library math tutor for her recommendations. Jamal got a B+ and Faith got an A- on Friday's test, so they're motivated. Jamal mentions how hard a time he's having keeping it a secret from his mom, but he can't wait to surprise her on Christmas.

"Great work studying," Jazmine says after an hour. "Now let's talk about the winter dance."

Some students let out a whoop of excitement.

Sebastian brought in two huge Fresh Direct bags of winter wonderland stuff from his mother. And some employees from set design wheel in more supplies that we can borrow. They even have a Snowman from a Hallmark-esque romance they filmed upstate.

Faith says, "Maybe I'll go as an ice princess."

Jamal says, "But you're not icy."

"So, I *am* a princess?" Faith asks.

"Definitely," Jamal says.

Faith blushes.

There's definitely a vibe of something more than a next-door-neighbor friendship. I look over at Jazmine because I want to glance at Sebastian. It takes all I have not to look at him.

Jazmine smiles and nods.

"But then what should we do for the Heat Miser section?" Nora asks.

"We can make some surfboards out of cardboard," Jamal says.

"Let me google how we could make palm trees," Jazmine says and holds up her phone with a DIY site giving instructions. "Oh, hey. These look pretty good."

"I saw these iron pineapple string lights at Essex Market over the weekend. Those would be perfect," Sebastian says.

Jazmine's head whips around, and she stares at me, her eyes narrowed.

"Were you at Essex Market this weekend?" Jazmine asks Sebastian.

"Yes," Sebastian says.

I try to kick him under the table, but I end up hitting Jamal, who looks over at Faith as if hoping she just kicked him.

Faith needs to put Jamal out of his misery. She said she likes him, but she wants him to work for it. And he should be aiming for a corner office, not the corner 3-pointer shot. The youth are much smarter.

"Really interesting." Jazmine leans forward and stares at Sebastian. "I'd never heard of Essex Market until I went there with Iris. How did you hear of it?"

Sebastian flushes, but he does manage not to look my way. "I needed to buy coffee, and Iris recommended Porto at Essex Market."

"Oh, you were there to buy coffee too?" Jazmine says sweetly to Sebastian but glares at me.

"I heard it's very good coffee," Sebastian says weakly.

"I hear their process reveals hidden flavors other coffee beans can't be trusted to have," Jazmine says.

"It's not that they can't be trusted," I say quickly. "It's just a confidential secret they don't want to share yet."

Suddenly the door opens, and Xavier enters with Colby, Bob, and Kevin, the latter all in dark-blue suits. And all have grim faces.

"Iris, can we talk to you for a moment?"

This looks very serious. Is there something more to the hack?

"Of course." I get up and follow them into Xavier's office.

The office is crowded, and Bob elects to stand next to Xavier. It feels like a meeting with the FBI.

"You can have my chair," I say.

"No," Bob says. His mouth is set in a straight line, different from his usually cheerful demeanor.

"Colby says you were the one he asked to hack into the New Mexico system and retrieve that PowerPoint," Xavier says. "And you tripped that trap to make sure it didn't seem like you."

Chapter Twenty-Four

Iris

MY MOUTH DROPS OPEN. I stare at them in disbelief.

"I did not hack into New Mexico's IT system and exfiltrate that PowerPoint," I say. "That's a ridiculous accusation."

"You can come clean now," Colby says. "I've told them all the truth. And I'm stepping down. But I feel it's only right that you step down too."

Have I entered an alternate reality?

"We don't blame you," Xavier says. "I know that Colby told you to do it and so you had to listen. But I wish you had come to me or at least confessed when I caught you in the closet."

"Kevin showed us that your credentials were the ones used," Bob says.

My credentials?

No way.

My heartrate accelerates—and not in a good way.

I stare at Colby. I have no idea why he's fabricated this story, but it's a complete lie. Is he trying to save Kevin?

"I didn't do it. And my credentials were not used." I stare at Xavier and Bob because they've got to be the sane ones still here. My hands shake. I stick them between my legs and bend forward.

"Colby?" Xavier asks, looking at his brother.

"I'm your brother," Colby says. "You're going to believe her over me?"

"I'm not resigning," I say, my voice low and hoarse. It doesn't sound like me. "I didn't do it. You can fire me, and I'll sue you for wrongful termination. There's no way you'll win."

Let's hope that's true. I just know that it wasn't me. There has to be a way to prove it wasn't me.

I have to find the person who did *do it.*

Xavier folds his arms. My gut suddenly feels funny. Bad funny.

Xavier knows Colby is willing to lie and cheat to get ahead. And it's far more likely that Colby had Kevin on his side than that he didn't.

"I didn't do it," I say. I hate that it sounds like I'm pleading. I straighten my shoulders, planting my hands on my thighs, and speak more firmly. "You heard Colby and Kevin in that room. They're in on this together. I'm being blamed, but I'm sure they hired an outside white hat hacker. There's even that partially executed agreement in the files. Why would that exist if it was me?"

Xavier first stares at his brother, but Colby smirks in response and shakes his head. Xavier eyes Bob with a quick sideways glance. The answer is almost an imperceptible nod. They're wavering.

"All right, let's hire an outside firm to investigate," Xavier says. "You'll be put on paid leave in the meantime. Here's the paid leave agreement Sebastian drafted."

Sebastian drafted? *Sebastian knew?*

My stomach pitches like I'm no longer on solid ground and the boat just hit a swell. My hand shakes as I pick up the terms. I look down to read them, but I can't see the words. *Sebastian knew?* I can feel tears welling in my eyes. *I can't cry.* I stare at the page, blinking away the tears, trying to look at the words swimming before me. But the only thing that's flashing in my head is *Sebastian drafted this.*

I almost miss Xavier's concluding sentence: "And if we find out you did steal the documents, you'll be fired." He takes a breath, and his tone lowers. "I expect honesty."

Fired. My face flushes.

I don't have much faith in an outside forensic firm if Kevin decides who is hired.

"Security will escort you out." Xavier thrusts his splayed hand towards the door.

I know I'm supposed to get up and leave. But my legs feel like jelly. My teeth clench as I will myself to stand straight and walk out, the paper clutched close to my heart. *How could Sebastian not tell me?*

Security is waiting for me in the hallway. The officer ducks his head, as if embarrassed.

Heat flushes through my body. How dare they accuse me. I stride ahead of security to the elevator. I'll see myself out.

And I'll figure out who the hacker is. Raphael knew something. Did he think he was going to be set up to take the fall? Was he warning me that I was being set up to take the fall with that "don't trust anyone" book?

If that was your warning, Raphael, be a little less opaque next time. What the—?

But Raphael was definitely terminated, so he must have figured something out—and they got rid of him. And now they're trying to get rid of me.

I've looked through all the files. There must be some clue I overlooked.

Reggie meets me in the lobby with my coat, my backpack, and various personal items from the top of my desk.

It is surreal.

And it's only when I'm standing outside on the street, holding a box of my personal effects, that the enormity of what just occurred hits me.

I was accused of hacking into the system to retrieve the Power-Points.

I've been *escorted* out.

That's my reputation—my ability to work in this industry. My stomach churns as I hug the flimsy cardboard box to my chest.

Kevin—who definitely orchestrated this—is in charge of the investigation to prove my innocence.

I lean against the stone building. It's cold and hard. A gray fog hangs in the wet air, and I didn't bring an umbrella again. The sky darkens. A drop of rain falls. I pick up my box and run to the subway entrance, down the stairs, and into the corner by the station booth.

I'm about to lose my job.

And Sebastian. Just when I thought I could trust him.

A wave of dizziness passes over me. I crumple back against the wall, but then pull away. It's probably not clean. Indeed, the white subway tiles are cracked and streaked with grime. The harsh glare of the fluorescent lighting above illuminates all of its flaws. I should have known Kevin was up to something. Maddie warned me. I thought I could outsmart him.

I want to lean against the wall. But I have to center myself on my own two feet. *"Here's the paid leave agreement that Sebastian drafted."*

I fall back slightly with one shoulder against the wall. *Get it together, Iris.*

The station attendant in his glass-paneled booth is helping a tourist with directions, speaking slowly and clearly into his microphone. She translates for the rest of her group.

I take a deep breath. I *will* figure this out yet.

Faith is still up there—she's going to think I forgot about her. I put my box down, trying to balance it on my feet so the cardboard doesn't get wet. I text her that I had a work emergency and we're still on for later this week.

I call Raphael again and leave him a message telling him what's going on, ending it with a desperate plea: "Raphael, I know you signed an NDA, but please figure out some way to tell me what you figured out so I can save my reputation. Kevin is in charge. They're saying the hacker used my credentials. *Please.* This is my career."

I pick up the box. How dare Kevin and Colby besmirch my name?

Did Sebastian know? Did he draft *my* leave agreement, or could that have been a generic agreement he drafted for anyone on administrative leave?

I clutch the cardboard box as my chest tightens in pain.

Please let it be that he just drafted the generic agreement—*not the one specifically meant for me.*

I shiver. *Please.*

I *can't* believe he drafted this for me and didn't tell me.

But is Sebastian a "straight arrow" who won't want to be with me now that I've been accused of fraud?

Accused of fraud.

I feel nauseated.

He fought with Melody when she stole a bathroom robe. I'm accused of stealing confidential company secrets. *"But I learned my lesson that company property was definitely not mine for the taking."*

I call Tessa because I might need legal counsel. She doesn't pick up, and I leave a voicemail message explaining what happened. Then I call Maddie. No answer. Same message. My voice cracks as I finish repeating what happened.

My finger hovers over Sebastian's name.

Did he draft this for me and not tell me? And if he didn't, what is he going to think? Is he going to believe them? Are we already over?

I want to call him. I swallow the lump in my throat, and my body flushes hot and cold again. I was just accused of stealing proprietary information, escorted from the premises. Will he believe me? What if he wants to break up? What if he does have some perfect ideal? I wasn't enough for Patrick. I don't think I can take Sebastian's rejection too right now.

I call my brother.

Chapter Twenty-Five

Sebastian

Faith keeps looking at the door to the conference room, but Iris doesn't return. It's very strange. We're basically taking turns staring at that connecting door.

No texts on my phone either.

We finish up for the day, and Jazmine says, "I know Iris would've come back if she could. That was all of company senior management, so it must have been a very important meeting. I'm sure she'll reach out later."

Faith nods but still looks disappointed. Jazmine gives them a voucher to take a car service home.

As soon as they're out the door, Jazmine and I turn to each other.

"What do you think happened?" she asks.

"Let's check in the bullpen to see what's going on," I say.

But the bullpen is grimly quiet. Everybody is head down, working.

"Did Iris come back?" Jazmine asks.

"No. It's like that story *And Then There Were None* around here," Hank says. "I think maybe she got sick. Reggie came and grabbed some of her stuff. Kevin announced she's taking a leave of absence."

What?

"A leave of absence?" Jazmine exclaims.

We back out and turn to each other in the hallway.

"What is going on?" Jazmine asks, worrying her lip.

"Iris wasn't sick." I call Iris again and then turn to Jazmine. "She's not picking up. It's going to voicemail."

"You guys are dating, aren't you?" Jazmine asks me.

"We are," I say. "But we'd prefer to keep it a secret at the office."

"I can't believe Iris didn't trust me to keep it a secret," Jazmine says.

"I don't think it's you *per se*. She wanted to keep it professional at the office."

But she did meet me in the supply closet. I can't grin like an idiot. I need to keep a straight face. I press my lips together. Especially when Jazmine is clearly feeling hurt.

"She definitely wanted to tell you. I'll ask Bob what's going on. And I'll keep calling Iris, although she seems to have disappeared with Raphael into the Bermuda Triangle," I say wryly. *Why isn't she picking up?*

"I'll talk to my boss," Jazmine says.

I walk down the hallway and knock on Bob's door.

"Enter," his voice booms out.

Is it me, or does he look older today? He seems rather gray and slumped.

"Did something happen to Iris, the deputy CISO?" I ask.

"You minded my words to figure out the office cooler chat. Company gossip travels fast," he says. "She's been put on leave while we figure out who hacked into the system to steal the company PowerPoints."

I don't understand.

"Isn't she the one investigating that?" I ask.

"She's the one suspected of doing it," he says bluntly, "so it's like a fox guarding a hen house, if she's the one investigating. Maybe that's why there hasn't been any progress."

"There's no way," I say.

But why isn't she calling me?

But then remnants of Colby's conversation with Kevin replay through my mind: *She's not going to want to do it again. I think she discussed it with Raphael.* Who else would talk to Raphael? And she leaned forward at that point as if to hear what they were going to say.

There's no way it's Iris. But what if this is me thinking I know a person, but I really don't? Like Nathan. Like my relationship with Melody. Has Iris been deceiving me all this time? I don't think so. I can trust my judgment this time. Her character shines through. When Iris and I figured out Raphael's clues. When she got angry on my behalf about Melody and I held her in my arms waltzing. Her head ducked, listening to Faith explain her solution to a math problem. There's no way Iris did this.

"Did you ever do any cybersecurity investigations at Capital?" he asks.

"No," I say.

"Kevin recommended a firm, but I've never heard of them, and I don't trust him," Bob says.

Kevin definitely can't be trusted.

"I can reach out to my former boss at Capital. She's done some cybersecurity investigations."

Back in my office, I call Iris again. Why isn't she picking up my calls? She's actively avoiding me. It doesn't make sense.

I call my former boss and send the list of firms she recommends to Bob.

My phone rings. I grab it. *Not Iris.*

Rupert says, "I proposed last night, and Lily accepted."

What? Yes. Not that it's a huge surprise. But I'm still very happy for Rupert.

"Congratulations!"

"I wanted you to be the first to know, and I'm pretty sure Lily is about to tell everybody at Banter & Books tonight. They're meeting to discuss the fundraising for the library that Iris's little sibling wants to build."

"Iris too?" I ask.

"I'm sure Iris will be there. It's her sibling's project. Lily just skipped out of here, saying everybody was coming. Her dad and I are enjoying drinks back here in my apartment. But I had to call you."

Time to get some answers at Banter & Books.

Chapter Twenty-Six

Iris

I'm first to arrive at Banter & Books, probably a record for me. The benefits of being fired. I thought about saying I couldn't come because, honestly, I want to go straight back out to Raphael's house in Brooklyn. But this is Faith's project. I can't ask them to do all this work and not show up.

Focus on helping Faith and forget about Dream—for now.

At least it stopped raining. A train runs on a track in the Banter & Books window display with book recommendations in each train wagon, including local authors like my friend, Bella. Round and around. Like the thoughts in my head.

In the other window, holiday-themed novels fall in a flurry of paper snowflakes. Like all my dreams crashing to the ground.

I push open the door and make my way through the velvet curtains that surround the door entrance to keep out the cold. Hanging plants and shelves filled with colorful books line the whitewashed walls. Holiday music plays in the background, underneath a cheerful buzz of conversation. It smells of cinnamon cider and balsam candles. This is really *not* helping.

I try to make myself relax into the vibe of Banter & Books, which feels like a harmonious mash-up of a café in Provence and a greenhouse. I take a deep breath and let it out. I have to relax for now.

I can't.

Escorted out…on leave…Sebastian drafting my leave agreement…runs on a loop through my head. *Focus on this meeting, Iris.*

The long table in the conservatory in the back is occupied. I grab one table off to the side, surrounded by peace lilies, the four French-blue settees around it empty. That won't be enough chairs, but I can pull some from the table at the back. I put my box down on a chair, Raphael's *No Trust* peeking out of top.

What am I going to do? I text everyone that I have a table.

Sebastian has not stopped calling.

I should call him back. But if he says we're done…that's it. I slump down into one of the chairs, feeling suddenly weak. I can't take that betrayal too—on top of losing my job. And if Patrick couldn't be faithful after dating for a year, what's going to make Sebastian believe me? We've only been dating for seconds.

Or if he's calling me as Dream's lawyer…

My eyes water.

The door chime rings, and Lily enters. She's glowing, her eyes bright and her blonde hair gleaming. She waves hello and bounces over. I quickly wipe under my eyes.

"Rupert proposed! We're engaged!" She hugs me. "I'm not sure I'm going to be able to sit down, I'm so happy."

"That's so great." My eyes fill up with tears. Because I am happy for her.

But I can't tell the gang now that I've been accused of hacking into the company system and I'm on leave while my conduct is investigated. I can't ruin Lily's happy moment.

"You're tearing up," Lily says.

"Happy tears." I hug her tightly back. "I'm so happy you found your true love. And Rupert is so devoted." *Good guys do exist.* I'm so glad Lily found someone, especially after losing her mom so young.

And Sebastian is his best friend.

Oh, no. I've got to text Tessa and Maddie and tell them not to say anything—we can discuss my voicemails later.

"Did you order anything?" Lily asks as she drops her coat on a chair across from mine.

"Not yet," I say.

"What do you want? My treat," she says.

A pint. Or two. But they don't serve alcohol.

"Coffee."

"Are you going back to work afterward?" she asks.

"I'm going to try to find Raphael again," I say.

She nods and walks over to the counter to order.

I text Tessa and Maddie.

I push my box under the chair with my foot and then cover it with my jacket. *My whole career.* Not now.

Bella arrives next. She hugs Lily first but then comes over to me, pulling off her coat.

"Thank you so much for donating your books," I say.

"It makes me happy to do this. I struggled for so long that it feels like this is the least I can do." She waves her hand dismissively. "I'll get some more chairs."

"I'll come with you." I don't want to be alone with my thoughts.

"So excited about Lily and Rupert!" Bella says. "I can't wait to hear how he proposed."

Tessa arrives next. Her glance meets mine across the room, and she gives me a short nod. She received my message not to say anything. She hugs Lily by the counter and then joins us.

"How's your case going?" Bella asks Tessa.

"Good. I'm figuring out who paid whom. Follow the money, you know."

A chill goes through me. *Follow the money*. That's right. They had to have paid this hacker.

I shake my head. But Colby probably paid her out of his own funds. Colby said the hacker got suspicious. Was that because she wasn't paid from company funds? That would be too big a tell. Still, there has to be a money trail. Somewhere.

We pick up a chair each and lug them back to our circle. Lily sets down a tray full of drinks.

The door chime rings, and I look up to see if Tessa or Maddie arrived.

It's Sebastian. And he's heading straight for me. Looking pissed off.

Chapter Twenty-Seven

Sebastian

IRIS IS HERE. A sense of relief washes over me. When Reggie said she was white with shock when he handed over her box of possessions, my sense of worry deepened. Especially because she wasn't picking up her phone. I don't like to think of her crying alone somewhere.

But she looks okay, if a little pale.

Those dirtbags. How dare they accuse Iris?

It takes me forever to cross the café and reach Iris. She meets me halfway.

"Are you okay?" I ask, gripping her arms. She feels frail—and wet.

"I'm okay," she says.

"We need to talk. Is there somewhere we can talk?"

"What's happening?" Lily comes up.

"Is something wrong?" Bella joins us.

"It's okay." Iris waves her hand dismissively. "It's something at work. Sebastian, let's talk outside." Iris gestures for me to follow her out the back door into the garden.

The backyard space has clearly been packed up for the winter, one iron table with two chairs abandoned in the bare trees.

Why didn't she return my calls? Why didn't she call me? I would have called her first thing. Her back is still to me.

Dead, brown plants wither in pots around the edge of the garden. She straightens her back and turns.

That one move undoes me. It's as if she's facing a firing squad. Doesn't she know I'm on her side?

I take her hand.

"Haven't you seen my calls? I can't believe they're accusing you of being the hacker," I say.

It seems as if her shoulders drop—as if she relaxes. She looks up at me, her eyes swimming in tears.

"Why didn't you return my calls?" I take off my coat and wrap her in it, pulling her into my arms. She clings to me and rests her head against my shoulder.

"I was afraid you wouldn't believe I wasn't the hacker. I don't know how they can accuse me. But Xavier seems to believe Colby. And then I was escorted out—" her voice breaks "—like I was a criminal."

I hug her, trying to give her my strength.

"Of course I believe you," I say. She holds me so tight. "They're crazy. Colby is just evil, and Xavier is blinded by the fact that Colby is his brother. Do you want me to resign in protest?'

"You would resign?" She stares up at me.

"This is too unjust," I say. "I didn't become a lawyer to work for an immoral boss."

She shakes her head. "You need to stay on the inside. Tessa was just talking about her case, and she reminded me about following the money. There might be a money trail. He had to have paid the hacker."

"Unless he used his own funds—like the way Xavier used his own funds for the ice skating."

"I know. But you know Colby. He's all about the money, while Xavier is all about the artistic idea. Also, if a white hat hacker was paid from personal funds, that would be a red flag—for the hacker."

"I can talk to Ernest or Aaron," I say.

"They also said that you'd prepared the paid administrative leave agreement," she says.

"What? I didn't prepare a paid leave agreement for you," I say. "You didn't believe that, did you? That I would have prepared that and not told you?" Did she really believe that? Did Colby and Xavier do that on purpose? Did Xavier suspect that there's something more between us?

"It would be confidential," she says.

"Okay." I run my hand through my hair, frustrated. "But I could have excused myself as having a conflict of interest."

"With my taking a leave of absence?"

"I'd have to include daily massages."

She chuckles weakly.

"I did prepare a leave of absence for someone in marketing who had a health issue," I say. "They must have used that one."

I look down at the top of her head.

"Is that why you didn't call me back? Did you think I was calling you as the company lawyer?" I practically bite out the words "company lawyer."

"You *are* the company lawyer," she says.

"I'm your boyfriend first," I say, kissing her on the forehead.

Her phone rings again.

"It's Jazmine," she says.

"You should pick up. She's also worried about you." I tug her over to the iron chair and sit down, pulling her into my lap.

"I'm okay," she says to Jazmine. "I'm in shock, I think. It all happened so fast, and it was so...surreal."

She rests her head against mine.

"Amelia's probably just saying she doesn't believe it because she knows we're friends," Iris says. "If anything, my being willing to climb through the window should not speak well for me." She half-smiles, and I hug her closer, relieved to see that. "Yes, I'm still coming to your Hanukkah party. I've already bought my gift for the Secret Snowflake exchange."

Tessa comes outside. "I didn't say anything, but Iris, are you okay?"

"I'm okay—for now," she says. "But *not* if my name isn't cleared." Her eyes are huge in her face, filled with worry and fear. "I have to find the hacker who did this."

"I'm looking for a lawyer for you," Tessa says. "But they might be expensive."

"I have the money I was saving for an apartment." Her shoulders droop. "I can't believe Raphael isn't calling me back." She turns to me. "Do you think he left because he was afraid he was going to get set up for this? I want to go out to his house again."

"Let's go over the clues that you have," I say. "You know he was sending you coded information, so let's try that approach first. If we go out there and he's abiding by this NDA, which came with a significant grant of money, he's not going to talk to you. Otherwise, he'd return your calls."

"You're right. I'm off my game." Iris turns to Tessa. "Did you tell Lily?"

"No, but you should tell them. Lily will feel terrible if she feels like you couldn't share this," Tessa says. "She and Rupert will be happy for many years, so it's not like her joy is going to fade."

We go back inside, and Iris explains to her girlfriends what happened. They're all upset, but mostly they feel helpless because nobody knows how we can prove that it's not Iris—other than finding the real hacker.

Iris and I soon take our leave because we're off to decipher the clues. I pick up the box of Iris's belongings, *Zero Trust* right on top.

Iris didn't trust me. I can't think about that now. But it hurts. She's not as deep into this relationship as I am. And that scares me. Because I've been here before. With Melody. And it didn't end well for me.

Chapter Twenty-Eight

Iris

WE'RE IN MY BEDROOM at my parents' place. My mom dropped off snacks like I'm a teenager, but both Sebastian and I are happily munching on the apple slices and cookies. We're both seated in my gaming chairs—I have two in case a friend comes over—by my desktop, with my monitors. It's actually a better setup than what I had in my apartment with Patrick.

I feel better now that we're taking action.

"Believe me, if I wanted to get a copy of that PowerPoint, there were a million ways to get it—and I wouldn't have been caught. Both the CEO and his assistant used their personal emails to work on documents at home, and they've failed thirty percent of our phishing tests. It would have been child's play to obtain their credentials and access it."

Fatma is purring as she sits in Sebastian's lap.

Total traitor.

She should be sitting in my lap giving me comfort.

"It also makes no sense that we'd want to publicize the hack by my tripping my own trap, especially since Kevin definitely didn't want to notify L'Etoile," I say.

"Exactly," Sebastian says. "But that's an appeal to logic, and I think we need to come up with conclusive proof. I like your idea of reviewing the clues Raphael sent—that we *presume* Raphael sent."

"What I think came from Raphael is a pot of honey and this book, *Zero Trust Networks*. I also received fingerless gloves, a calculator, and an ergonomic mouse."

"A calculator? Is there some value you could calculate?" Sebastian asks. "I sent the mouse."

"Did you send the specialist too?"

"Yes. You kept rubbing your wrist. It seems to be better now. You don't rub it as much, and you're not wearing the wrist brace."

He noticed I was rubbing my wrist. My heart is melting. I shake my head. *Focus on the investigation.*

"Okay, so I set up a honeypot. I was planning to do it anyway, but I think that's a clue from Raphael. The calculator was rather basic. And then *Zero Trust Networks*. But that's where I found the two presentations—in a folder in Raphael's backup files labeled Zero Trust. I think I've used the two clues."

"Do hackers have code names?" Sebastian asks.

"Some do," I say.

"So could one of the hackers have a code name having to do with honey or calculating quickly or anything like that?"

"That's a definite possibility," I say. "But it doesn't spark any names off the top of my head. And Raphael said I'd be able to figure out the clues. He said that as if it was going to be easy."

"What exactly did he say?" Sebastian asks.

"Are you acting as company counsel at this moment?" I say. "Because I don't want to get him in trouble with the NDA, if he signed it before this point."

"No, I'm acting as your boyfriend," Sebastian says. "My loyalty is to you."

He says that so easily. No pause at all. I tear up.

"Okay, Raphael said something to the effect of…he didn't think he should tell me verbally what he found because Kevin wanted to know who else he had told. He said I'd figure out the clues. Then he talked about this book I gave him, *The Code Book*. But I gave it to him when we visited his house last December, so his referencing that was out of the blue. I thought he was trying to change the subject."

"What's *The Code Book* about?"

"It's the science of secrecy from ancient Egypt to quantum cryptography. It starts with these stories about how the Greeks foiled the Persian War by sending covert messages." I pick up the copy on my bookcase and hand it to Sebastian as I recount the story about the messenger Raphael mentioned. "If we think he was being deliberate referencing *The Code Book*, I should look for covert messages—because I don't feel like a pot of honey and *Zero Trust Networks* are really covert messages. They don't involve any decoding. Except that the book title was the folder name, so I guess that's some decoding."

"But the messenger story didn't involve decoding."

"No. It definitely didn't. That involved shaving a head. There's a term called yak shaving in cybersecurity, which refers to focusing on the main task and not being distracted by nonessential projects."

"Or maybe it's more like something hidden in plain sight, but you need to know the key," Sebastian says.

I stare at him. A shiver goes through me.

"That would be totally Raphael," I say. I pick up *Zero Trust Networks* and flip through it.

Letters are underlined. Very faintly, but definitely.

I show Sebastian. We copy them down.

"Given the Greek messenger story, it should be something relatively simple."

"I don't know," Sebastian says. "I wouldn't like to have my head shaved just so people could read a message written on my scalp."

I ruffle his hair. "I wouldn't like you to shave your head either." I study the first chapter of *The Code Book* where the messenger story is recounted and try one of the methods listed there: rail fence transposition. No go. Next, I try the Caesar shifter, which was used by Julius Caesar. I replace each letter with a letter three places down in the alphabet.

Priya@priyasnowleopard.com is revealed.

We stare at the written words.

"What do you think it is?" Sebastian asks.

"I think it's the email address of the white hat hacker," I say. A huge weight feels like it was just lifted off my chest.

Chapter Twenty-Nine

Sebastian

IRIS EMAILED PRIYA, BUT she hasn't received a response yet, so now I'm doing whatever I can do here at the office. To be honest, doing this kind of investigation is one of the reasons I like practicing law. But it would be better if the stakes weren't so high and Iris's career didn't depend on it.

I step into Bob's office. He doesn't look very restored from a night of sleep. If anything, he looks worse.

And indeed, he immediately says, "I didn't sleep a wink last night. I have a bad feeling about what's going on. I thought Iris was telling the truth. And I wasn't brought in on Raphael's departure, which makes me suspicious. As the GC, I should definitely have been consulted about his termination."

"Do we have a copy of Raphael's NDA?" I glance at the stack of folders on Bob's desk.

"We've been given nothing, but I was told he signed one by Colby and Amelia."

"Why don't we release Raphael from his NDA so we can get the truth about what he discovered?" I ask.

"That's a good idea. I'll talk to Xaiver and insist that we need to do that. I'll ask HR to contact him," he says. "I'll also ask HR for copies of whatever he signed. This is part of Legal's purview."

Whether Xavier agrees will show whether he really wants the truth.

Back in my office, I call my former boss and ask if she can recommend employment counsel for Iris. The calendar shows Ernest is out. I call Aaron and ask him if he can come to my office.

I gnaw on my lip. Given that Hank deleted Raphael's files, Kevin might have confided in him. Hank might be a weak link whom I can question. But that didn't seem to be their relationship during the conversation I overheard.

Aaron knocks on my door and comes in, taking a seat. He's carrying a mug that says, "I'm an accountant, not a magician."

"I like your mug," I say.

"My latest gift from my Secret Snowflake," he says. "It seems especially apt. If only I could conjure up some more budget cuts for Colby."

"I'm investigating this white hat hacker situation, given the company's potential liability in an employment lawsuit." It's true enough. "If there was an outside white hat hacker, they would have been paid. Has that been recorded anywhere?"

"Jazmine is really upset." Aaron opens up his laptop.

We pore through the financial statements. It's certainly not recorded under third party payments or outside contractors.

"Ernest mentioned that he found more money at one point because Colby had recorded something incorrectly. Do you know anything about that?"

"I recall him mentioning it," Aaron says. "The company paid an invoice, and Colby said he should have paid it instead. Ernest would keep records of that."

"Even if Colby told him to delete that?"

"Yes. For his own sake."

Aaron opens the accounting files that underlie the recent executive PowerPoint presentation for L'Etoile.

Nothing.

Aaron purses his lips. "Let me check this other folder." Aaron clicks on another folder called Backup. It's password protected.

That seems like a good sign, even if we can't get in.

"We can ask Ernest," I say.

"Let's try Mother," Aaron says.

"Mother?"

"I'm pretty sure that's his password. He's always saying how he doesn't need a password book because it's not like he'd ever forget his mother."

Iris would have a heart attack.

And there it is.

An invoice from Snow Leopard White Hat Consulting.

With Priya's email address.

Ernest saved the documentation that Dream paid this invoice, and Colby then reimbursed the company.

"Wow," Aaron says. "I just got chills. This is like a smoking gun. Does it save Iris?"

"They might still claim it's Iris's company," I say. "We're closer to unraveling all the lies. I need to search the New York State corporation database to find out who owns Snow Leopard White Hat

Consulting." *And I bet it's Priya.* We save the document to our own files, and I print out a copy.

Bob knocks on the door. "Xavier agreed to release Raphael from his NDA. Can you come to my office? We need to talk in private."

That doesn't sound good.

Aaron and I stand to leave, and I follow Bob into his office. Bob slumps in his chair. His pallor is not good. He excuses himself as he takes some pills with a glass of water.

"We found the money trail." I show him the invoice.

Bob stares at it. "I don't believe Colby forgot this payment. That's not Colby. He wanted this person to think the company was paying for their services."

"Exactly," I say. "Which makes it unlikely it was Iris."

Bob sighs. "I'm not as surprised as I should be. I was worried one of them would go off and do something half-cocked because they thought the company was at risk of closure. But I thought it would be Xavier, not Colby. I thought Colby was the more logical one and wouldn't pull a crazy stunt like this."

He picks up the invoice and the record of Colby's repayment. He shakes his head. "At least Colby has resigned. But Xavier has made it clear that he's blaming me for this and he expects my resignation—after I fix this. I'll recommend that he appoint you as GC. I should have done this kind of legwork before accepting Colby and Kevin's accusations."

He stands. "I'll tell Xavier now what we've found."

I should feel happier, but he really doesn't look well.

"Are you sure?" I ask. "We can wait. Are you sure you're okay?"

"Yes, I'm sure. And I'll feel a lot better once I've done this. I've been considering retirement for some time now, in part for health reasons. That one time you came in and I shoved the papers into a drawer—that was me doing calculations on my income streams if I quit."

His phone rings. "I'm going to take this, but I'll talk to Xavier as soon as I finish."

I leave his office and return to mine.

I'm going to be the General Counsel?

I want to call Iris, but until her name is cleared, it's not a position I can necessarily accept.

I call her anyway, but she doesn't pick up.

> Iris: *In meeting with lawyer. Lawyer just called Bob, and Bob and Xavier are coming over. It looks good. Don't worry. Will call you when it's done.*

I wish Bob had invited me to the meeting. But it's probably for the best. My loyalty is to Iris.

My dad calls and says he's in the neighborhood and asks if I want to meet for lunch outside. Perfect timing. Work can wait until I hear from Iris.

THE CAFÉ IS A small brick-walled establishment with black-and-white photos of Paris on the walls. A narrow passage between a dark wooden counter lining one wall and tables for two on the other side leads up to the counter in the back. We both order black coffees with milk and sugar and some French bread sandwiches.

We sit near the front window, even though there's a slight chill from the door.

Dad looks good. A lot better than Bob right now. And Bob is ten years younger. Not the best omen for taking over his job.

Dad even has a little bit of a tan from all those long walks with Pepper. Or it could be the cold.

"Thanks for taking the time to meet me," he says. Formally. He sips his coffee.

"Dad, you don't need to thank me. I'm happy to see you. What are you doing in the neighborhood?"

"Your mom wanted to see the latest exhibit at the Whitney, but she ran into a friend, so I excused myself so they could talk freely," my dad says with a smile.

I snort.

"She's thrilled that you're dating Iris. You haven't seen her lurking outside your apartment, have you?"

I stare at my dad. "*Is* she lurking outside my apartment?" It's not outside the realm of possibility.

"Not yet, but she will be if you guys don't show up soon to say hello as an official couple. She's worried that you're fake dating, like at Baby Love, so she'll stop setting you up."

"Iris and I are definitely dating," I say.

"That's good." My dad nods. "Also, I have a friend, a CEO, who is looking to hire. I have the highest respect for her. I was very impressed—"

Not again.

"Bob told me today that he's planning to resign and that he'll recommend me for the General Counsel position." I need to nip this new appeal by Dad in the bud now.

"You're going to be the Dream GC?" he asks.

"Yes," I say. "Providing the CEO approves. So, can you give up on my going into finance?

"This was a GC position," my dad says.

My mouth opens.

"It was?"

He nods, a slight smile peeking out.

I grin. "You're serious?"

"Although there is also a finance position open too, so, you know, I was going to offer that too. But if you're the GC of Dream Studios at your age, you're obviously a success and doing what's right for you."

I stare at him. *He's finally accepted my career.*

"Your mom told me to stop pushing you to do finance. And Annabelle told Neville that his son needed to grow up or get out, and Neville isn't talking to me, so maybe I've been blinded by rose-colored glasses in my view of finance. You actually seem happier in your career than your sister," my dad says. "She's furious that she is going to have to spend her vacation here cleaning up Nathan's mess. But at least we caught it in time—because you warned us that he can't be trusted."

They caught it in time. Again. At least my warnings helped.

"Oh, no," I say. "I should call Annabelle. Is she okay?"

"I told her Neville and I would do it."

"Can you handle that?"

"I can and I will," my dad says. "Maybe I was hoping she would come back here. I should've stepped in earlier. She said that at least now she can attend some of the holiday parties in London before she flies home for Christmas."

"I wish she would move back," I say. Annabelle flies home frequently because of the New York office and New York deals, but it would be even better if she lived here.

We talk about the dog park renovation, and then my father says he knows I have to go back to work because I keep checking my phone.

"I'm sorry," I say but don't mention I keep scanning for updates from Iris.

"I'm sure I did it to you when you were a child, which is even worse," he says.

"Can I ask you to do a huge favor for me?" I ask. "It's a Christmas present for Iris."

Chapter Thirty

Iris

MY LAWYER—ONE OF TESSA'S friends—and I meet Priya at a corner café in midtown across from Carnegie Hall. The windows have been spraypainted with snowflakes and green pine boughs. Inside it's relatively empty at this hour. In the corner sits an older woman reading a newspaper; a family speaking French sits at another table. My lawyer reviews Priya's agreement (signed by Kevin) with Dream Company to make sure they can't proceed against her.

"The job was pretty straightforward, except for your traps. They were very sophisticated. I was bummed I got caught by them," Priya says. "That's when I thought—this team obviously has some serious cyber credentials. I did a search and saw that Raphael worked there. But I still wasn't suspicious—until Kevin had no interest in how I got in. Absolutely none. He totally zoned out. He clearly just wanted the PowerPoint."

She sips her coffee.

"I'm pretty good at reading people, because hacking involves so much social engineering. I called Raphael, and he was completely unaware that I'd been hired to do this, which makes sense if I'm pen testing, but once I told him they asked me to get the CEO's

PowerPoint, he was like, *I don't know, That doesn't seem legit.* Then I sent him copies of the two PowerPoints I'd exfiltrated."

She hands those over. They're the two documents I found in the file titled Zero Trust.

"He said you'd set up the traps and he was going to talk to you, that I shouldn't do anything further, and that you guys would reach back out to me. That's the last I heard before you emailed me. But he also emailed me last night, asking me to talk to you because he was no longer working at Dream and had signed an NDA."

Thank you, Raphael. Raphael did intend to tell me. And he did get my message.

Priya then shows us a copy of the company check she received. She also agrees to join us at our meeting with Dream Company.

I am in the clear.

THE VIEW OF MIDTOWN from this law firm's conference room is very different from the view we see from our offices in Chelsea. *Ha. Our offices.* Not so much anymore.

"They're here," my lawyer says. Priya, my lawyer, and I take our seats at the conference table in a row facing the door.

Bob and Xavier enter. We stand and shake hands across the table, but the atmosphere is still frosty—at least from our side. Xavier smiles and tries to make some small talk, but my lawyer shuts him down pretty quickly by saying we're delighted they could join us on such short notice to discuss the false allegations against her client.

"Yes, we agree that they were false," Xavier says hurriedly.

"Raphael will be here momentarily. He's been released from his NDA," Bob adds.

"Great. Then this should be relatively smooth," my lawyer says.

Priya shows her agreement and the check to Bob and Xavier and explains that she was the one who did the hacking. Bob confirms that Colby authorized the check payment and then replaced the funds. "Sebastian and Aaron found these documents."

My heart warms to hear Sebastian's name.

"I am deeply sorry," Xavier says. "I'm sorry I didn't believe you—and I'm sorry for how we treated you. Colby has resigned. I fired Kevin when Bob showed me the check and the hacking agreement."

Kevin is out. A wave of relief flows through me—I'm thrilled that I don't have to ever see Kevin again.

"I just couldn't believe my brother would go that far and lie to me. It's clear to me now that he wanted his mole—Kevin—to stay in the company. Maybe he couldn't give it up or maybe for the misguided reason that he thinks he needs to protect me from myself. That I don't have the head for finance or for political machinations. And maybe I don't."

His body sags against the chair, but then he straightens.

"Because I really couldn't believe that he would lie to my face like that. But that's neither here nor there. I'd like to offer you the position of CISO. I'll hire a separate CIO, and you'll both report directly to me."

CISO! I'd be Chief Information Security Officer of Dream Company! At my age.

"I also expect you to pay my legal fees," my lawyer says.

"That's a given," Xavier says.

"I'd be happy to accept," I say.

"We'd be happy to negotiate the terms," my lawyer says.

"Yes," I say, "pending the negotiation of terms."

"Great—welcome on board, CISO," Xavier says.

Raphael arrives and explains how Priya called him, and he agreed with her that it seemed suspicious. But when he confronted Kevin, Kevin said Colby had authorized it. Still, Kevin offered him a severance package as long as he signed an NDA, noting they needed to cut costs to make their proposal competitive for France. It was a year's salary, so he took it.

He hadn't thought I would be framed for the hacking job. But he also wanted to make sure I had all the background on the hack so I could deter any future attempts. And leaving these clues didn't violate the written text of the NDA, although maybe it was not quite consistent with the intended spirit. But then, Colby and Kevin didn't want to involve lawyers in drafting his NDA, so the language was not as precise as it should have been.

There's a round of handshaking and goodbyes. Bob and Xavier leave. It's Raphael, Priya, my lawyer, and me.

And it all hits me.

At first, I can't say anything because I'll cry. But finally, I choke out, "Thank you so much. It really means the world to me that I have my reputation back."

I duck my head. It's embarrassing to be so unprofessional.

Priya pats me on the back as I wrestle to control my emotions.

"I'm sorry I left you to face that. I really didn't think Kevin would frame you, but he's crazy. Did you figure out all my clues?" Raphael asks.

I explain what I figured out. "How did you send me those presents?"

"I left them with my assistant and told her I was your Secret Snowflake and that I wanted to make sure you still received your gifts," Raphael says. "So I asked her to send them via inter-office mail."

"She didn't say anything when I asked her," I say.

"She definitely liked the secret mission aspect of it," Raphael says.

"Raphael, where are you going to work?" I ask.

"I'm considering Shooting Stars," Raphael says. "They're a start-up, so I'd be coming in as CISO there. They're building their information security team. I did enjoy the time off, though. I'm worried this will be twenty-four-seven, and that might be a problem with my mom's care. As you know, I have to make sure she takes her medicine and gets to physical therapy. I explained that to the CEO. She said it's about working smarter, and they want people to have outside lives."

"I'm relieved you have an option." I pack up my bag. "My brother's friend works for Shooting Stars and is very happy there."

I say thank you to my lawyer as she sees us to the elevator. She waves off my gratitude. And she promises to get me great terms for my new position.

"We should celebrate and catch up with dinner and drinks," Raphael says. "How about La Bonne Soupe?"

"That sounds great. Let me just call my boyfriend," I say. "You guys go ahead. I'll catch up."

I stand off to the side on Seventh Avenue and 57th Street. Across the street is Carnegie Hall. Next to me a newsstand is covered in lottery ads, the yellow typeface glowing against a blue background.

As Priya and Raphael cross 57th Street, I call Sebastian. He picks up on the first ring.

"It's all resolved," I say. "And I was appointed CISO! CISO! Reporting directly to Xavier. Kevin is gone!" I am practically hopping.

"I've been appointed General Counsel," Sebastian says. "Bob resigned."

"Wow," I say.

"Wow," Sebastian says quietly back.

I take a moment to absorb this. *We both made it.*

"I told my dad, and he said he understood that law was the right career for me—even before this position."

"Oh, Sebastian, I'm so happy for you," I say. "I'm going out for drinks with Raphael and Priya. Come join us!"

"I can't leave yet. Bob wants to walk me through stuff right now," Sebastian says. "I'll join later. Or I'll see you at Jazmine's party."

"It'll probably be lots of infosec talk, so not so fun for you anyway, but I'll definitely see you at Jazmine's."

We hang up. I stare at the traffic whizzing by on Sixth Avenue. A car cuts in front of a bicyclist. The bicyclist stops short, the back wheel rearing up, but the rider stays on board.

That's how I feel. My career was almost upended, but I managed to stay focused on proving my innocence. And I did. *Whiplash. Escorted out.* That still makes me cringe inside. But now I'm CISO. *CISO.* But can I trust Xavier? He's Colby's brother. I still can't believe Colby and Kevin tried to frame me. Will Colby still have some in-the-background influence? And that might be even worse because it won't be up-front.

I think Xavier is now determined to prove to his brother that he can run this company on his own. And this is a career opportunity I can't pass up.

And Sebastian is the General Counsel too. It's perfect. I turn to catch up to Raphael and Priya. They've disappeared from view. A burst of wind picks up an empty plastic bag, which swirls in the gray sky. It dips and turns in the wind, filled with so much air that it looks like a ballon. The joy inside of me bubbles up. The bag darts along, buffeted by the wind, until it gets snared by a light pole.

I run to catch up to Priya and Raphael.

Chapter Thirty-One

Sebastian

IRIS SOUNDS SO HAPPY. And this time she called me immediately to tell me the good news.

A new artwork has been installed in the High Line. Only the back is visible from my window, but my dad and I briefly walked through the park after lunch, and we checked it out. It's a pastel-hued floral mural with "Thank You Darling" styled in bright bubble letters, by Dutch artist Lily van der Stokker. Appropriate. I feel grateful and relieved that it's all worked out.

I call my dad. "I'm General Counsel. The CEO approved it."

"Congratulations! That's great news. I'm happy for you," he says.

And he does sound happy for me.

My mom gets on the phone. "I haven't called you, but I'm so thrilled you and Iris are dating. I like her. Are you guys going to come over for Friday movies? I hope you bring her."

I can't get a word in.

"Oh, yes. Your dad just reminded me. Congratulations on becoming the General Counsel. Wow! That's quite a title," she says. "Now hopefully you can come and talk to one of my classes about being a lawyer. Will you have more control over your schedule?"

"Maybe Iris and I can each come in. She's the new CISO," I say.

"It's like an alphabet soup," my mom says. "But you guys are really a power couple. It's good that you were both promoted. Much easier."

"I'll ask Iris if she wants to come over on Friday."

We talk more, my parents passing the phone back and forth, until I say I have to go because I'm meeting Iris at a party.

Jazmine's studio apartment is packed with people. I make my way through those congregating in the hallway, excusing myself as I slip through, and drop off my Secret Snowflake gift in the box decorated with blue paper and snowflakes in the living room/bedroom corner. Two people are having a conversation, wine glasses in hand, over the box.

I say hello to Jazmine. She tells me Iris went to the kitchen to fill up the ice bucket. Jazmine's queen-size bed is pushed against the wall with a mountain of coats on one side and some people sitting on the edge like it's a couch facing the official couch. A small Christmas tree fills one corner. A set of red, green, and black candles sits on the short bookshelf by the north wall in a wooden candleholder, ready for Kwanza at the end of the month. A menorah is in the center of the dining room table, surrounded by a feast.

"There," Jazmine says. "She's at the food table by the windows."

Iris looks up and smiles at me. I'll never get tired of seeing that light beam.

I pass through more people, saying hello to the ones from work I now know, so it takes me a bit of time.

Finally. I go to kiss Iris hello, but she backs up and whispers, "Too many work people here."

I kiss her quickly on the cheek instead.

She nods.

"Did you have dinner?" Iris asks. "Jazmine is an amazing cook. I left space for her latkes."

"I had lunch with my dad, but I love latkes."

Jazmine's latkes are deliciously crunchy and flavorful. Our work colleagues are much more cheerful. There's a feeling that the storm may have passed because Xavier made another speech, telling everyone the company is not going to be shuttered.

Jazmine claps her hands together and thanks us all for celebrating the first night of Hanukkah with her.

"I want to read a passage from one of my favorite children's books about Hannukah," Jazmine says. "It's called *The Hanukkah of Great-Uncle Otto* by Myron Levoy. I loved this book as a child, and I want to share its message about love."

Jazmine reads a passage about how, on Hanukkah, one light becomes two lights the next night, and then three lights the third night, and that's how kindness spreads. One kind act begets another.

Jazmine tears up as she reads the passage. Iris slips her hand into mine and squeezes. I squeeze her hand back.

Jazmine lights the first candle. She then invites everyone to pick out their secret snowflake gift.

Iris unwraps her gift. "The movie *Pillow Talk*. And it's from..." She looks at the back of the card. "You?"

"One of my mom's favorites," I say. "I was passing by Barnes & Noble, and they had it in their sale DVDs."

"I like your pillow talk," she whispers.

"Do you?" I ask. Suddenly, I understand Wim. I want to go home right now with Iris and explore some more pillow talk.

"What did you get?"

I unwrap my gift. It's body soap.

"We can find a use for that too." She winks at me.

Yes, I definitely want to be a caveman, pick her up, and go home right now.

"How was Raphael?" I ask.

"He was good. Thank you for suggesting that he be released from the NDA," she says. "I gave him back his copy of *Zero Trust Networks*, but he said I could keep it."

Aaron and Jazmine are cuddling in a corner. *Lucky.*

I understand it's a work environment thing and that dating a coworker can impact her professional reputation negatively, but still. Kevin is gone. Hank is an idiot, and I don't want to live my life catering to his narrowmindedness. I worry it's something else. I want to shout from the rooftops that we're together now.

Especially because Ernest keeps putting his hand on Iris's arm, and I'm stuck here as a neutral observer. At this point, it's not exactly fair to Ernest either.

He tells us he was out of the office today because he was interviewing for another job—but don't tell Jazmine.

"Still, if you guys were both promoted, it doesn't seem like they're closing us down, right?" Ernest asks. "That would be cruel."

Iris and I look at each other. It's not entirely past them.

"Xavier never thought they were going to close us down," I say.

"Well, it was incredible for Colby to step down to save money for the company—his brother's dream company—so that maybe they won't close us down. The New Mexico CFO seems like a good guy," Ernest says.

"Is that what you heard?"

"Colby implied that at his good-bye party with accounting," Ernest says.

Iris frowns.

Jazmine joins us at that moment. "I'm so glad you're replacing Kevin." She hugs Iris. "And Ernest, there's someone I want you to meet." She winks at me.

"Jazmine, everything is delicious, but I'm going home soon," Iris says. "The last 48 hours have been such an emotional rollercoaster. I'm wiped out."

"Take some latkes," Jazmine says. "And some babka. Don't leave it all for me to eat."

"I will. Thanks again for inviting me."

"Well, you understand the meaning of kindness begetting kindness. I'm going to donate a copy of this book to Faith's library. By the way, Nora has been helping Faith pick out books to buy, and they're so excited. Faith says it's like Christmas came early, and Nora says it's like Eid al-Fitr."

"I'm so happy to hear that," Iris says. "I need to call Faith and coordinate for the winter dance on Friday. I forgot."

They hug goodbye, and Jazmine pulls Ernest over to meet another woman.

"Are you really tired?" I ask. "Are you going to go home?"

Iris smiles at me. "I don't have any more energy to socialize, but I do want to celebrate at your apartment with you."

"I'm just going to slip into something more comfortable," Iris says as we enter my apartment and hang up our coats. She picks up her backpack.

"Did you bring a change of clothes?" I ask.

"I should," she says. "Getting up at six a.m. to rush home and change is not ideal."

"You can borrow my sweatpants now if you want," I say.

"I picked up something on my way over to Jazmine's." She leaves the living room.

I want to suggest again that she move in, but it's probably not the right timing. *Remember, she didn't fully trust me.* But hopefully, now she does. And if she wants her own apartment, I should respect that. But it makes sense for us to share an apartment. I pour us both some wine and swirl the red liquid in my glass.

"Do you want to do some cooking?" Iris asks as she walks back into my living room.

I blink.

Iris is wearing an apron. *And nothing else.*

She winks at me. "Do you still think aprons fall into the same category as socks?"

"Definitely not," I practically growl. I grip the counter. It takes all I have not to cross the room to her. All words seem to have deserted me.

She raises one eyebrow, a very satisfied expression on her face. She knows she has me completely enthralled.

I can't hold back and pick her up, swinging her around. "And yes, I definitely want to heat someone up."

She wraps her arms and legs around me. "I do like a man who can cook."

"I think you're going to be very happy with what we're serving tonight."

I walk us both into the bedroom, and she hugs me tighter as she closes the bedroom door with her foot.

Chapter Thirty-Two

Iris

THE NEXT MORNING, AS we enter the office elevator and Sebastian presses the floor for Dream Company, Xavier joins us.

"My new GC and CISO! Great to see you both here so early," Xavier says. "Did you run into each other at Starbucks?" He nods to our matching Starbucks cups. Xavier presses his floor.

I ended up not going home, so I'm actually wearing the same skirt from yesterday with a sweater of Sebastian's, the sleeves rolled up so it looks less formal, over a T-shirt. We were able to buy underwear and the T-shirt at the CVS near his apartment.

Sebastian glances at me. It is true that I don't want to lie to my boss. Especially not after being accused of subterfuge.

"Not exactly. We're dating," I say.

Sebastian flashes me a relieved smile.

"You're dating?" Xavier asks, his voice rising.

That's not a happy tone.

"Let's go to my office," he says.

I glance at Sebastian, and he shrugs, biting his lip. We're silent for the rest of the elevator ride.

The dull gray metallic doors open. We follow Xavier past the movie posters and down to his office at the end of the corridor.

Inside, there's a blackboard covered in white chalk handwriting, various ideas outlined, trophies and deal toys on a shelf. Film scene stills cover the walls, along with framed review clippings of Dream's first success.

Xavier shuts the door behind us and gestures for us to take seats.

He paces back and forth.

This is not good. *Not again.*

"I can't have a GC and CISO who are dating." He clenches his jaw. "I need unfettered loyalty to the company, and I'll worry you won't serve as a check on the other. I made a mistake starting a company with my brother. And as we all know, I was blinded by my loyalty to him and my belief in him. I want a fresh start. One of you needs to step down from this executive position. You can keep your original job, of course. Or if this is just a passing fancy, you can break up, and I'll take your word that it's over. But it has to be really over."

I stare at him. My stomach drops, the buoyant balloon I'm floating in taking a sharp nosedive.

"I don't need an answer now. I'll let you guys discuss and decide." He walks towards his desk. "It would be easier for me if I could appoint Hank as CISO, because otherwise I need to look for a GC. But I also was really impressed with your investigation and the way you followed the money, Sebastian, but was that just to clear your girlfriend?" He holds up his hand. "Don't answer. Even if you think your relationship didn't influence you, I'm sure it did. Just like I wanted to believe Colby. You can both leave."

I can't believe this. How could Xavier set such a condition? Is that even legal?

I stand. Sebastian doesn't look at me.

I can't step down. He can't step down either.

I walk to the closed door.

He'll step down, right? I mean, it's a lot easier for him to get a GC position than it is for me to get a CISO position. And what if all the craziness I just went through leaks and other companies think that's why I stepped down?

But Sebastian was so excited about his dad finally accepting his career choice.

There's no good solution.

We exit and stand in the hallway.

"Should we discuss in my office?" Sebastian asks, his tone formal.

Chapter Thirty-Three

Sebastian

We enter my office. It is still devoid of personal effects, but I did bring in a framed photo of Iris and me from our bike ride that I planned to display once Iris gave the okay.

"You were right that we should have concealed our relationship," I say. "Maybe we can prove to him that we're both honorable and not about to defraud the company. He doesn't need to worry about this conflict. If he works with us in these senior roles for a while, he'll realize this."

"So you're suggesting we put our relationship on pause—'break up' for him—and then see if we can persuade him down the line?" she asks.

"No, I don't want to break up," I say immediately. I don't. I can't.

Her eyes are sad, and she looks away. "I don't think we can lie to him about our relationship. That wouldn't inspire trust."

"You're right," I say. "There has to be a solution other than one of us stepping down or our breaking up."

"I don't want to step down," Iris says. "This is an amazing career opportunity for me—and if I'm realistic, it's one I may not get again because cybersecurity is so male-dominated. And by the time I prove myself at another company, it'll be time to have kids and I'll have to step back. And I definitely can't work for Hank. He'll make me do all the work, but he'll take all the credit."

"You can't step down," I say. "There has to be a third way."

She squares her shoulders and stares at me. Does she want me to step down? But...

I do have a fallback. My dad's company. My chest feels tight.

"You can't step down either," she says. "Not when you've finally earned your dad's approval."

I exhale. She's not suggesting I work at my dad's company. She's not Melody.

I nod. "It's not just about my dad's approval. I also took this job because I wanted to work in the film industry—and because Bob said I'd be the GC in two years. And it's not exactly easy for me to get another GC position. Though, yes, I could find another job and hope again that I could prove myself and eventually become GC. But there's no guarantee. There has to be a third way."

The GC position my dad mentioned. But I don't want to be a nepo hire. Iris has made her opinion of nepo hires very clear.

Her shoulders slump. "I don't think there's a third way. And the thing is"—she swallows—"one of us could give up the management position and we could keep dating, but it would poison our relationship. That person would always be bitter. Not immediately, maybe. But what if the person who gives this up never makes GC or CISO again? That's definitely going to fester." She sighs. "I just got out of that relationship—where my career was resented. Patrick missed that signing opportunity for me. I can't do that again."

"What are you saying?" I ask.

"I'm saying there's no good solution." Her eyes, brimming with tears, meet mine.

"Are you saying we should break up?" I can't believe this. Isn't she willing to fight for us? She's not even thinking this through. "I can step down."

"No, you can't. Because I can't let you. And what will your dad think? If you do that for a woman? When he wants you to be some cold financier type?"

"My dad wants me to be happy. I think that's what he just realized. *You* make me happy."

"And you make me happy. I've been floating these past few days," she says, wiping her eyes. Her phone beeps. "But let's end it on this happy note. I don't want to watch you have regrets and become bitter. I don't think I can survive a betrayal like that again." She walks over to me and reaches out to hold my hands.

I turn away. This is not what I want.

"We're under a DoS attack. I have to go," she says from behind me.

A denial-of-service attack. Ironic. I feel like I'm under a *denial of our relationship* attack.

I turn back around. "I can't believe you're not willing to fight for our relationship."

There's a knock on my door, and then Bob sticks his head in. "Ready to meet again?"

"We have another DoS attack. I was just telling Sebastian." She walks out the door, past Bob.

"Can you give me a few minutes and I'll meet you in your office?" I say to Bob.

How can she switch so quickly into professional mode? I feel like the floor was just pulled out from under me. *We broke up.*

Another woman who is willing to give me up. Not willing to go the distance.

Another woman who isn't willing to fight for me.

And the thing is, love requires that. I've seen it in my parents' marriage. It means facing tough times together. My parents' marriage has definitely had its ups and downs. My mom has been frustrated with how much my dad works. My dad hasn't always felt appreciated for all the stress he lives with. I don't want to date someone who calls it quits at the first sign of trouble. Or give up the GC position for that either.

But she's also right. That if I did give up the GC title, and if I never got promoted again and I was always Associate General Counsel, wouldn't that bother me? Or if I took the GC position my dad mentioned, could I prove myself—and ignore the whispers that I got the job because of my dad?

I stare out the window at the choppy waves of the Hudson River. I have to be honest and say I'm ambitious enough that it would bother me if I was never GC or if I took a job and my colleagues viewed me as a nepo hire like Hank. Maybe it wouldn't—maybe I'd be so happy with Iris that I would think it was worth it. But can I tell that now? We've only been dating for three days.

She's right. There are no good choices.

Chapter Thirty-Four

Iris

WE WITHSTOOD THE DENIAL-OF-SERVICE attack. And Hank is actually doing some work now that he's afraid I'm going to fire him. But he's definitely not a happy camper. That's fine. Neither am I. At least my job requires total concentration. I can't think about the fact that Sebastian and I are breaking up.

Because there is no other choice.

Hank stands. "I don't think I've ever sat for so long before."

Definitely not a real gamer.

He stretches.

Jazmine: *Are you going to the Secret Snowflake reveal later today?*

Whoops. I forgot to open the gift that was on my chair earlier today. I was so focused on making sure we survived.

Me: *Yes, I think we're okay now.*

I open the gift. It's a baseball hat that says "I'm the boss." Well, that definitely rules out Hank as my Secret Snowflake.

"Are we allowed to leave now?" Hank asks, a mocking tone in his voice.

"Yes." I stare at my monitor, but I don't see anything.

I was so happy with Sebastian. Maybe I wouldn't be bitter about stepping down or finding another job. Is Dream Company really my dream? Because I'm not sure I'm totally over the accusation and being escorted out. That was more like a nightmare. I woke up in a cold sweat last night after dreaming that Kevin proved that it was my credentials that stole the PowerPoints. I had to remind myself that he'd lied about that.

I call Raphael and leave a message, asking him if he knows of any other companies hiring.

HANDMADE DECORATIONS OVERFLOW THE conference room Christmas tree. A red and green paper ring garland loops around it. The little siblings spent Monday afternoon crafting holiday ornaments, and clearly some of those have been added to the tree.

Sebastian is off in the corner, talking to Anita. She looks delighted. Sebastian looks like he's trying hard to appear jolly and like he's not hurting—after being hit by a truck.

I did that to him.

Should I have pretended there is a third way? That's not really me—to not face up to reality.

Jazmine comes up to me. "Aaron is late, and he already knows I'm his Secret Snowflake. But I have to tell you something."

"What?" I ask.

"I had to draft a policy today prohibiting executives dating and also prohibiting relationships between HR and any other functions because we supervise them. So, I told Xavier Aaron and I were dating, and he said one of us has to leave. I know I'm not supposed to know about you and Sebastian, but did you know this? What are you doing to do?"

"He told us the same," I say. "What are you going to do?"

"I said he needed to give me a month to find another job, but I would resign."

"You did? But you really like it here," I say.

"I like Aaron a lot more." Jazmine grins.

I stare at her. *How can she be so sure?* They also just started dating. Is it really that easy a decision for her?

"There's Aaron." Jazmine lights up. "I'll go tell him again I'm his Secret Snowflake. He said he's also going to look for another job, so I don't have to quit. But you know, with all the rumors of the company closing down, everybody started searching for new jobs, so really, Xavier shouldn't be setting ridiculous, outdated conditions. I've been dealing with so many people bringing competing offers. It's a total mess."

Aaron looks over, and his face brightens when he sees Jazmine.

Sebastian still isn't looking in my direction.

Patrick used to find me in the crowd and sing directly to me, "I love you. You're the only one for me."

But I wasn't.

But Aaron seems like a more dependable guy than Patrick. And I thought Sebastian might be...but now we've fumbled at the first hurdle.

Jazmine excuses herself to talk to Aaron, and I make myself a hot chocolate. The desserts don't tempt me at all. I have no appetite.

Amelia walks in and does a double take when she sees the tree. She rushes over but then stops and seems to take a deep breath. She turns away. She must see that what Jazmine said is right—that now the tree gives off a true holiday feel.

Ernest bounds up. "I'm your Secret Snowflake."

"You are?" I ask.

"Yes. Did you guess?"

"No," I say. "Because I'm yours. What are the odds?"

"You're mine?" he says. "I think that means we're soulmates." He winks.

Soulmates. My eyes can't help searching for Sebastian. To cover my inattention, I say, "Or at least Secret Snowflake-mates."

"I was afraid you guessed when I told you I knitted. You seemed so taken aback," he says.

"That's because my ex knitted," I say. "I love the gloves. They're perfect for wearing in the office, especially on weekends, when there isn't much heat."

"I picked the green to match your eyes," he says. "And then I sent the calculator as a clue."

I blush.

"Those gifts met the spending cap, but then I heard about your promotion, so I couldn't resist buying the *I'm the boss* hat," he says. "And thank you for your gifts. I should've guessed it was you when you included that gift for my mom."

"Did she like it?" I ask. Sebastian is completely ignoring me. Has he accepted that we need to break up?

"She loved it," he says. "The Florida guidebook was another great gift. And I can always use more coffee."

He takes a big breath.

"Anyway, I just accepted another job, so if things don't work out with that guy you're seeing, I hope you'll give me a second chance.

Because I won't be a work colleague anymore. And obviously, if you're the CISO here, I can see that you wouldn't want to date some junior in the accounting department in the same company. I mean, I'll still be a junior in this new company, but I won't be in this one." Ernest loosens his tie slightly.

Ernest is a bit like a sweet puppy dog. And that's the type I was determined to date.

But the one I *want* is Sebastian.

He's talking to one of the women who works in production. She laughs and touches him on the arm. She must be his Secret Snowflake.

Odd that Sebastian never mentioned his secret snowflake gifts. Were they something special?

He's smiling at Anita and the woman. The color is returning to his face.

That's good.

I don't want him to hurt. And I definitely don't want him to return to Mr. Single Sebastian because he doesn't think he's worthy of love. He's worth all of it.

Isn't he? Worth giving up this job?

Chapter Thirty-Five

Sebastian

IRIS LOOKS SO CUTE. She's clearly been in the middle of a cybersecurity incident because her hair is in some sort of weird half ponytail/half bun on top of her head, strands escaping from every direction. But she hasn't looked my way once.

My chest hurts.

Ernest is staring at her like he's completely besotted.

I turn back to my Secret Snowflake, whose name I already forgot. She's asking me why I didn't wear the Santa tie she gave me to the party.

Because it didn't even occur to me?

She's pouting and hits me on the arm.

Might as well nip this in the bud.

"I was promoted to General Counsel yesterday, and that wasn't the impression I thought I should convey," I say.

She steps back.

Maybe that was too harsh. But Iris is now smiling at Ernest, and this woman is not the one I want to be talking to.

Iris turns and leaves the room with Ernest.

That's that, then.

I stand on a ladder and hang the paper snowflake from the gym ceiling in Alice Walker High School. Iris is helping Faith create a tropical island in the other half of the room. She's fixed her hair, and she's listening intently to Faith's instructions.

"I thought you were dating Iris," Jamal asks. "Did you guys fight already? You haven't talked to her once, but you keep looking over there."

This kid is way too perceptive.

"We're in a bit of a cool period." I climb down the ladder and maneuver Frosty the Snowman into its designated place.

"What's that?"

I run my hand through my hair frustrated. "I'm not sure. We're not allowed to date under company policy."

"Companies can do that?" Jamal's eyes widen.

"They can fire you if you don't abide by an internal policy, so basically yes. One of us has to find another job."

"That's tough. But shouldn't you be talking even more, then, showing her that you're good enough? That's what you told me to do to win Faith, and it worked." Jamal grins. "I still can't believe she agreed that we could date and she'd go to this dance with me. Of course, I have to keep up my grades." Jamal narrows his eyes. "You leave this to me. I got you."

Uh-oh. Jamal is typing away on his phone.

"I think I'm okay. I'll talk to her later when we can be private."

"No. It's much better if you talk to her in public—that way you both have to be nice to each other."

I don't want to ask how Jamal knows this.

Faith comes over. "I think we need some help putting together the Tiki bar that Dream sent over. Iris is figuring it out, but she probably needs someone to hold the pieces in place while she screws them together. Sebastian, do you think you could help? I need to explain how to make the DIY palm trees to that group."

Jamal gives her a thumbs-up. "Let's go."

As we walk over to Iris, I take a quick look around. The gym already looks amazing, and we're not even finished decorating.

Iris is muttering to herself as she is inserting one piece into its slot.

"Faith sent us to help," Jamal says.

She glances up and stills when she sees me. I hate that reaction.

"That's great," she says. "I actually have to run back to work, but I wanted to see the library Faith set up, so if you guys can put this together, Faith can show that to me before I have to leave." She stands.

The old work excuse. I've used it myself.

"Sure," I say—because I can't say, "*Let's talk, here, in this gym while setting up a Tiki bar.*"

Iris practically runs away.

"Boy. You're really in the doghouse," Jamal says. "This is beyond my abilities. You should talk to your guy friends who have girlfriends. You need help."

I'M FIRST TO THE Grey Dog restaurant. I stopped by the bullpen on the way out, but Iris was already gone. Only Hank was still sitting there. He made some snide remark about how now that's she's the boss, she's leaving before five. She definitely can't work for him.

They seat me at a table next to the Christmas tree, which has been decorated with plastic orange slices, candy canes, multicolored lights, and gold balls. A pirate sits at the top instead of an angel.

Zeke and Rupert arrive at the same time.

"You're looking rather glum for a guy who just started dating someone and made General Counsel," Zeke says. "Tessa says congratulations."

"General Counsel for two days." I tell them about the ultimatum and Iris's response. "It has to be me who gives up my job, I know, but man." I close my eyes. "I've been so focused on this goal for the past year. My dad has finally accepted my career choice. And I'm not even sure she's as invested in this relationship as I am. She was so quick to say we should break up." I think she cares about me. Because she opens up to me. *Can I read Iris, or am I just looking for what I want to see?*

"I hope I'm not betraying confidences, but Tessa said that Iris seems head over heels for you," Zeke says. "That she was really impressed by the two of you going off to investigate the clues."

"Tessa said that?" I ask, hope expanding in my chest.

Zeke nods. "But don't tell anyone in case I'm not supposed to disclose that."

"Lily also commented on how close you guys seemed when you left Banter & Books together. That she was so happy Iris found you," Rupert says.

The waiter takes our orders. I order my favorite taco dish and a beer.

"And it's your life, not your dad's," Rupert says. "Believe me, I know. I definitely conformed too long to my grandfather's expectations."

"It's not like Sebastian hasn't been living his life," Zeke says. "He did become a lawyer."

"But I thought you said that Iris won't accept you giving up your GC position," Rupert says. "At least she's not Melody, pushing you to work at your dad's company."

"I feel guilty because I have a ready-made position there. I could make him happy, make my sister happy, and maybe even make Iris happy because it won't look like I'm stepping down. I'm just going to work for my dad's company."

"But *you* won't be happy," Zeke says. "Then you will resent Iris. Don't do it."

"But I could do it for the short-term. Help my dad deal with Nathan and then find another job."

Rupert shakes his head. "You'll end up disappointing your dad more. He'll get his hopes up. He's finally accepted your choice. Don't do it."

The waiter sets down our beers.

"Iris is more important to me than any job. I can get another job. I can't find another Iris."

"You know, Shooting Stars is looking for a GC," Zeke says. "They're expanding rapidly now after their last string of hits. Although they've previously survived on angel investors, they're now looking to ramp up and get some venture capital funding, so I met with the CEO. I can put you in touch. Their GC is retiring, just holding on until they find a replacement."

A chill goes through me. This could be perfect. There *is* a third way.

"My dad also knows of a possible GC position, but I didn't want to get the job because of him, so there's also that."

"Apply for this one first, and then if it doesn't work out, you should ask your dad for help," Zeke says. "A company is not going to hire a GC based on connections. There's too much liability on the table."

"This position sounds perfect. I'd appreciate it if you'd put us in touch."

"Definitely. I'll send an email right now, connecting you guys. Cheer up," Zeke says.

"Weren't you the one telling me about those Hallmark movies where love conquers all?" Rupert asks.

I scoff. "If you're going to quote Hallmark movies, I should warn you that now is the season to watch out for flannel-clad bearded men wielding axes who live in small towns seducing city women away from their wealthy corporate boyfriends."

Rupert backs away. "It sounds like an invasion of Vikings."

"I have to talk to Iris." I signal the waiter for the check. Her phone goes straight to voicemail. Again. Like when she didn't trust I'd have her back. I need to tell her in person that there's another option.

"And you used to make fun of us for rushing home to our girlfriends," Zeke says.

I grin. "Now that I've seen so many Hallmark movies, I think you definitely need to rush home and keep them warm."

Chapter Thirty-Six

Iris

I text Faith that I'm so impressed with the library she created at her school. She came up with the idea, asked for help, and saw it through to the end. Jazmine was right about asking for help and not doing it alone. I look up to see Liam waiting for me at the Central Park reservoir. I'd grabbed my workout gear from the office and asked him to meet me for a run.

"Shooting Stars is looking for cybersecurity employees," he says. "I asked my friend."

"Raphael was offered the CISO job there," I say. "Should we start?"

The water is dark blue-gray, and the sky is completely overcast, obscuring the setting sun.

"You need to stretch first," he says.

"Are you sure you're younger than me?" I ask.

"I'm younger but wiser. I watch you make mistakes and learn from them," he says. "Like when you pulled your groin muscle and then moaned about it for months."

"Thanks a lot. Do you think giving up the Dream CISO job is a mistake?" I ask. "And that groin injury was really painful."

"Not necessarily," he says. "But you have to be happy with whatever you choose."

I stretch my leg out, using the green bench for its height, as Liam reaches to the sky with his hands. Little sparrows hop near my feet, searching the ground for crumbs. They flutter away.

The plaque on my bench reads *His Path*.

What is *my* path?

Isn't this my dream—to be the CISO of an entertainment company? I'd resolved not to be with a guy who can't support my dream.

I should be happier, then.

Liam gestures with his head. We jog north on the brown dirt path, side by side. Liam is matching his stride to mine. I'm definitely in worse shape than I used to be. We started jogging together in high school because my dad didn't want me out at night alone. Liam was scrawny back then but still tall. He's a good partner because he's quiet, allowing me time with my thoughts. I wipe my runny nose with my sleeve. It's cold, but I'm warming up now. I let my hood fall back.

Through the bare trees, the buildings of Central Park are visible to the west. Patches of green grass under crumpled brown leaves line either side of the path. Farther uphill on the east side is the reservoir, with its one-way running path.

Down here, the path is wide, with plenty of space for people to walk or run in either direction.

Do I think Sebastian is the one? And if he is, isn't that worth giving up this job? It's just a title, in the end. Maybe Jazmine is right—that it's an easy decision. If I got this CISO title at such a young age, I can do it again. But I won't find another Sebastian.

Sebastian sitting in my room, totally supporting me.

Sebastian coming out to Dyker Heights.

The ergonomic mouse.

"My loyalty is to you."

Liam glances at me. "We need to do this more often. You're getting slow in your old age."

"Old age." I harrumph. But I pick up my pace.

We turn the wide corner to a view of both the lit-up brown, beige, and white buildings of the East Side and the gray metal skyscrapers in midtown lining the southern view. The clouds cover the tops, only the blinking red warning lights on top visible. They're so tall, reaching for the sky.

But would I want to live in one?

No. I definitely prefer my Lower East Side neighborhood, where everyone looks out for each other. Or the community on the Upper West Side Lily cultivated with the garden and the library.

Liam and I haven't been running lately because I'm always working.

This is the time for me to advance my career, but I also don't want to spend my thirties in an office staring at a screen.

We jog down the east side of the track, passing the Guggenheim, its façade one of the most recognizable landmarks in all of Manhattan. Not long now to go. I'm definitely breathing heavier than Liam, but I just have to put in that last push.

My sneakers crunch on the gravel. We pass a couple walking hand in hand and someone with AirPods talking out loud on a call.

We turn again. All I can hear is my harsh breathing and my feet hitting the dirt on this narrow path on the south end, hemmed in even more by parked police cars. A police station is somewhere around here. And finally, we're back where we started. We walk it off.

"Did you decide what to do?" Liam asks.

"I'm going to call Raphael and see if he needs a Deputy CISO at Shooting Stars," I say.

"For what it's worth, I think that's the right call. I like Sebastian," Liam says. "And they *escorted* you out, Iris. They shouldn't get the benefit of your expertise. They sound like a bunch of idiots. And now they're setting rules about who you can date. *Just no*. Let them promote that Hank guy. And then we should hack into their systems and—"

"We work for good, not for evil," I say, resting my hand on his arm.

"It's still a fun fantasy."

I perch on the green metal bench—the *His Path* bench—and text Raphael.

"You need to stretch again," Liam says.

I dutifully get up and do so.

Raphael calls me back, incredibly enthusiastic. "I just called Shooting Stars, and you can interview right now. They're going to be there late tonight. Where are you? Their offices are right by Columbia University."

"I'm sweaty and in workout clothes," I say. "But I'm at the reservoir, and Liam lives by Columbia."

"You can shower at my place and then go," Liam says.

"I don't have clothes."

"You can borrow my girlfriend's clothes. They should fit."

"Okay, I'll be there in an hour," I tell Raphael.

I stare at Liam. "You have a girlfriend?" I punch him playfully. "I can't believe you didn't tell me."

"It's early yet. And introducing her to the three of you is not for the faint of heart."

"All the more reason to introduce her. She shouldn't be faint of heart. You're the best brother ever."

"I'm also your only brother," he says.

THE WINDOWS OF THE Shooting Stars offices overlook 110th Street. The H-Mart sign and the green subway globes glow across the street in the dark.

"The ISP seems to have contained it for now," Pearl says, running her hand through her curly hair. Shooting Stars was in the middle of a denial-of-service attack when I arrived, so they interviewed me about what steps I would take, using the real-life scenarios, relaying them via Pearl, the junior member of the two-person team.

"You want to make sure you continue to monitor your other network assets," I say. "Sometime hackers use distributed denial of service attacks from multiple hosts to deflect attention from their intended target. Make sure you look out for other anomalies or indicators of compromise."

"I will," she says.

She's very earnest and clearly talented, if swamped, at this under-resourced information security department.

The CEO smiles at me from across the conference room table. I'm never good with guessing age, but I looked up her bio on my way over here. She's in her early fifties, attractive, and well-dressed in a crisp cream suit.

"It's lucky you came when you did," Christy says. "This wasn't the interview I planned, but you definitely passed the test with flying colors. Thank you for helping us out. I'm glad Raphael recommended you come in."

She leans forward. "As you can see, we desperately need to hire more people. I guess I was hoping we were flying under the radar and wouldn't be subject to attacks like the bigger companies, but we're a good target because we're so vulnerable. Pearl keeps giving me vulnerability reports."

"Those aren't just to scare you. They also help us react faster," Pearl says.

"I hope you will consider joining us as Deputy CISO," she says. "The job is yours if you want it. Given that you were just appointed CISO at Dream, maybe you don't want to be a Deputy CISO."

A phone beeps, and Christy checks her phone.

"And it looks like I might be able to fill another spot on our executive team," she says. "I love it when a plan comes together." She shakes my head. "Anyway, the job is yours. I'll have HR send you the written terms, and you can decide."

"Thank you so much," I say.

"I thought Dream was doing well, but it seems a lot of employees are leaving. We're certainly getting a lot of inquiries," she says.

"My understanding is the situation is good again, but there was a concern that L'Etoile was going to close the company down," I say.

"I presume you've met Sebastian Davies in Legal? What do you think of him as a lawyer?"

"Is Sebastian applying for a job?" I ask. My heart does a little flip. He's also trying to stay together.

"Yes," she says. "I expected him to apply sooner, after I talked to his father."

"His father?"

"His father recommended him. I know his father from back when I worked at my last film company, so I thought he might know some good lawyers I could entice over."

"Sebastian is a smart lawyer." I give an example of Sebastian's analysis when we were dealing with an intrusion a month ago. "But we're also dating, so I'm not impartial either."

"And you both don't want to stay at Dream and work together?" she asks.

"The company prohibits our dating," I say.

She nods. Her phone beeps, and she checks it.

"I have to go, but it was a pleasure meeting you." She leaves the room, saying thank you to Pearl and asking her to call with any updates.

She nodded. Would this company prohibit our relationship too? Probably, right? I need to talk to Sebastian.

He's willing to quit and find another job!

We might succeed.

My whole body feels so much lighter.

Pearl offers to see me to the elevator. I pick up my coat and bag and find my way out of the building. It's dark outside, but the shops are lit up on Broadway. College students congregate outside a bar, deciding whether to go in, while two figures in hooded coats with large backpacks scurry by.

I was too quick to dismiss Sebastian's plea that there had to be a third way. Maybe Patrick was right, that I am too quick to put my career first. But to see Sebastian become bitter—like Patrick did... I definitely didn't want that. But Sebastian isn't Patrick.

This is the perfect solution. I already know Raphael and I work well together, and it gives me more of the work-life balance I want. And hopefully Sebastian will take me back. And he doesn't have to quit his job at Dream, but I am so grateful he also looked for another job.

I need to see him in person.

Chapter Thirty-Seven

Sebastian

The tiny Christmas tree on my coffee table looks a bit lost in my apartment, especially with all the socks clipped with wooden clothes pins to the branches. Maybe I should have bought a bigger tree. Should I put on some music? Probably not. Then it will look more like I'm trying to seduce her rather than sit down and talk.

I can't wait to see Iris. It's now so clear to me that this is the right choice. If only I'd realized that immediately. Even if I don't get this job at Shooting Stars, I'll find another job.

The doorman buzzes to let me know she's on her way up.

I prop open my front door and pace in the hallway. What if she doesn't take me back?

The elevator opens, and she steps out. And we both just stand there, drinking each other in.

"I'm so sorry I was such an idiot. I'll change jobs," I say quickly.

"You don't have to. But I know you're trying. I just interviewed for a job at Shooting Stars, and the CEO mentioned your name. I applied for the Deputy CISO job there—Raphael is CISO, and they offered it to me, and it's perfect for me," she says without a breath.

"What?"

She smiles. And I'm so happy to see that grin that I just reach out and pull her into my arms.

"Can we just hug for a minute?" I ask. "It seems like we're back, and I wasn't sure we would be, and I just want to hold you."

I hold her tight and bury my face in her hair. It smells of peony. And she squeezes me right back.

We finally release each other—sort of. I don't release her hand, and instead I pull her into the living room.

"You bought a Christmas tree," she says.

"A small one. We should get a big one together." I pull her down to sit on the couch next to me. "But wait, you don't have to give up CISO to be Deputy CISO. I'll leave Dream, and you can stay there. Our being together is much more important than the job or that title. I'm sorry I didn't realize it immediately."

"No, I had to realize it as well. And that you were right—there is a third way. And actually, reporting to Raphael is perfect. I already know that we work well together, and we will get to build our own department. And I'll hopefully have a life as well. And the Shooting Stars CEO is so cool. I like her much better than Xavier. You can stay at Dream."

"Okay. I should cancel my interview, then. But only if you're absolutely sure. Because I want to support what you want. You don't have to leave Dream."

"Liam was annoyed I was staying at Dream, given how they treated me. But Shooting Stars hasn't called you to cancel the interview?" she asks. "They know we're dating. She asked me what I thought of you, and I said I couldn't be unbiased because I was dating you. I didn't want to say we'd actually broken up. And I said there was a no-dating rule at Dream."

"You sure you don't want to think about it overnight?" I ask.

"I'm positive. I feel good about this."

I pick up my phone. "I can text her now that I can't interview for the job since we're dating." I text that message to the CEO.

"Why is your Christmas tree decorated with socks? Is this to make the point that you really like socks?" She touches one. "Why are they numbered?"

"Not quite," I say. "I prefer to think of them as stockings. You should respect the role of socks as a very laudable Christmas gift."

Iris faces me on the couch and a serious expression crosses her face. *What now?*

"I want to apologize that you felt I wasn't fully on board with this relationship." Iris holds my face between her hands. "I love you." Her face softens.

She loves me. My heart feels full.

Her thumbs trace my cheekbones. "I love you. You're the most amazing guy. You were so completely in my corner during this whole horrible crisis, and you even made it fun. I was completely devastated, and then sitting with you in my room, figuring out Raphael's clues, I was actually having a good time. It should have been one of the scariest moments of my life because my whole career could have gone down in flames. And yet, I was happy. It's because you were there for me. I feel so lucky that you want to be with me. And I'm sorry I was scared." Her beautiful hazel eyes brim with tears. "I love you."

"Don't cry." I brush a tear away with my thumb. "Please don't cry. It hurts me so much to see you cry. I love you so much." I do. It's overwhelming how much I love her.

I enfold her in my arms. We just hold each other tightly, and then I kiss her. And it's like we're finding each other again, but with a deeper knowledge of our strengths and our frailties and with the confidence that this will last. But it's also worth celebrating now and not taking any of this for granted.

My phone beeps. I ignore it. It beeps again. I should've silenced the thing. We ignore it.

When we finally break apart, we grin at each other.

"So the socks—sorry—stockings?" she asks.

"It's a scavenger hunt for you," I say.

Her eyes light up. "Really?"

I nod. I don't want to ever let her go.

"You should check your messages," she says. "In case it's your family or something."

I pick up my phone and silence it at the same time.

"It's the CEO from Shooting Stars. She says that they definitely don't have a no-dating policy because her husband works there as a film director, and they started the company together. She hopes I will come for the interview tomorrow."

"You should go, then, if you want," she says.

"I do. I'm not happy with how Dream treated you either," I say.

"But you don't think this is another weird Colby/Xavier situation?" she asks, her brow suddenly furrowed.

"My father spoke very highly of Christy's integrity, so I don't think so." I text back that I'll be there tomorrow to interview, as planned. "It turns out my father knows her and recommended me. But I don't think they'll hire me based on that alone."

"Not for a counsel position," she says.

Iris turns the first sock upside down. Out drops a chocolate chip. At least it didn't melt. She pulls out a Levain Bakery napkin.

She looks at me quizzically. "Okay, Levain Bakery chocolate chips. Not what I was expecting, but interesting. Definitely yummy."

"Open the next one." Have I made this too obscure?

She pulls out a photo of the Emerald City house in Dyker Heights. "Is this like a tour of every place we've visited? I love it."

She turns over the card. On the back is written:

"Emerald City exists in the magical land of_ _."

"Oz," she says.

She reaches into the next sock and pulls out a picture of Rudolph the Red-Nosed Reindeer.

She smiles at me, but it's more of a "this is cute" expression.

I can't wait until she figures it out.

The next sock has a picture of a Yuletide cake. Her brow furrows. She clearly thinks I need some help in making scavenger hunts.

She opens up sock number five, which has a photo of the Hudson River.

"We should glue all these into a scrapbook," she says. I love that she's trying to make the best of what she clearly thinks is a random assortment of memories from our relationship so far.

Sock number six has a photo of my bicycle. On the back, I underlined the b faintly. She holds that picture for a moment. And then she looks back at the clues which are all lined up on the table.

"L for Levain Bakery, O for Oz, Oh cool. Love. But R for Rudoph, so not V. Unless is this supposed to be Vixen? But how does Yuletide cake fit in? Lovy. Or is it an *e* because you eat a Yuletide cake? But this is clearly Rudoph. The nose is glowing red."

I tilt my head, but I don't say yes or no.

Clue number seven is a photo of the Rockefeller Christmas tree, and clue number eight is an abbreviation for Christmas.

"Xmas?" she asks.

I nod.

She writes down the first letters of all the words on a legal pad on my coffee table.

LORYHBRX

She glances at me quickly, her eyes widening. "Caesar's cipher?"

I kiss her on the forehead. She quickly figures out the letters that are three letters behind these.

I LOVE YOU

"I love you," she says.

"I love you," I say. "Exactly."

She puts her hands to her mouth and just stares at me. "This is so unbelievably romantic and perfect for me."

"You're unbelievably perfect for me in every way," I say.

Chapter Thirty-Eight

Epilogue - Iris

THE BAR IS CLOSED for Christmas Eve as we celebrate, family and friends only. The napkins are now crumpled, the dishes cleared, just empty or half-full cups of coffee or tea and dessert plates left, as everyone leans back, satiated, away from the tables decorated with red tablecloths and candles.

Our parents' meeting went well. Our moms definitely clicked, and our dads were chatting. My siblings definitely get along with his sister, who flew back from London for the holiday week.

It feels weird not to have Lily here, but she's with her dad, Rupert, and his family. She and her dad used to join us, after her mom passed.

"I can't believe you're both working for Shooting Stars," Liam says. Xavier did not take it well when both Sebastian and I resigned—even though it was because of his ultimatum. He promoted Jin Ae, at least, as I recommended, and asked Bob to return.

"No work discussions," Sebastian's dad says, and Sebastian and his sister both look at their dad in surprise. "I'm not such an old dog that I can't learn new tricks."

Sebastian raises his glass to him. Sebastian then wraps his arm around me, and I snuggle into him.

My sister's son, Jack, climbs into my lap. "Auntie Iris, how is Santa Claus going to leave us presents? We don't have a chimney."

"What did your mom and dad say?" I ask, having learned my lesson previously.

"I didn't ask them yet. I just thought of this," Jack says.

"I think you had that same question when you were younger, Iris," Rose says. *Phew*. She's listening in, and I'm not about to contradict whatever they told Jack.

"Your building has a fire escape, right?" I ask.

Jack nods.

"Santa Claus uses the fire escape and climbs in through the window. In fact, he prefers that," I say.

"That's how I met Iris. She was trying to climb through a window," Sebastian says, and we share a smile.

"That makes sense. We should leave some carrots on the roof for the reindeer," Jack says.

"Okay, we can go up." My parents recently renovated the roof to create a deck space. "Sebastian hasn't seen it yet, so we can show him too." I turn to Sebastian. "Should we tell your mom we're going to the roof deck?"

Sebastian laughs. "No. But she still wants us to see their apartment's roof deck."

Sebastian and I hold hands as we walk up the staircase to the roof, following Rose and Jack.

The top door is bolted shut, and it takes a few seconds for Rose to slide it out.

"Maybe we should just leave this open," Jack says. "I bet Santa would like stairs even more. Do we have this on our roof, Mom?"

"Yes. We can do it at our place too," Rose says as she opens the door. A burst of cold wind and wet snowflakes greet us. I pull up the collar of my coat.

Some high rises tower in the distance, but mostly we are surrounded by other flat rooftops, some with gardens or patio furniture and others left bare, all covered with snow. The faint sound of Christmas music from the bar down the street murmurs in the distance whenever someone opens the door. The city is slumbering, like in "'Twas the Night Before Christmas."

Jack places the carrots on a table, and then Rose hurries him off the roof, saying they have to get home so the kids can go to bed on time. She adds, "Since they're going to be up at five a.m. anyway."

I hug her goodbye.

It's just Sebastian and me on the roof. He pulls me in for a hug and a kiss. I wipe the snowflakes from his hair. He kisses my nose.

"There was a snowflake there," he says. "We should probably go soon too."

"Okay, just let me get Fatma," I say.

"Fatma?" he asks.

"I do want to live with you," I say. "And she comes with me."

A huge smile spreads across Sebastian's face. "That's the best Christmas present ever."

Then he tilts his head and his brow furrows. "Was there some kind of parent-approval test that I had to pass?"

"No. You passed that when you came over and helped me figure out Raphael's clues and my mom brought us snacks."

A FEW CHRISTMAS TREES remain at the tree stand around the corner from Sebastian's apartment. The snow is falling more thickly now, swirling in the soft glow of the light from the lamp post. Fatma is *not* happy to be out in the cold and is meowing in her carrier.

"Should we get another Christmas tree?" Sebastian asks. "I think you have more ornaments than we can fit on my small tree. And now they're only twenty dollars."

"But how will we get it home? We're already carrying my stuff." Or rather, we both have backpacks, and I have the cat carrier. Sebastian is carrying my box of ornaments.

"We can load it up on a Citi Bike and wheel it over to my apartment, and then I can carry it in," Sebastian says. "As long as you can carry your ornaments."

"Let's do it," I say. Sebastian goes to unlock a Citi Bike as I examine the last few trees.

The vendor is from Canada, and he's happy to sell us a tree. He's leaving soon so he can be home with his family. We agree on a skinny seven-foot tree. After he cuts three inches off the bottom and ties it all up, we balance the tree on top of the handlebars and the bike seat.

Sebastian wheels it down the street as I walk alongside. The snow is still coming down softly.

"I always love walking by the Christmas tree stands because it smells so good and makes me feel like celebrating the holidays," I say.

Sebastian winks at me. "Then I hope the fact that I smell like tree sap will definitely lead to some celebrating when we get home."

THE BALSAM FIR TREE stands tall in the living room. Fatma meows as she explores the apartment. I hang her stocking—in the shape of a cat paw—on the cabinet where we've decided to hang the stockings, and then I follow Sebastian into his bedroom. *Our* bedroom.

I like the way he's decorated it. It has a very modern feel. The bed is a queen, in pale wood. Above it hangs a color photo of the ocean. A black-and-white photo of a street in London hangs above his dresser.

"My sister took that photo and gave it to me last Christmas," he says.

"She's cool. My siblings liked her as well," I say.

Sebastian smirks. "Your brother was definitely friendlier this time."

"Well, he was being protective initially, but he likes you."

I open Sebastian's closet.

"Hey, no peeking," he says. "Are you looking for your presents?" He pulls me into a hug.

I kiss his cheek. "Do I *have* presents?"

"Of course," he says.

"When have you had time?" I ask.

"It helps to have a retired dad."

"Your dad bought my Christmas present?" My eyebrows rise.

He nods.

"Well, that rules out lingerie," I say.

Sebastian grimaces. "Definitely. Anyway, I like your cat pawprint underwear." He scoops his shirts out of a drawer. "You can put your clothes here, for now."

"That's perfect," I say. "I only brought a few things anyway, since we're going back to my family's house tomorrow when my sisters' kids come over in the afternoon."

I unpack one of my backpacks and put my clothes in the drawer and my toiletries in his bathroom.

"So is my present at your house?" Sebastian asks as we return to the living room. Fatma has curled up on Sebastian's couch.

"You want a present?" I ask, pretending I don't have one.

"I'm sure you didn't have time to get one." He pulls me into a hug. "You're my best Christmas present."

"I made you one. Plus, I bought these." I pull out two stockings from my other backpack. One says *Sebastian*, and the other says *Iris*. "I thought I should give these to you tonight because maybe Santa will fill them. If you've been good."

Sebastian hugs me. "Like I said earlier, I've been very good this year."

We hang the stockings next to Fatma's.

"By the way, what are we going to tell our kids about how Santa gets into the apartment? We don't have a fire escape or a fireplace."

My mouth opens. "Are you talking kids already?"

"Not anytime soon, obviously. But that Baby Love trip was more dangerous than I realized."

"He parks his sleigh on the roof and comes down the stairs?" I suggest. "Or his sleigh hovers outside each window while he climbs in?"

"I do like your imagination," he says. "Should we open one present now?"

"And you were making fun of my peeking," I say. "But yes. But how do you know I have more than one present for you?"

He points at my still-full second backpack. "I think that holds the presents."

"It could be presents for Fatma," I say.

"I don't have a present for Fatma." He grimaces.

"I bought an extra gift for you to give her," I say.

"Thanks. I should have thought to buy her one. Close your eyes while I bring out your gift."

I sit on the couch and close my eyes. Fatma jumps into my lap and purrs. The door to the bedroom opens and closes. Sebastian's steps sound like he's carrying something heavy.

Sebastian kisses me on the forehead. "You can open your eyes now."

A huge box wrapped in green with a little box on top sits under the tree. I pull out a wrapped shoebox from my backpack, which is now looking a lot less full, and put it under the tree.

Fatma sniffs the package as I pull the wrapping paper off the big box. It's an IKEA flatpack holding a dresser that matches the one in his bedroom.

"Did you know I was going to say yes to moving in tonight?" I ask.

"I hoped you would," he says. "And if not, even if you were just staying over a few nights a week, you should still have your own dresser."

"I'm excited to spend every day with you," I say.

He kisses me quickly, teasing me with the promise of more to come.

"Now this box..." He hands me a small box with a bow on it.

I open it up, and it's a necklace with a silver snowflake pendant. It shimmers in the light.

"It's perfect." I put it around my neck, and Sebastian closes the clasp, his fingers tracing the silver chain, making my heart flutter.

"You have to open your gift now," I say.

He unwraps the red and green paper and then lifts the lid of the shoebox. He pulls out a mason jar with popsicle sticks inside. He scoots closer to me on the floor. He pulls out the first stick and reads it. *Thank you for supporting me and helping me figure out Raphael's clues.*

He pulls out another: *Thank you for being perfect for me.*

He chuckles at the next popsicle stick: *LORYHBRX.*

"I'm not going to even attempt to say that out loud. But I know what it means. And maybe it's now time to show you how much I love you."

"I love you too," I say.

He gently sweeps my hair off my forehead and, holding me tight, kisses me.

I don't think sleep is on tonight's agenda. But then, Santa doesn't need to stop here because we've already received the best Christmas gift: Love.

THE END

I hope *My Secret Snowflake* left you with a warm, fuzzy feeling. The New York Spark world continues with *My Rock Star Neighbor,* a fake dating romantic comedy: When a wary rock star and a cynical reporter fake date to bury a scandalous rumor, will true love be exposed as the real story?

FREE NEWSLETTER EXCLUSIVE BONUS!

For your own Icebreaker Bingo sheet (the New York holiday edition) and a bonus epilogue for fans of Rupert and Lily, sign up for my newsletter at https://books.kathystrobos.com/MSSmore

Chapter Thirty-Nine

About the Author

Author Photograph by Parin-
yarat Cutone.

Kathy Strobos is an award-winning author living in New York City with her husband and two children, amid a growing collection of books, toys, and dollhouses. She took a break from working as a lawyer to write romantic comedies and get in shape. Born and raised in Manhattan, she loves writing about New York City and the accomplished heroines who live and fall in love there, amidst its vibrant energy and the aroma of homemade chocolate chip cookies. She is still working on getting in shape.

Also by Kathy Strobos
A SCAVENGER HUNT FOR HEARTS
PARTNER PURSUIT
IS THIS FOR REAL?
CAPER CRUSH
MY BOOK BOYFRIEND
LOVE IS AN ART
MY SECRET SNOWFLAKE

TRANSLATIONS
EN BUSCA DEL TESORO DEL AMOR
MEIN BOOK-BOYFRIEND
MEU AMOR TRAVESSO
MUZIP AşK
MY MISCHIEVOUS LOVE (KOREAN)

Chapter Forty

Acknowledgments

THANK YOU, AS ALWAYS, to my lovely readers. It makes me so happy to know that my books are bringing joy and comfort to readers around the world. I treasure all the positive reviews. Thank you for enjoying my books and taking the time to write a review.

Thank you also to my ARC team, my newsletters subscribers, the librarians, book bloggers, bookstagrammers, and booktokkers who recommend my books and help me find my audience. You make it possible for me to follow my dream of being an author.

Thank you also to the bloggers of Rachel's Random Resources for such heartwarming blog tours.

Thank you to Caroline L. for the plot inspiration and for our friendship since high school!

Thank you to Guy M. for sharing his cybersecurity expertise and for reviewing several manuscript pages. Our talk helped so much with my plotting. Thank you also to Ketsia Elie and Meghan Smith for sharing their IT/IS expertise and helping with plotting. Thank you also to Victoria Walker and her husband James for sharing their cybersecurity expertise and correcting my text. All errors are mine.

Thank you to Kathy Lopez for coming with me to visit Dyker Heights—that made it so much more fun!

Thank you to my mom for cooking dinner for the seven of us out in Fire Island, leaving me free to polish my manuscript.

Thank you to Rob B. and his daughter for sharing their memories of Fatma with me.

Thank you as always to my critique partner, Giulia Skye. I'm so grateful for all her insightful suggestions. I can't imagine being an indie author without all our weekly encouraging emails.

Thank you also to my critique partner, Ellen Gilman, who was absolutely adamant that the scene where Iris finds Patrick cheating had to be cut because it made her feel too sad. I'm so thankful for all her thoughtful edits.

Thank you to Amy Chan and Krysteena White for their comments on the original first chapter.

Thank you also to my RWA-NYC critique group (Ursula Renee and Laurel Anne Raven) for their comments on the initial chapters.

Thank you to Linnea Sinclair for the invaluable advice she provided in her class last summer and thank you to Steve Kaplan for his comedy class in 2021 where I first pitched this idea.

I also want to thank the members of the Romantic Novelists Association Indie Chapter and Romantic Comedy Chapter; our monthly Zoom chats are so helpful, and I look forward to them every month.

Thank you, as always, to Emily Poole of Midnight Owl Editing (my developmental editor and my line editor), Sharon Coleman (my story editor), and Jenny Rarden of Stormy Edits (my copy editor and proofreader) for making my story the best it can be.

Thank you also to my cover designer, Lucy Murphy, of Cover Ever After. I love my covers. Thank you to Tenna Nørgaard

Landsperg of Tenzian Creative for helping finalize my covers while Lucy was on maternity leave.

Thank you to all my friends who cheer me on. Your support means so much to me.

And finally, thank you to my family, who encourage me and put up with me disappearing to write at my computer.